To all those who listened to my endless rambles of ever-changing plot ideas and supported the whole "I'm writing a novel" thing from the beginning. Your unwavering enthusiasm and appreciation for the characters in this story, as well as the story itself has done more to get this book finished than I can express in a short, condensed dedication. Thank you.

Manipulation is Humanity's most honest behavior.

BLOSSOM

All running and playing beneath the heavy heat of the sun, children filled the park while their mothers—women cradling purring babies with pinched cheeks and sore bellies—sat on knitted picnic blankets along the sides, sipping on bubbling white wine and eating salted crackers with softened slices of warm cheese, watching their daughters prance and swirl with light dresses billowing around their boyish hips, plastic dolls tucked to their sides as squealing giggles ripped from glossed lips, reminiscing of a time when they were so ignorantly blissful, stupidly innocent, unaware that one day, such a thing would be turned sour, like the sticky juice of peaches whose pits were filled with squirming maggots. So unaware of the void that had been left in the center of the Town, gaping and cold.

His white sneakers kicking up loosened pebbles, Adam Hall ran the perimeter of the park until he took a sharp turn down the wooded path and cut through the haze of green pine, becoming enveloped by the trees alongside low rumble of white noise created by a nearby stream where cold, foamy waters cascaded over moss-covered rocks. He stuck to the right of the path, passing a detailed sign of the trail system that would weave deeper into the woods and headed toward his usual turn-around: an old, wooden bench engraved with the initials of one of the founders of the Town, dated back to the mid 1800's. Upon seeing this bench near, he then slowly came to a stop, taking a moment to calm his heart while shallow breaths tightened the muscles of his intercostals.

His hands placed toward the back of his hips with sweat trickling down his temple, matting the hair at the back of his head to his neck, with the stream now a distant rumble, there was no one else on the trail and the silence that transpired around Adam besides the thumping of his heartbeat alongside the muffled music in his ears made the sudden snapping of a thick branch all the more painfully loud.

Yanking the cords from his ears, he snapped his head over his right shoulder, looking into the seemingly endless abyss that washed over the rocky trail such as the ocean over sandy beaches, feeling goosebumps crawl up his back as delicate as a spider's legs weaving tightly knotted webs along his spine, turning cartilage to stone. And despite the sunlight that cut between the leaves, Adam suddenly felt as if the bold shadows were stretching towards him with the intentions of snatching him; ravenous, impatient from hunger.

Before he could dispel such anxieties, such childish notions, there was another snapping of a branch and overhead, birds dug their sharp talons into the chipped bark of aching branches. Singing a sweet lullaby, a warning.

One

Virginia. Surrounded by stacks of messy papers covered in red ink and grades put in the system from years past, deep within the stone walls of the Behavioral Science building with smoke clouded the ceiling— pierced by streaks of yellow light that shone through a cracked, dirty window at the back of the room, revealing the dust that lingered against the corners of the desk and collected between the pages of untouched books, detailing where some had been pulled from the shelves— that's where Henry Williamson sat, hidden away behind closed doors and tightened blinds, tipped back in the wooden chair which creaked beneath his weight.

Glossy black shoes propped up against the desk, a cigarette hanging from between his lips before he took a long drag, he scrunched the bridge of his nose against the piss-taste of burnt paper and the foam filter. Watching the grey dissipate and linger in front of his mouth with a slow exhale.

His frame was that of a crow. Or, rather, a starved wolf. Ropey muscles forming a lean angle to his movements that stood just under six feet with narrow shoulders, his ribs became harshly outlined beneath his sternum as he stretched back, muscles aching from the cramps left to become even tighter within the spongy tissue between the columns of his spine due to sitting nearly ten hours straight.

Compared to the youthful, strong composure held by his younger years, his presence had become sharpened by the years. Now 47 and having been of the Bureau's most prized Special Agents for the past twenty three years, anyone who knew him back when he first joined the Bureau would describe Henry's state as having aged such as the withering of a leaf against the harsh cold of winter as even the gray that streaked the roots of his raven black hair had begun to highlight the wire-like texture of his thick brows. He smoothed back fallen strands with long, calloused fingers, lost in the haze of smoke that suffocated his surroundings, filling his thoughts with the rush and euphoria of nicotine before kicking his feet from the surface of his desk and leaning forward with a sharp thud to tap the excess ash of his fifth cigarette. Flecks of grey collecting at the bottom of the tray: the remains of his self destruction.

Pushing himself up from the wooden chair with a slight groan, shrugging on his black coat and hurriedly collecting the minimal amount of things he carried with him such as the bent and weathered pack of Marlboros he kept shoved in his pocket, the lighter he had discarded onto his desk and his book bag, which carried neglected papers he had long ago promised to hand back to his students in a timely manner, he then gulped down the last bit of the black coffee he had poured for himself upon the arrival to his office—bitter grounds sloshing at the bottom of the Bureau-imprinted mug—and swiftly locked the door behind him.

By the time he had arrived back at his apartment from the droning bore of evening traffic, an hour spent with his head back against the seat and smoke filling the air a powdered white until he cracked the window open (Henry always found himself smoking more when he was bored, something he anticipated would end up killing him, give him a heart attack or suffocate him in his sleep, but then again, perhaps that was a good thing), the sun had already dipped behind the surrounding buildings.

Standing in the doorway, he observed that the five-hundred square-foot space was saturated in hues of indigo and cobalt blue. A single patch of sunlight remaining stretched over a single square surface of the hardwood floors in front of where he stood. Scrunching his brow, staring into it, thinking if he were to step into the center of the bright canary yellow portal that he'd be transported to somewhere anywhere from where he was, however, Henry dropped his bag by the coat rack and merely closed the door behind him. Locking it, then moving around the light with exhaustion already infecting the slowing movements of his bones.

Located straight back from the entryway, to the right of the kitchen and snug between the hallway and his bedroom, the fluorescent white lighting of his bathroom flickered above the mirror when he first flipped the switch. Henry glanced up at it, strands of black hair neglected to be pushed back from his forehead before kicking his door shut.

The wall to his right was lined by a single sink, mirror, toilet and a silver trashcan, where empty pill bottles littered the bottom. As he undressed, first unbuttoning his white collared shirt after yanking his loosened tie from around his neck and pulling his black leather belt from the loops of his trousers in an almost mechanical manner, Henry faced a faded lime green tub with both a bath and shower nozzle; stepping beneath the stream of hot water that clouded the small room with a fog as thick as the smoke from his deadly habit.

His spine curving while his hands lifted to press against the tile wall, letting the water splash over the tense muscles of his shoulders and back, Henry gently lifted his chin so the hot water hit his cheeks and released the air from his lungs. Closing his eyes and feeling the heat melt into him while his thoughts began to swirl. The sound of gurgling water splashing down the drain filling his ears.

In the next moment, a moment of self-indulgence, he allowed for his fingertips to drop down the middle of his pecs, where sparse chest hair matted down from the stream of water, and trail down to between his hips. Finally satisfying what first felt like the craving for a cigarette between his fingers.

At this time in Henry's life, everything had become a sort of agonizing routine. As addicting as his taste of cigarettes, he went through this routine slowly, barely able to keep up simply keeping himself alive by eating and drinking more water than what was included in his coffee. Not thinking too hard on it, however, his temples sharp with a looming headache that had been relieved temporarily, after finishing his shower, towel drying his hair before wrapping it around his narrow hips, he moved to the kitchen and grabbed a single serve packet of instant oatmeal from one of the cabinets.

Tearing into the packaging, pouring its contents into a bowl, the microwave buzzed and whirled with bright yellow lights. The motor roaring, the oats burping free of trapped air until the timer went off and Henry proceeded to extract the pale, creamy contents of his dinner. Then, reaching above the fridge and sliding a half-filled bottle of whiskey onto the counter, unscrewing the cap, bringing its lips to his own, he took exactly three painful gulps.

Dressed down in a black t-shirt and plaid boxers, sitting in a slump against the couch and flipping through endless channels, he settled on a nature program which showed the techniques of predators hunting down their prey. Holding a pillow to his chest and laying on his side, watching the sight of ripping flesh and spattered, pooling blood until almost three hours later, when his hand found the remote once more; having failed to lull himself to sleep and finding himself only more numbed from the booze which he had set next to the now-cold and cemented oatmeal.

Truth be told, he couldn't even *think* about sleeping. So, shrugging back on the coat he had tossed onto the coat rack and grabbing his keys, Henry locked the door behind him. Crossing the line between the blueish shadows of his apartment to the peach-yellow reflection of beige walls in the dimly lit hallway.

Blowing smoke from his nose, he watched the neon sign above him sparkle dreamily with the message: **HAPPY'S BAR AND STRIP, GET HAPPY!** While biting on the end of a cigarette. Two blocks away from his apartment, his gaze that of no emotion, with an exasperated exhale he then pushed open the entrance, where blue, red, and purple lights soaked his figure. The static noise of men's calls and girls egging them on with teasing whispers, squeals and laughter drowning out his thoughts.

It smelled of cigarette smoke, booze, throw up and perfume. Sweat slick on the backs of men's necks which craned to watch the women in front of them. Henry rested his elbows against the countertop once he reached the bar.

"What can I get you?" The bartender slung a dish rag over his shoulder while asking the question he had repeated countless times within the hour, glancing at Henry's cigarette when he placed it back in his mouth but deciding not to say anything. Even beneath the dark lighting, he could see just how deep the lavender streaks were beneath this man's eyes, or how... Thin and pointed he looked. Sickness oozing from his presence like the puss that leaked from inside a tumor.

"Just a black Russian, please." Henry fished his wallet from the breast pocket of his coat, puffing smoke from between his teeth as the words he pushed from his lungs in a near shout cut through the pulsating music.

"You got it."

Not even five minutes passed before the man slid the dark caramel-brown drink over to Henry, the ice clinking and crackling inside the clear glass.

Henry smiled, then turned and rested his back against the counter with the spin of his heels. While pressing his drink to his chest, ahead of him, raised onto a platform littered in green dollar bills, a young woman in strawberry hair, black lingerie, and lifted red heels swayed her hips with a dreamy, deliberately stylized movement of her hands up the flesh of her hips before burying them in the bouncy, heavy curls that fell around the roundness of her face.

The lights casting shadows over her figure, Henry watched her with a fixated gaze, raising the glass and taking two large gulps. It burned down his throat before replacing the numbness of his cheeks that the whiskey had caused, worn away by the passing of time and his metabolism.

In his distraction, he had hardly noticed that next to him, a woman had slipped against the counter and was looking at Henry with a lift of her brow. He only glanced down when he felt her brush up against him—whether an accident or not—it caused him to squeeze his hand around his glass just a bit harder.

Through the hazy, smoke-filled red lights, she pushed herself up on her toes once seeing she had caught his attention and smiled. "I've seen you around."

After a few seconds of simply watching her gauge his reaction, finally, he shook his head. "No you haven't."

"Are you here alone?" She changed the topic quickly, discarding the opener to the conversation as if it was just that: an opener, something to start with.

Now, for the meat of why she had walked toward him after spotting his lean, tall, sharp figure through the crowd of overweight, sweaty men that pawed at her.

Henry took another drink. "What's it to you?"

"I guess just curious, wanna know what I'm up against." With a shrug, her fingers found one of the buttons of his coat, and Henry looked down at her hand, his heart skipping a beat. Leaning closer to her, inhaling the sweetness of her perfume, he suddenly decided he liked it the best out of all the ones that had filled his lungs since walking inside. With bright, summer squash hair, one side tucked behind her ear, it was also evident from the stiffness in its length, how sharp and exact it was that she had recently gotten it cut; the edges curling inward just above her shoulders. Letting the strands fall between his fingers, meanwhile, she watched him observe its softness, how light and delicate it was, his knuckles brushing her cheek while he tucked the other side behind her ear and earning a shiver down her spine before she tugged at his coat. "If you don't have any prior arrangements, how about we take this a little more private?"

Henry blinked, his touch lingering at her cheek, before nodding.

Back at his apartment, stumbling inside the darkness, Henry kicked the door shut with the heel of his boot. His hands placed on her hips, they had begun to kiss in the elevator. She tasted of white wine and apples, her skin soft as his nose brushed her cheek. Pushing back her hair again, holding her face with his hands, he tilted her body up against him so her weight nearly fell against his.

This was something he had been so hungry for that he hadn't even noticed it building, pushing at the seams, until now as it overflowed from his touch.

His skin hot and itchy and his clothes tightening, he shoved the woman—who's name he hadn't bothered to learn—onto the stiff mattress of the bed that remained unmade from the last time he had really slept in it, almost a week ago, listening for a moment to the sound of her breath. It was ragged, distraught, and she gulped down the smell of smoke from his apartment. Then, his hands reaching around her ankles, he yanked her back to him. Promptly beginning to undress her while muttering, "take off your shirt." With a gruff tone that remained laced with vodka.

Obeying, she peeled her shirt from her arms then unclasped her bra so she lay naked on his bed, the cold causing goosebumps to cover her body and her nipples to harden.

After all their clothes lay in a crumpled pile, Henry finally lowered himself into her, the echo of his night table's drawer snapping through the silence, followed by the slick slap of latex alongside thick grunt that pushed itself from his lips to hers while they tangled their limbs. Burying his face in her neck, she wound her hands through his hair, and Henry found sanctuary in her warmth, in the bubbly noises she made, the squeals and sighs, in the gentle words whispered against his temple as if they were long-lost lovers, not complete strangers. She enveloped him with welcoming arms; coaxing him deeper, and deeper into the darkness. Yet, even as his muscles ached and tightened, her delicate touches left Henry only increasingly aware of the void in his chest, left empty and all the more... Hungry.

The next morning, Henry shot his hand out and silenced his alarm. Nuzzling his face into the pillow, his temples pounding heavily with a slight hangover.

A tired groan muffling itself into the cold fabric, he turned his head over his shoulder to see that the woman, whose face blurred in his mind but the feeling alongside taste of her skin lingered, had slipped from his bed back into the night. The only evidence she had been there being the lingering smell of her perfume against the sheets and a strand of hair left against the pillow.

Henry pushed himself up against the headboard, peering down at it before his calloused fingertips grazed the soft, cotton pillowcase cover and he picked it up, proceeding to twist the thin strand around his finger until it broke.

His black hair disheveled, tangled with tight curls bound around his ears, without being slicked back it held a thick wave to it and fell over his eyes. Sticking up on the sides from where he had slept on it. Rubbing the sleep from his eyes, the craving for a cigarette led his hand to fall over to his nightstand, grabbing blindly for the bent pack he kept for such reasons until he successfully bit down on the end, sparking the lighter under his thumb and breathing in the heavy mix of smoke and ash. Looking toward the windows, it was still dark out, the sky painted a dark blue and grey.

Lips remaining pursed around the cigarette, taking another long puff, Henry then kicked his legs from the tangled web of sheets, his bare feet landing against cool hardwood floors as he snatched his underwear from where they had been tossed over the edge and trudged to the kitchen while pulling them on, going to pour the dusted grounds of coffee from a half-empty bag into a plastic filter, filling the water tank before flipping the lid down and watching the black liquid begin to trickle through and fill the glass pot.

At first, the noise muffled, he couldn't hear that his phone had started to ring, but with the realization, Henry ran over to the pile of clothes that still lay on the hardwood floor on the way to his bedroom, wrinkled and stinking of his cologne and alcohol. His hands fumbling to find the pockets, he finally yanked the screen to his cheek before the ringing stopped. "This is Henry." He exhaled, standing back up and pinching the bridge of his nose with a sigh of frustration.

"Agent Williamson." The deputy director spoke in a clear, distinct voice. Henry swallowed the lump in his throat, but didn't say anything. "I have a case for you."

Two

Dread filled Henry's belly, but then, a rush of adrenaline--excitement--made goosebumps crawl all up his arms. "Do you really think that's a good idea?" He muttered, dropping his hand, staring forward. It was all making him nauseous, and needing of a drink. And he didn't even know what the case was. "I mean, I thought I was done."

There was a slight hesitation in her tone, but she continued. "Small town, two kids, young boys, dead within the past month. Locals haven't seen anything like it, so the Sheriff called for backup. Barely on the map." Which meant: *If you fuck up, not much liability, so no pressure.* "We have all the files and information you'll need waiting for you with the Sheriff's department alongside a car at the airport where you'll be dropped off. The guy you're gonna look for is Norman Green. He would like to schedule a meeting for tomorrow morning, at this local diner. If you're up for it. Might be good to get you back out there."

Looking up from where his gaze had fallen to the floor, it felt as if he was almost out of breath. "Y-Yeah? Yeah. Sure."

There was a pause. Henry looked at the phone to make sure the line hadn't gone dead before she continued. "Great. Your flight is at 10:00. Don't be late. I'll give him a call to let the station know you'll be coming in for consultation then send over some more details—"

"Wait—" Henry hurried his words, catching her before she hung up. "What about my work here?" He asked in reference to the rest of the semester he had been assigned teaching classes.

"Don't worry about it."   *why?*

Henry blinked, hesitating, then finally responded with a simple, "yes, ma'am," while considering asking, *why me? I thought I was done. I* was *done.* Still, he held his ~~retired~~ tongue and the line then went dead with a hollow beep, the time blinking at him dauntingly, reading 6:30 a.m. An hour later, he managed to leave for the airport.

The drive barren outside the city, small houses and broken down fences passed in a blur, becoming soaked in a hazy mix of hazelnut brown hues and peachy oranges as the sun rose higher and Henry neared his destination. At that hour, he parked in a nearly empty lot, waited almost two hours in a nearly empty airport and grabbed bitter, thick coffee from one of the vending machines as well as two small pouches of salted almonds and roasted cashews before boarding a nearly empty plane. Shoving the plastic in his pocket, when he took a sip of the coffee, Henry couldn't help but cringe from the taste of thin cardboard; the contents lukewarm from sitting in the pot since the previous day.

Almost seven hours later, spinning from the parking lot of an old gas station, with a slight turn of his wrist, the silver-rimmed watch he wore with a tightened black leather strap ticked steadily toward 6:00 in the evening. A foam cup of steaming black coffee next to his right hand, it was his fourth since he had hit the road, sweetened by two sugar cubes and costing him only a dime and two cents, the sugar cubes melted at the bottom of the cup. Gooey and sticking to the sides like syrup. Nonetheless, they didn't help much with the taste and perhaps as he tilted his jaw back to fill his mouth with the hot liquid, Henry was looking for something sweeter. Welcoming the juxtaposing tastes.

Driving, his eyes wandered into the evergreen trees. The blurring green light reflecting the sun, which reached high into the coral blue sky, fresh rain dripping from sharp pine and onto dew-covered asphalt from the previous day's afternoon shower. One hand still wrapped around the softened foam cup, the heat radiating into his palm, he admired the nature that engulfed him long before he passed the welcome sign of the Town;

awestruck by the immense beauty before taking another sip of his drink and setting it back down. It all made his stomach twist with a sense of nostalgia that overcame him like waves. Nostalgia for something he didn't even know he was missing.

Upon his arrival at the Evergreen Hotel, sitting in the 1976 Monte Carlo the Bureau had, as promised, sent him, Henry rested his head back with the window slightly cracked. Letting the smoke that trailed from his chewed cigarette escape into the springtime air before finally pushing himself from his seat and crushing the cigarette beneath his heel, grinding the ash into the damp, fresh rain that still beaded against the weeds growing from cracked cement. Then, quickly grabbing his bags from the back seat and making his way into the golden-lit lobby where flames licked up the brick walls of a fireplace and emitted a soft, charming glow through the space—the walls adorned with hunting photos, fishing trophies, stuffed animal heads and a timeline of the Town's history —Henry moved up to the mahogany, polished wood countertop and checked into his room, which was to be on the fourth floor, room twelve.

The key he was given slightly bent from use, an etched silver with the room number carved into a small pendent connected by a silver, looped chain, it didn't budge the golden, round knob to his door the first time. Yet, with a grumbled breath, his nerves pinching, jiggling the knob, reinserting the key, jiggling the knob, reinserting the key, on the third try the lock slipped.

His shoulder already aching from the weight of his bag pulling against the stiff connections of his pectoral girdle, Henry turned on the light with a huff. Scanning his eyes over his surroundings and taking in the space he would be residing for... He didn't know how long.

To the left of the entrance was a narrow countertop with a small stove, the grease stained microwave plugged in next to a slightly discolored, yellowed coffee pot. Passing the breakfast bar that separated the two sections of the room, directly opposite to the bed, which was pushed up against the same wall in the middle of the room, was a tall dresser and tv bolted to the wall above it; next to which was a small rectangular desk with the chair pushed in.

Crossing the same raspberry red, frayed carpet that lined the hallways, Henry set his bags down at the foot of the mattress, rusted springs squeaking in a slight protest against the weight as his eyes caught the sight of a bible placed on the nightstand closest to the window. With a squeeze of his jaw, his back molars aching, he paused for a moment before walking over to it. Then, with a sharp slam of the wooden drawer beneath the top of the nightstand, he tossed the leather-bound book with grand, golden-inscribed letters out of sight.

Shooting pain throbbing at his temples, moving back to the bed, Henry proceeded to pull four bottles of second-grade booze out from where he had wrapped them in cotton t-shirts and pushed them between neatly folded suits. Accompanying himself within the private confines and the sweet nectar of a plastic bottle of Smirnoff Vodka, Jack Daniels, Captain Morgan, and Jim Beam Bourbon Whiskey until successfully drinking himself to sleep while outside, resembling thick droplets of blood or clotted masses of brain that spooled from empty skulls, seeping into the cracks of old cement until scrubbed away by suds of pink soap, shimmering pools of rain reflected the blinking yellows, reds, and greens of street lights hanging over empty intersection against the asphalt as cool breezes washed through the mountains such as water does over a jagged shore and the trees moved in synchronized waves.

At first glance, The Town seemed like every other. Its suburban landscape, however, had become infected. Below sharpened blades of green grass that bent under the weight of heavy raindrops, worms wriggled and dug through damp soil, establishing intricate systems of rot; intertwining the roots of tall-standing trees and invading overgrown weeds, harboring all the people's secrets, filling with blood and pulsating such as the empty womb of a woman overcome by a withering sickness. And unknown to the stranger who slept under a heavy blanket of ash and liquor, but this sickness had also nestled itself —as real and consuming as her organs—within the girl who wandered the streets of the Town. Flickering yellow lights shining through bounds of thick white locks, she could feel it inside her, sliding into her belly, residing alongside the trauma that coated her tongue like honey; sweet as ripe tangerines but bitter against the back of her throat like coffee grounds.

Three

Pills rattled inside yellow bottles and caps popped with a snap of the safety lock. Spilling into an empty palm, Henry looked at them for a moment with disdain, observing the four different kinds, each of which seemed to counteract each other in a blended chemical effort to treat a similarly complex set of issues. Tilting his head back and letting them fall into his mouth, he washed them down with cold black coffee, closed his eyes, and squeezed his trembling fingers into a tight fist with white knuckles.

Having woken that morning shaky, out of breath, and with a headache, cold sweat slick against his chest and forehead, sitting forward with his hands clawing at the stiff hotel sheets, his brows scrunched, he shook the dreams from his head and gulped down breaths of air. Looking to the clock and realizing he had slept in later than normal, attempting to calm the heavy thump of his heart, with the shaky light of a morning cigarette, Henry held his head in the center of his palm, rubbing one of his temples with the careful stroke of his thumb.

After shoving the array of bottles back into the plastic bag alongside his tooth brush, tooth paste, a comb and pain killers, Henry tucked his white collared shirt into his black pants and slipped on the black coat he had packed with his other suits; smoothing back his hair with flat palms while walking from the bathroom and exiting his hotel room.

Moving from the elevator, he could smell the thick aroma of breakfast foods sizzling and smoking, bubbling in pans with flames heating the stovetop cast iron containers with oils burned into the rims.

The hotel restaurant bustling with guests who poured in from their rooms within the allotted time of 8:00 to 10:30, during prime time, a long line had developed along the assortment of self-serve trays filled to the brim with greasy, caramelized sausage links, scrambled eggs drowned in melted cheese with green onion sprinkled sparsely over bright, sunshine yellow yolk, still gooey from undercooking, crisp—nearly burnt—bacon trimmed with squishy fat, and cardboard-tasting flat pancakes.

Passing the chaos and making his way outside where the sun had risen over the tree-line, Henry trapped himself in the heat of his car. The light shining through the windshield, causing him to slip silver-rimmed shades over his eyes.

Filled by the scent of warm coffee and the sweetness of buttered pie fresh from the oven, just as anyone would expect from a diner in a small town, laughter muffled the sound of coffee dripping from machines while impatient fingers drummed irregular beats over polished, cream-colored countertops.

The Diner was mainly occupied with high school students, occupying their time discussing homework, the upcoming football game, the end of year formal, who they were going to ask out and who they hoped was going to ask them out; their voices muffled by the rest of the noise while they drank malt shakes and ate greased fries with fidgety fingers, savoring the salty taste of thick ketchup melting against their tongues. Bubbling laughter spreading their lips wide, amidst this crowd, with rosebud red lipstick stains smearing against a clear straw, Blossom James sucked on an iced one-pump vanilla, almond-milk latte, sitting behind a half-finished tuna sandwich on whole-wheat bread and a pile of greasy, parmesan-dusted garlic fries.

Her shoulders hunched slightly toward the table of the booth she had hidden herself behind and her leg bouncing, she was buzzing with an almost wired energy. Listening intently to spiraling conversations held by those around her who battered from topic to topic, boredom itched beneath her manicured nails and her attention floated restlessly. She clasped her fingers over her knuckles, blemished white, and squeezed them tight in her lap, turning her head to across the cash register where she then spotted two girls from her class.

One, Emmerson May, stuffed the last of her fries into her mouth, wet lips dripping with oily saliva. She was a small girl with blushed cheeks, black hair, and a small arch to the tip of her nose. Side-parted bangs that once hung just above her brows now too long, she twisted her hair into tightly wound dutch braids that fell over her shoulders, making her look younger than she was. She had turned eighteen at the beginning of February.

However, despite the pixie-like, cuteness to her features, she was also a girl who took three pills every morning to treat her depression then three more at lunchtime; crunched into cocaine-fine dust which powdered the sides of her malt shake like clockwork. And as she leaned over the counter, picking at the crumbs of food on her plate, licking smeared ketchup from her fingers, seated to Emmerson's right, Bethany glanced over in a disgusted fashion before pushing a couple of napkins her way with a sigh.

Redirecting her attention back to the book she had spread between the fingers of her other hand, the crisp pages ripped and bent at the edges, the binding loose from how often she handled it in such a way, after finishing the paragraph she was on, she then wrapped her hand around the perspiring glass cup of a strawberry milkshake. Taking a long sip of the sweet cream-swirled filling through a striped blue and white straw before scooping some of the melted down whipped cream onto her tongue.

Curly, coffee dusted brown hair that stuck out with frizzy ends, wearing a plain white t-shirt tucked into ripped, high waisted jeans, she propped her untied converse against the metal footrest ring, avocado socks bunching around her ankles.

The bell had chimed again as Emmerson went to lean over to Bethany and whisper something, yet, turning her head over her shoulder and looking at who had just entered, Bethany wasn't paying any attention to what she had to say. Instead, she nudged Emmerson with a sharp knock of her elbow. This cut Emmerson off from whatever she was saying, causing her to mutter an uninterested, "what?" Before she followed Bethany's eyes.

Blossom's heart skipped a beat.

Leaning her shoulders forward with a newfound, peaked curiosity and rush of excitement, spotting the tall stranger that looked as if he had stepped through a time portal from the forties, she continued to watch even while everyone, including Bethany and Emmerson, had gotten back to their usual business.

The man had a certain athleticism to the way he carried himself. Narrow shoulders held straight by a strong posture, his chest tapered to lean hips and with a sharp pointed nose, dark eyebrows shadowed over lavender bags beneath his eyes.

High-set, hollow cheekbones curving into a strong jaw, age had streaked gray in the roots of his black hair, highlighting an M-shaped hairline with sparse silver strands swept back toward round ears, the tops slightly blushed.

Memorizing these features in awe, Blossom tilted her head to the side. The bounce in her knee stopping and her hands becoming relaxed. Slowly, however, she began rolling her finger over the rim of her glass with contemplation, curiosity lifting at her brows and teasing her lips open just enough that a small sigh escaped her lungs.

Stirring her straw through clinking, half-melted ice, she was transfixed by the FBI agent.

She wanted to crack him open like an egg, spool through his brains, his guts, and burrow herself deep inside his roughness. As if there was a safety to it all.

A home in all that damage.

Pushing the door open, the chime of the bell caused a few to glance over at him with absent-minded notes of suspicion flashing over their narrowed gazes, but Henry merely looked over to the nearest empty spot at the front counter. Walking over to where the sound of heels against tile cut through the background noise of water splashing against ceramic plates, washing smears of solidifying ketchup, cold eggs, crumbs of bacon and the remnants of clumped jelly doughnuts down open drains.

Moving from around one of the silver coffee machines and frozen yogurt dispensers, a tall woman with thin fingers and a narrow frame made her way over to Henry. Honey-white hair curling around her ears, bouncing with a thinned lightness over her shoulders, she wiped her palms against the front of her ketchup-stained, grease-smeared apron. Wearing the Diner's signature dress—a pale avocado green with pine collars—there was a rag tossed over her shoulder and two pens tucked into the left breast pocket. Pulling the black one into her right hand, clicking it, her hip bumped against the counter while she silently tugged a leather notepad from one of her pockets. "Morning, stranger." She then glanced at Henry with raised brows. "What can I get you?"

Henry leaned forward. "Coffee. Please."

"Any food?"

"Not yet. I'm meeting the Sheriff. Norman Green?" He slid his hands forward, one palm covering his knuckles while he sat against the stool. "Has he come in yet?"

Clicking the pen once more, the front of the notepad slapped closed with a quick bend of her finger. "Haven't seen him... But, you're the Special Agent, aren't you?" She squinted.

"Henry Williamson." He extended his hand, allowing her to shake it.

"Sophie. James."

"Pleasure to meet you, Mrs. James."

"It's just Sophie. No Mrs. Not since the Mr. skipped town."

"Alright." Smoothing out his tie after retracting his hand and adjusting his seat, Henry gave Sophie a slight, uneasy but earnest smile, which she returned before turning against her heel. Reaching under the counter and pulling out a mug that matched her dress.

After filling it to the brim with fresh coffee, she turned back to him, sliding it forward.

Henry lifted the drink to his top lip, breathing in the thick aroma of the dark roast before taking a large gulp as Sophie watched him.

When he lowered the mug back down, she shook her head, muttering to herself, "terrible.. To think someone thinks they could do those things to those boys and get away with it... *Here.* Nothing bad has ever happened *here.*" To which Henry shrugged, feeling the heat of the coffee in his palms. His hands were almost always cold.

"Quiet town, friendly neighbors, you'd be surprised."

"How so?"

Speaking plainly, taking in her responses, he thought for a moment then let out a quick breath. "No one *expects* anyone, especially within their town, their neighbors, to be capable of something as *horrible—*" Henry exaggerated himself, attempting to sound decently normal so she would stop staring at him like she was actively piercing out his eyes, "—as murder. So, of course, people look outside of themselves long before they ever suspect..." He trailed off, about to take another sip of coffee before finishing. "Someone of their own. And the killer is of course, just as aware of this."

Sophie's brows dropped into a stern expression. His appeal didn't work. "What are you suggesting?"

"Only that I'm here to help." Henry looked down, shaking his head slightly and attempting to present himself has convincingly as he could. "And I'm going to try to the best of my abilities to find whoever did this. By looking at any possible angle."

She opened her mouth to respond, but before she could say anything more the bell chimed again, redirecting her attention to the front of the Diner, where an older couple walked in, their arms linked.

The man took off his hat and waved over to Sophie with a smile that told Henry they were regulars, and not to be ignored. Pressing her lips into a fine line, Sophie patted the counter, silently excusing herself and leaving Henry alone with his coffee.

After taking care of Mr. and Mrs. Jones, Sophie moved into the back of the Diner and delivered their orders. Coming back out, that's when she saw that Blossom's gaze had fixated upon the FBI agent—Henry —and felt her nerves pinch. Coming up behind her, she attempted to pull her attention away. "Blossom. Blossom, please—" Grabbing the plate from in front of her daughter with a shake of her head, there were still a few fries left, still gooey with sauce, smeared around the edges of the ceramic blue. Blossom's eyes shifted and as if she was knocked from a trance, her hands fell to her lap. "It's rude to stare." Her mother then grumbled.

"Who is that?" Blossom asked, absent-mindedly picking the dirt from under her nails.

"*That…*" Sophie glanced over her shoulder at Henry. He had one elbow propped against the countertop. His nose hidden under the rim of his coffee mug, he took a long sip. "Is Special Agent Henry Williamson. With the Bureau."

"What's he doing here?"

Sophie stopped cleaning the table with her rag, brushing loosened strands of her hair from her forehead with her knuckles. "You know exactly why he's here. Norman called for help with those two boys that died."

"Huh." Blinking, her shoulders leaned against the back of the booth with a slouched posture, Blossom crossed her legs under the table and continued to pick at her hands. A gentle frown forming on her lips as she pretended not to care about the information her mother was conveying. However, hushing her voice, she looked up at Sophie. "Do they think there's a connection?"

"I'm sure they're going to look into every possible scenario, but, please."

With a glare, Blossom looked back up at her. "What."

"Stay out of it." Sophie urged with a lifted sympathetic brow, as if to say, *if you ever keep out of other people's business once in your life I'm asking for it to be now. Be thoughtful.* But didn't say anything more before beginning to walk off.

"I wasn't done." Blossom spoke with underlying hostility. As soon as Sophie turned and set the plate back down in front of her spiteful daughter, Blossom grabbed one of the leftover fries, plopping it in her mouth with a smile as her mother rolled her eyes, leaving with a snatch of her rag from her shoulder.

The corners of Blossom's lips remaining curled upward, she sucked on her finger, swirling her tongue around her knuckle before pulling it out with a gentle *pop!* And grabbing what was left of her sandwich; chewing thoughtfully on the gummy, mayo-drenched tuna and doughy whole-wheat bread while the Special Agent looked around The Diner. Lost in a haze of unfamiliarity, a fish out of water.

Four

Looking down at his watch, Henry finally turned his head as the bell went off a final time and Sheriff Norman Green stepped inside. With dusty brown hair—an espresso blend of aged grey and features that nearly resembled Peter Cushing—he pulled a pair of shaded, silver-rimmed sunglasses from the slanted bridge of his triangular nose, revealing deep-set eyes and flat cheekbones that hollowed out into a square jaw. Dressed in a blue collared shirt tucked into black slacks, the sleeves rolled up and the first few buttons undone to combat the warmed weather, a golden badge engraved with *Sheriff,* then his name was pinned above his left breast, the sunlight glinted off the carved edge. Stepping from his seat, Henry extended his hand.

"Sheriff Green?"

"Henry Williamson. Nice to finally meet you." Norman responded with a smile, shaking his hand firmly before clearing his throat and motioning toward the counter, where Henry had left his coffee. "Have you ordered yet?"

"Just the coffee."

"How are you settling in?" His voice was deeper than Henry's, but smooth. It was easy to listen to, rounded, such as his features were warm.

Henry cringed slightly at the attempt for small talk. "Just fine, thank you, but, if you wouldn't mind us getting to the murders," Then cut to the actual thing he wanted to talk about, discarding any social graces perhaps he should have exercised. "I heard there's two bodies, so far?"

As soon as the words had left Henry's mouth, a tint of green flushed through Norman's cheeks and a flash of dismay took over his expression. "Perhaps we should discuss this away from..." His eyes wandered to the surrounding customers, the teenagers, who without a doubt would listen in to the gory details, their eyes already shifting over to the two men.

"Of course." Henry nodded, following as Norman then led him to one of the booths on the side of The Diner.

Two menus alongside one of the pots filled with coffee, an extra mug hanging from her finger, Sophie headed their way with a strand of her hair falling from behind her ear, her demeanor completely different than that of which she had approached Henry with. "Hey Norman." She tugged out her notepad after sliding the menus forward. "What can I get you today?"

While she poured the coffee, Norman didn't even pay attention to the menu. Instead, folding his hands out in front of him, he leaned back with a smile. "One of your *delicious* steaks, Sophie, please."

Henry glanced down at his watch with the flick of his slender wrist, noting the time. It was barely past 7:00. Looking up to see that Sophie had begun to blush, he frowned, then grabbed one of the menus. Opening it to bold letters, dull tones and small illustrations inside some corners, he proceeded to read through the pies: honey, cherry, blackberry, blueberry, maple, raspberry, peach, strawberry, mulling over the sound of each of them in his head until his stomach rumbled.

"Are you in the mood for some food yet?" Sophie looked at Henry with the tilt of her head. A second later, she noticed the nearly-empty mug he had brought with him to the booth. "Besides more coffee?"

"How would you say the raspberry pie is?"

"A classic, especially when paired with some of our vanilla bean ice cream." She tapped the corner of the notepad with her pen.

"I'll take it"

"Great, those will be out in a few." She reached over, grabbed the menus from the table, then turned.

Watching her walk away with steady strides before disappearing to the back behind swaying, grey doors, Norman echoed a small, "thanks, Soph." Before pulling out the folder he had brought— first, having tucked beneath his armpit— then from beside his thigh, setting it in front of Henry, who reached into it and pulled its contents out: about 30 photos, 15 from each crime scene and with them, the reports on the evidence collected and information about the victims. "Andrew Clemmington and Luke Roberts. Both eighteen, seniors at the high school." Henry nodded for him to continue. "Andrew, the first, was found beneath the high school bleachers by one of the teachers. Stabbed in the spine and surrounding areas. Luke..." His voice thickened by the acidic information that laced through it, he paused. Henry bit the inside of his lip, glancing up. "Luke was found at the playground by his house. His wrists bound behind him around the pole to the swing set. We found both tied using pink ribbon." He paused. "He had been stabbed, like Andrew, but then had his throat slit. That's what killed him."

"Interesting. And how far apart were they?"

"Andrew was killed on the 24th, found March 30th, Luke on the other hand was found on the 1st, not twenty-four hours after the accident. One week later." He spoke of it as if Luke had simply fallen down the stairs or had been involved in a tragic car accident.

Running his finger down the lines of one of the reports, coffee stains on the edges, Henry tapped the papers then let them fall back to the table, reaching into his pocket and lighting a cigarette. Norman observed the smoke that lifted from the sizzling, thin paper rolled over filtered, yellow-stained foam and after a few moments of silence, spoke up again, hesitantly asking, "do you deal with a lot of this stuff?"

"Not anymore."

"Not anymore?" Before Henry was able to say anything, to his relief, Norman waved his hand. "What I mean, is... May I ask about your first time... Dealing with this type of thing?"

"You mean a possible serial killer?" Henry felt his nerves pinch slightly at the taste of the term rolling from his tongue, mixing with the bitterness of lingering coffee and sucked in another lungful of smoke, looking down at the photos, allowing the uncomfortable silence to wash through him like a flash of heat.

In the next few seconds, Sophie returned with a black tray, carrying a messily sliced piece of the raspberry pie, syrup swirled over flaky surface with heavy crust and smearing onto the plate like droplets of blood; melting against the scoop of vanilla bean ice cream alongside Norman's thick, fat-trimmed cut of steak.

Setting the tray down on the edge of the table, she began to distribute the plates onto the photos when she realized what they were and the color in her face seemed to drain just as quickly. There was a gentle pause in her movements, which Norman responded to by carefully taking the plates from her hands, but with nothing other than the slight catch of her breath, Sophie continued. Giving a weak smile to Norman before tucking the tray under her arm and leaving as Norman quickly thanked her.

Continuing to inspect the photos while digging his fork into the food that had been set in front of him—teeth scraping against metal—Henry chewed the gummy and warm raspberry flavoring, a slight hum of delight escaping him toward the sensation of the food melting against his tongue. Then, setting the fork back down, metal clinking against the glass plate, he wiped the crumbs from the corners of his lips with an off-color napkin; clearing his throat before finally responding to Norman's lingering question. "It wasn't my case, but there was this guy... Early thirties, so he was around my age at the time, and he had killed nearly five people in one night. Then the next night he killed another two people. After that he went dormant for three months." Meanwhile, after Norman sawed through the thick-cut steak with a dull knife, cracked pepper dusting the plate, mixing like dirt into the blood that poured from the spongy tissue, he proceeded to shove piece after piece into his mouth. Henry glanced at him, knitting his brows together—creating an indentation of hesitation alongside deep thought—while rolling his tongue over his teeth and picking back up his fork, pushing the clots of raspberry filling around the plate. "When we caught scent of him again, even though we had a profile and narrowed the list of suspects, three people died. Two girls and their neighbor: a sixty year old retiree who was making his wife toast and eggs when the guy decided to walk in through the garage and stab him four times. He escaped, leaving the wife, but we caught him in the street and he was shot by the police who were sent to apprehend him. My superior wanted me to see what it was like—to go to one of those crime scenes and see the mayhem—so I went, and..." He scrunched his nose.

There was a metallic taste in his mouth, but he swallowed it down and despite the gruesome details he was speaking of, Norman noticed his eyes were clouded over, fixated on the pie that he scraped the fork through, spooling the innards from, picking at the bleeding juices that stained the ice cream a light pink. "I don't think I'd ever seen that much blood before. In each of the two houses, he left such destruction like a bomb had exploded." His stomach turning, Norman dropped his fork and knife. "The girls were having a sleepover, and the younger one's parents had gone to the grocery store just twenty minutes or so before. It was the first time they..." he clenched his jaw. Norman looked at him with wide eyes, a smear of red from the steak glistening on his bottom lip and his body rigid, as if someone had just gutted him. "It was the first time her parents let them stay home alone. Ages thirteen and fourteen. One was found in the bedroom while the other was in the bathroom. I don't suppose they knew either one had died before they were attacked."

"*Fuck.*" Norman muttered under his breath.

"I don't think anyone realizes how much that fucks with a person, having to witness that kind of destruction and mayhem." He added quietly. Then, leaning over, Henry scooped another bite of his pie into his mouth, allowing silence to transpired between them once more.

As Norman had relayed to him, Andrew, the first, suffered multiple stab wounds on his chest and back; four chipping his ribs and puncturing his lungs. There was an open gash along his forearm, presumably a result from him attempting to defend himself before turning and trying to crawl away, when the killer continued stabbing him along the spine and between his scapula. Moving on through the report, Henry found that Luke was found by eleven-year-old Lizzie Thomas.

With a leash wrapped tightly around the palm of her hand, she had been walking in pursuit of her dog's wagging tail when, at first, she spotted the swarm of flies that buzzed around what looked like a mannequin. Her mother had just started allowing her to circle behind the house via the trail that led toward the woods, veering toward the remote playground on the edge of the tree-line and located right next to a small baseball field. But then, Lizzie caught the sudden stench of rotting meat and instead of a mannequin, she recognized the ivory skin—

torn and battered with flowering bruises—to be that of Luke Roberts. Just as quickly as she had thought the latter.

His throat cut so deep his spinal cord lay exposed for maggots to eat away at its tissue, his chest turned into what looked like slabs of meat or ground beef, his flesh had become littered by numerous stab wounds that tore through bone and cartilage. And without any sign of life or consciousness, he stared into Lizzie's eyes with a pale, fogged gaze; darkness seeping from his mouth, spreading his lips back as a large, hairy spider squeezed through the yellow of his teeth.

At approximately 10:16 am, the Sheriff's station received a call.

"The killer most likely realized that he wasn't going to die right away and got impatient, so he slit his throat as a final act." Henry scratched his chin while Norman continued to eat rather than look at them, already having spent hours trying to dissect whatever information he could. "A way to get it over with."

Periodically taking sips of his coffee until the black sludge at the bottom smeared against his bottom lip, Henry looked up at Norman when he nodded at the images and asked, "can you see a pattern? Between the two? Or could we possibly be dealing with two people?"

"No, it's definitely one guy. From what I can see with the photos, the wounds are consistent, but I'll be able to confirm that with the autopsy."

"Frank, our medical examiner, is working on it."

"Perfect—That being said, the killer is developing a relatively consistent track, yes. But it's interesting. You can see..." Henry slid Andrew's photos in front of Norman. He grimaced. "He was sloppy with this one. With the first one—Andrew—he didn't do as good a job as he wanted. So, he goes after Luke." His fingers moving to Luke's photos, he tapped twice, causing ash to smear on the surface of the glossy finish. He wiped them off, cursing under his breath before poking his cigarette bud into the remaining surface area of his leftover pie. It sizzled. "He's gained confidence. Only, he's more impatient." His eyes widening, he then leaned forward almost excitedly. "Norman. He's nailing down an almost *weekly* routine, right? Luke was found last week. So. He's going to be craving it now, that rush, like a drug."

"What are you saying, Henry?"

"He's not done, and you very much have a serial killer on your hands, Norman. Better yet, we'll have a fresh body on our hands in..." He waved his hand as if doing a rough calculation, his lips gently pursed. "A week or two with my arrival. He might try to hold back, or slow down to veer off and cover his tracks. But give him two weeks max, and he's gonna slip up. He won't be able to hold it back anymore, this craving." He pressed his lips together, thinking for a few seconds. "And depending on how well we do with this next body, he may start to play around. Experiment a little bit. Get risky, try something new. Try to extend the high, if I indulge in the metaphor."

"You talk about this as if it's a druggie getting another hit, or an alcoholic trying to abstain." Henry understood it all too well. "We have a fucking *murderer,* and you say *better yet?"*

"I'm only trying to give you a framework for this stuff, Norman, please." Henry grabbed his coffee, tipped his head back, and gulped down the remaining black sludge. A shiver crawled up his back. "I mean no offense."

"I hope you're wrong."

Henry shrugged.

The clock nearly striking 9:30 a.m, Norman wrote mangled notes along the margins of one of the reports while Henry drank the fresh coffee that Sophie poured for him in passing; two more cigarette buds poking from the crust of his pie. The ice cream completely melted down.

Leaving half his steak to go dry by his left elbow and ordering a sprite about fifteen minutes ago, Norman lifted the clear liquid to his lips. Letting the fizzling bubbles ease the churning of the contents in his belly as well as the unsettling sense of sickness that left a distaste at the back of his throat. Setting down the cup, his phone then began to ring.

The muffled noise distracting Henry from the work, he watched him press the phone to his ear.

"This is Norman." He looked down. "Yes, we're just wrapping up. We can be there in twenty, does that still work?" Then, finishing the conversation with a quick, "thanks. see you then. K. Bye." He shoved the phone back into his pocket. "Frank's got the report ready."

Henry set down his pen and lifted his brows. "Great."

Leaving a tip for Sophie on the table, Norman tucked his wallet away and began walking toward the door while Henry stood from the booth and pulled back on his jacket, which he had taken off forty-five minutes into their meeting, his eyes trailing forward while smoothing out the sleeves.

Sitting lounged against the cushion, having finished the last of her food, Blossom now stirred murky, coffee-stained ice at the bottom of her cup, tucking loose strands of her blonde hair behind her ear before making eye contact with Henry. When she did—continuing to pinch her fingers around the bitten down, mangled straw—her eyes were sharp and intent, cutting right through Henry as clean as a jagged icicle while the corners of her lips lifted into a gentle smirk, mischievous and daring. Henry raised a single brow, as if asking, *who are you?* However, with a small shrug of her shoulders—exposed by the puffed short sleeves of a sheer, button-down, collared crop top she wore over a peach spaghetti-strapped cami and tucked into contradicting black skinny jeans, pink socks visible from beneath the poorly laced black combat boots—Henry got the sense she was telling him, *well, you'll just have to find out yourself.*

Exhaling from his nose, he then felt the corners of his lips begin to reflect Blossom's smile. Yet, as if having just escaped a deep trance, in the next moment he pressed his mouth into a fine line and turned away, catching up to Norman with the flash of her smile reeling over and over in his mind like a broken tape.

Five

Winding through the trees for merely five minutes before entering a boxed parking lot where straying birds pecked at spilled, stale bread crumbs and flocked across patches of grass—hanging onto the swaying branches of trees before flying off at the startling sound of the cars' engines—Henry pulled up into the nearest space to the entrance, three over from where Norman parked.

Closing the door, he squinted toward the sunlight.

Made of grey concrete, the Hospital looked almost like the Academy back at Quantico. It was tall, with massive sections connected by narrow walkways, shaped like a college campus with a fountain and small, dying rose garden in front of the entry.

Making their way inside, automatic doors ushered them into a chamomile, vanilla scented room facing the main nurse's desk, which was decorated by two vases of multicolored flowers on either side, occupied by a pudgy, older nurse who wore a light purple set of scrubs and worked on the computer while her younger—thinner— counterpart continued to be distracted by paperwork.

Glancing up at the men when they arrived, the younger one, wearing black scrubs with sandy brown hair, smiled at them and asked, "Norman! So nice to see you. Are you here for Frank?"

"We are." Norman turned to Henry, who pressed his lips into a half smile and nodded in a polite manner. "Debbie, this is Special Agent Williamson. He's here to help with the investigation." Then, he motioned to the older woman, who had rested her chin against her knuckles and cautiously observed the stranger. He didn't blame her. "Judith," Norman greeted.

"Have you guys gotten any suspects yet?" Judith's voice was layered by a bitterness that made Henry lift his brows. He removed his eyes from the woman and instead looked at Norman, who answered her scolding question quickly, the room growing stale.

"We're working on it."

Debbie turned her chin against her shoulder, almost hissing at Judith, "be *nice.*"

Judith, however, responded with a scoff and Henry turned away, slowly beginning to walk the perimeter of the entrance, following the hallway into the waiting room. It was empty. The fireplace was on and so was the tv, flipped to a cooking channel. About half-way back to where Norman still stood, talking to Debbie, out of the corner of his eye he noticed a man in a white lab coat and a name tag labeled *Dr. Arnold, F. phD. M.E.* step out of a side clinic, hurrying over to them in a slight jog.

"Are you the FBI agent?" He slowed to a stop.

"Henry Williamson. And who might you be?" Henry asked, despite having read his name tag. The man reached out, hurriedly shaking his hand with a folder tucked beneath his armpit. He smelled of spice and cologne.

"Frank Arnold. Pleasure to meet you."

"I assume you're in charge of the body." Henry then inquired, watching Frank carefully.

He looked around, almost jokingly saying, "guilty." Before stuffing his hands into the pocket of his white jacket.

"Then... You're the man we want to see." Henry responded, stiff, not cracking under the pressure of the well-intentioned joke.

Frank smiled with wrinkles forming at the creases of his eyes. Wearing thick, silver-rimmed glasses, they seemed a bit larger than natural and he nodded excitedly, taking an audible breath in as Norman, who cut his conversation with Debbie short, made his way over to them. Redirecting his attention away from Henry, Frank then tipped back on his heels. "Norman, how's Stacy?"

"She's fine, just a bit frazzled because of... You know. She's having a hard time letting Nathan, or even Maggie out of the house. Especially Nathan."

"Completely understandable."

"I tried telling her—"

Henry cut the two off. "You have the reports?"

Frank unshielded the folder under his arm and handed it to Henry. "Sure thing."

His temples beginning to throb with a dull headache from the brightness of the hospital lights, Henry bent his head, pinching the papers and sliding them about halfway out in order to read what they were.

As Frank had told Norman on the phone, they were the autopsies for both the boys, including a list of evidence collected off the bodies and sent to the lab for testing and diagrams showing the lengths, depths, and locations of the wounds. He closed the envelope. "Can you take me to see them?"

Frank narrowed his gaze, glanced over to Norman, then nodded. "I suppose if you don't have a weak stomach, then it's fine with me."

After they entered the sterilized room, Henry looked around. Surprised at the fact it didn't smell like rotting flesh like most morgues, it instead smelled like... Bleach and... Metal. Clean. He grabbed a set of gloves from a nearby box while Frank pulled out the two bodies, swinging metal doors, clanging locks, the sound plastic zippers being pulled down all painfully loud. Latex wrapping tightly around his fingers as he snapped the gloves around his wrists then took off his coat, rolling up the sleeves of his white collared shirt and giving a more relaxed look, he then walked over to the body closest to his left. Through the blurred plastic, he could see that the boy's eyes were closed, but his mouth was open. His jaw cranked, locked open by rigor mortis that bared his teeth. Frank reached over beneath him and grabbed the metal zipper, opening the bag.

The smell of decomposition, though not as bad as it could have been, filled the room almost immediately. Henry breathed it in, unfazed, while Norman blinked and took a step back. Cursing under his breath, "I swear, it only gets worse." He muttered.

Finally fanning through the pages in the folder, printed on the front with a photograph, taken when he was alive, was the name *Luke Roberts.* Henry turned to the body, pulled the plastic wrapping away as if unveiling a gift. Then, flipping through the report with glazed eyes, quickly reading through the extent of the damage in order to match with those of which were in front of him, he dropped the folder on the floor by his feet. Rolling up a chair from one of the desks to where Luke's body lay.

Carefully, Henry began pulling the plastic back enough to inspect the wounds with more detail, including the loose flaps of flesh that covered the nicks of bone.

His tongue rolling over his bottom lip in concentration, the longer he worked, with Norman and Frank observing closely, they had no problem understanding why Henry chose to become a Special Agent.

He pushed his fingers in between Luke's teeth, forcing his stiff jaw open to search for any traces the killer might have left behind the gums and under the teeth. Picking at the corpse like a bird picking at its dinner, a crow, ten minutes passed before he lifted his hands; his review of Luke's autopsy report completed, blood clotting against his plastic gloves, the discolored liquid—thick and cold—smeared against his palms, and swiveled the chair over to Andrew. Starting the same procedure over again.

He fit the job perfectly, almost too perfectly. [1].

On the way over to Andrew, he smiled at the other two, baring his teeth until turning his back to them. And though a slick, cold sweat broke out on the back of his neck out of discomfort due to the way Henry looked at them like a kid looking back at his parents after hurriedly beginning to unwrap presents on Christmas morning, Norman believed that the killer, whoever he was, had a worthy adversary.

"Frank?" He hushed.

"Yeah?"

"Want anything from the vending machines?"

"I'm good."

"Sure? Not even coffee?"

Frank pouted his lips in thought in a slight pause of contemplation, then nodded. "Coffee, yeah. Thanks."

Norman, giving two pats on Frank's back, then began to walk to the door when he turned his chin to his shoulder. "Williamson, coffee? It's shit, but it's Joe."

Henry didn't respond.

Frank and Norman flashed glances, and Norman just nodded, wondering why he even bothered asking.

Ten minutes later, Norman returned with three coffees, two black—three milk pods for Frank—and one already with cream and sugar poured in it. Opening the door, he set the cups down and saw that Henry had already zipped back up the bodies, the stench of slowed decomposition and bleached wounds once more sealed behind locked metal doors.

Still sitting in the chair with the files in his hands, Henry flipped through them, looking up from beneath a slight lift of his brow after hearing the door close behind Norman. Slapping the folder closed, he then made his way over to him.

"Thanks."

"Sure, find anything?"

Taking a swig of the coffee, Henry grimaced. Norman had been right, it was *shit*. But, it was Joe. "Not really, it's still too early. But you can tell by the depth of the wounds that it's definitely one person, like I thought. So of course, that narrows the list of possible suspects."

"Even if we had five, it would be better than zero."

"I need fresh evidence. I need a fresh body, boys." Henry pressed his lips together and looked over at Frank, who tiredly grabbed his coffee, poured one pod of milk into it, then stirred using the wooden stick Norman had poked through the lid's opening. Shaking his head out of dismay. "And thankfully," Henry added, "the clock is ticking." Before sliding the reports back into their folder.

Frank separated from the other two early. Locking the door behind them, he shook Henry's hand, then continued down the hall to check on the labs he ordered earlier, which was in the other building—connected by a narrow staircase and hallway lined with windows—while Norman and Henry, who already finished half of his coffee, Norman only about twenty-five percent, headed back toward the entrance. Passing the nurse's station, Debbie had gone on break, and the two bid goodbye to Judith. She eyed them, but grumbled a quiet, "have a nice day!" Which they couldn't decipher whether it was supposed to be sarcasm or passive aggressiveness, or both, or whether she was being genuine.

Regardless, once outside, Norman glanced to Henry. "That's just Judith, don't take it personal."

Pulling a cigarette from his pocket and lighting it, with an exhale, Henry responded. "I never do."

The hospital was surrounded trees, and if you didn't know any better, it could feel as if you were hours away from the next sign of civilization. When, really, just about a mile or two through heavily wooded Evergreens, you'd find yourself in the center of town.

Moving across the parking lot, unlocking the trunk of his patrol car, Norman then pulled out a small filing box with red tape cut—ripped—and curling around the edges of the lid. In handing it to Henry, who bit down on his cigarette, he began to explain, "the recorded statements by the parents of the boys and some friends we managed to get a hold of. Plus, their transcripts. There's a copy of everything we have at the station in there that you'll need to get caught up." While Henry felt the weight of it in his hands, peering inside with the slight raise of his knee in order to stabilize it against his abdomen. "Tomorrow I'll show you what we have in the evidence locker, aside from what you saw today from Frank." He continued.

After moving around his car, setting the box in the passenger's seat, Henry moved around the front. Pacing back to Norman, who began to look off into the distance. "Are the addresses of the families in there?"

"Sure. All of their personal information, too. Why?"

"I want to stop by and speak to the parents myself. This doesn't have to do with the statements. I've just found by speaking to whoever I can directly, I can help them feel a little more comfortable with my involvement. In the investigation."

Norman mulled it over. "Yeah, sure. I just don't want them to be overwhelmed, it's all so fresh, but..." He let out a heavy exhale. "You don't need to explain yourself. Whatever you need to do, I understand completely."

"You're more than welcome to come with." Henry offered.

Norman waved. "I have to file those reports back at the station and check up with my team's progress. I'll scan the notes we took today, start getting a list of anyone with past records put together like we talked about, and be all ready for tomorrow."

"I appreciate it."

Henry glanced down at his watch. It was 1:30 pm. Then, getting into his car and watching from his rearview mirror as the Sheriff pulled out of the parking lot behind him, he tossed the lid of the box to the ground and pulled out the first set of papers on Andrew Clemmington.

Six

Parking along the curb, Henry crushed his cigarette into the asphalt beneath the heel of his polished shoe and shut the door. Glancing toward the sky—which began to turn grey with the nearing of an afternoon storm—when out of the corner of his eye, he noticed that across the street, an older woman walking her dog had stopped to watch him. Straightening his shoulders and turning his head, when he looked at her she began walking again, but didn't smile or wave. He frowned slightly, keeping an eye on her for another few seconds while she passed him, then walked around the front of his car and up the steps to the Clemmington's house.

They lived amongst a row of other houses with nearly identical floor plans, ten minutes away from the high school. The park visible through a small separation in the trees, connected by the street, Elizabeth— Andrew's mother— walked into the kitchen after letting Henry in, surprise turning into warm hospitality as she asked, "can I get you some coffee? Tea?"

"Coffee would be lovely, thank you." He hung his coat by the door.

"Any cream, sugar?"

"Just black."

Grabbing a tall grey mug, she wore a knitted beige sweater—though it was warm outside—with blue jeans; brown hair falling just over her shoulders.

The house filled by the aroma of baked, cinnamon spiced apples and root vegetables, moving down the hall and proceeding to look around, Henry scanned over the framed photos along the wall of Andrew; some taken during his childhood, others from school pictures, the rest of him with the family, when Mrs. Clemmington interjected again. "He was a great kid."

"I'm sorry for your loss."

Though his comfort wasn't so... Comforting, or reassuring, Mrs. Clemmington uttered a small, "thank you," before walking back over with his coffee. Having picked up one of the photos, Henry set it back down. Taking a courtesy sip. It had a hazelnut twinge to it, an aftertaste of sweetness like the flavored coffee beans soaked through the plastic filter hadn't been washed away completely, causing him to bite down a slight cringe and set the mug down on the shelf beside the photos.

Turning to face Mrs. Clemmington, who hovered behind him, unsure of what to do with her hands, she played with the hemming of her sweater as he asked, "can I see his bedroom?"

There was apprehension in her tone when she finally responded with, "sure," but she gracefully—quietly—led Henry up the stairs and to the right, pulling a key from above the frame to unlock the door before waiting outside, allowing him to move past her.

The bed, covered in stiff, unmade plaid sheets and askew grey pillows, was pushed up against the back wall next to a tall dresser where old trophies collected dust. Scattered comic books poking out from beneath, giving the space the feel of a twelve year old boy who failed to grow up, Henry quietly slid Shakespeare's *Hamlet* off the dresser and thought to himself, *how poetic* while ruffling the pages under calloused fingers. Then, setting it back down, he walked to the other side of the room where the closet was, on his way asking, "where's your husband?" And causing Mrs. Clemmington to lift her head; unable to look into the room for long.

"At work. The Evergreen Hotel… He's a cook."

"I'm staying there."

"Oh!" There was a slight lift of the tension before it settled back down over them. Henry opened the closet, pulling a few boxes down and rummaging through them. Attempting to find anything that Norman's team could have overlooked. "When did you get here?" She asked.

God, Henry hated small talk.

"Last night."

She nodded. But then with a slight hesitation, stuttered, "I'm sorry—but—may I ask why you're here? Sheriff Green already came around... And I thought he'd simply give you everything I told him the first time."

A small smile cracked Henry's stoic expression. Conveying transparency, *humanity,* and attempting to make her a little more comfortable, he relaxed his shoulders. "Well, Mrs. Clemmington, your son—Andrew—was, as far as we're aware, the first. And... It's important to know everything we can about the *first* because it can help build an idea of how the killer is going to go about the next victim, or choose the next victim."

"Oh?"

"So, if I haven't made it clear before now, I'm very appreciative of your openness toward me and I'm sorry I have to bring this stuff up again for you. I understand how difficult it must be to talk about it."

"I just want to help." Mrs. Clemmington urged, almost cutting Henry off.

"And you *are.* So thank you, again." When he looked back at her, she was rubbing her fingers over her knuckles, nervously squeezing her hands together. After a pause, he redirected the conversation back to where he wanted it. "Did Andrew have any friends you knew about?"

"A few. But none too close. He tended to keep school and home separate."

"What about romantic relationships? Anyone he got close to?"

"He uh—yeah, he went out with a few, three or four girls, but they weren't all that serious. Only brought one, Becky Stephens, home."

There was a small bookcase in the corner, where a lava lamp shone a warped, dim light on top of a stack of magazines. The silence stretched through the room bigger, and bigger, squeezing the walls until it felt like something was going to burst. Henry didn't notice as much as Mrs. Clemmington, however, he could feel the muscles of his neck tense under the watchfulness of her eyes. "There *was* this one girl—I'm not sure if they were really *together,* you know, but I heard rumors. About her."

"Rumors?"

"Not so pleasant ones, I mean, kids these days will say anything, but I was never comfortable with hearing about her. Didn't like he was hanging around her."

"What was this girl's name?"

"Blossom. James."

Blossom James... He mulled over the taste of it in his mouth. Repeating it in small chants through his head as the image of bright, colorful flowers bloomed through his thoughts. He imagined bees swirling dizzily around his head, pollen dusted and honey coated fingers pulling apart decayed flesh. Suddenly the bees were flies. The honey red. Blood.

Mrs. Clemmington struggled to form her words in an appropriate manner before she continued. Henry blinked. "I don't mean to raise any suspicion. I don't want to throw her under the bus. She's just... Trouble." Exhaustion was evident in her tone. *Where to start with that girl...* She sighed. "She holds something dark. I don't know what it is, but she's no good." She waved her hands.

"How do you mean?"

Mrs. Clemmington huffed and suddenly Henry could see her back in high school, her lips shiny with bubblegum gloss and cotton candy sweet against her tongue, a cheerleading uniform tight around the body she now wished she had, spreading rumors about anyone who crossed her path yet pretending to be America's sweetheart in the process. A class-A princess, gossiping queen.

"She has a... *Reputation.*"

"Do you think she could have anything to do with your son's murder?"

Her skin suddenly flushed with a sickly green shade, as if she wasn't just talking to the school principal, the word *murder* sticking like glue. Ah, *yes, your son is dead.* "I don't know. I couldn't say. She's *weird—peculiar—* certainly, but murder?" She finally responded, her gaze becoming lost. "Anyway, I hope no girl in this town could be capable of such a thing…"

"You're probably right. The nature of the crimes—" That's right, *your son is now simply a statistic. The child you birthed no more than a number. A dot on a line graph. No more important than last year's bake sale numbers.* "—indicates it's most likely a man. Very rarely do we ever see women committing such…" He looked her up and down, noticing the pale, grim expression on her face. "Atrocities. But it's best to check all the boxes and talk to anyone who may have known something to help us understand what could have led up to your son's death, including those he spoke to. So if Blossom has any information, we need it."

"Like I said, I don't mean to throw her under the bus or cause any suspicion. I just didn't like her hanging around my son, is all."

Blonde hair flashed in Henry's mind and taffy pink lips twisted into a provoking smirk.

"Of course." He squeezed the muscle of his jaw.

Silence filling the room, she gave a half smile and opened the door wider, as if to say, *we're done.* So, Henry smoothed out the front of his suit and walked back down the steps with his hand wrapped around the railing.

Once they reached the front entrance, he turned back and extended his hand out to her. "If you think of anything else, call Sheriff Green and he'll pass it along to me, or you can ask to talk to me directly."

"Thank you."

Then, beginning to make his way back to his car, he suddenly turned back. "Any chance Blossom James is related to the woman--Sophie--James, who works at The Diner? The place at the edge of town?"

Her hand already itching to close the door, Mrs. Clemmington tilted her head slightly and blinked. "Well, yeah, she's Sophie's daughter."

"Huh." Henry looked at his shoes. "Thank you." He then waved, and Mrs. Clemmington finally closed the door with a nod. Locking both the deadbolt and handle. Something so small, something before she hadn't thought to do, but now with the blinds drawn and the porch lights off, she retreated into the isolation of her home.

After visiting Luke Roberts's house and speaking with his parents—asking who he could have been meeting at the playground just a five minute walk from their house in the dead of night—Henry pulled into the hotel's parking lot. The warm light radiating from inside, reaching over into the glove compartment on the passenger's side and taking out his spare bottle of medication, he popped three, dog kibble-sized pills into his mouth. Throwing his head back to down them with the leftover coffee he arrived with; three cigarettes still sizzling in the murky leftovers of clumped ash. Black streaking the sides of the yellow-stained foam, when he swallowed, *hard,* the ash stung the back of his throat worse than alcohol, nearly making him throw up. His neck strained, Henry coughed and cringed, shuddering against the taste before throwing the bottle back into the compartment, slamming it shut, and turning off the engine; the darkness that surrounded the car no longer being fought off by the blinding white headlights, submerging him.

Two hours later, he put the hotel phone back down with the beeping of the dead line droning in his ears, having just ordered room service for a single bowl of Kellogg's Pops Cereal. Standing next to the bed, Henry then looked over the sprawled contents from the box Norman gave him back in the parking lot of the hospital, all the while the tv buzzed with colored, hazy captures of recorded interviews with both boys' sets of friends, their family members, three girls—including Becky Stephens, who claimed Andrew was more interested in her than she was of him and that he never really got over the breakup —alongside a tape of Norman and his team going through the houses of the victims.

Combing a hand through his hair, Henry pulled the two-finger glass of bourbon whiskey from the bedside table and finished it; hints of vanilla, caramel, honey and oak leaving a smokey tint to his next breath. Due to the simplicity of his order or perhaps the fact that the Hotel's staff had ample time to put it together considering the time, it wasn't long before he received his makeshift dinner.

After pouring himself another bourbon and sitting with pillows propped against his shoulders, coffee going cold beside him, earbuds in, he held a folder between his hands. Absent-mindedly reaching into the white bowl of Pops and crunching down on the textured puffed flakes, the sugary sweet flavor melting into a chewy corn as he smoked himself—and drank himself—to sleep in between bites. Allowing the energy of this place… The Town, to seep into the marrow of his bones. Slowly becoming as familiar as his own childhood, yet distant and strange.

Seven

Eight days later, entering the wooden, cabin-like interior of the station, yellow light poured over Henry and the smell of fresh coffee replaced the thick dryness of swirling ash at the back of his throat. He slung his jacket over his arm, biting down on the foam end of the bud between his teeth and moved past the wine-red brick of a fireplace to his left, where stacked magazines were sorted over a glass coffee table and two leather arm chairs were placed.

Walking from around the front desk, holding a silver coffee tumbler close to his chest and wearing a thin, pressed charcoal grey button up shirt tucked into navy blue jeans with the scent of sandalwood, lavender, black pepper and oak moss coming from the witch-hazel based aftershave he applied before arriving to the station, Norman spoke clear and eager. "Morning, stranger. Get breakfast yet?"

Turning his head slightly, Henry cracked a smile despite the coldness in his eyes. "Morning, and no, just coffee."

"Still not a morning person?"

"I suppose not."

The idea that perhaps the Agent merely sustained himself on caffeine and the ash from his nicotine addiction being reinforced, he nodded. "Well, if you get hungry, there's some in the fridge. Not much, but Abby brought in some of these Cinnamon-Pecan buns—made them herself—and muffins. Had to put some aside for you to keep the other boys from wolfing everything down."

Following him back to the conference room, Henry recalled the first time he walked into the station and how Norman had told him about Abby, the girl who worked the front desk—attempting to fill the gaps of their conversation by telling him, *"we always joke with her that she looks like a lawyer and that's what she should be doing instead of herding us around all day, but she's a sweet girl,"*—which made him wonder if he spoke of every woman he encountered like that or if there was possibly something more to his charm.

Piles of reports scattered next to yellow notepads over the surface of the polished teakwood table, black smeared ink scribbled along the faint blue lines, when Henry passed the box of Twizzlers that lay next to the unplugged coffee machine (a sticky note stuck to the pot that read: *I'm broken :(sorry!*) he, as usual, traded his cigarette for the hollow and textured candy. Tearing off chunks as it melted against his tongue, chewing softly on the strawberry, artificially flavored corn syrup, alongside wheat flour, sugar, cornstarch, Red Forty and soy lecithin while Norman moved toward the table, pulling out a chair.

With a single window that overlooked the trees (as everything in the Town seemed to do, wherever you went) a cool light filled the room and the two cardboard boxes Norman and him had been working on remained in the center of the table. The first time he had been in the room, it was clear they hadn't used it for some time.

The white board at the opposite wall becoming littered by autopsy photos, crime scene photos as well as portraits, the two continued their work until lunchtime, which passed with as much excitement as watching water boil. The tension between the FBI agent who radiated a frenzied appetite for deviancy and the small town, disheartened Sheriff slowly spilling over into acute agitation as Norman fought against the urge to ask him if all the fanciful protocols and wandering hypotheses—near similar to the ones he had spewed during his first day—were actually helping. Just as Norman's blood pressure spiked and his temples began to pinch with a looming headache, there was a soft knock on the door.

After introducing him around the station, standing in the conference room, Henry told Norman he went through the files the previous night, to which he asked, "notice anything?" And Henry nodded toward where he, before his arrival, put pictures of the boys up.

"Nothing more than what we discussed at the Diner. But the first thing we need to ask is, why?"

"I thought we were already asking that."

"Not in that *way. We need to look for what separates them from anyone else, and for specific qualities that'll possibly help up narrow the pool of potential victims. Much like looking at the qualities for a significant other, the victim portrays... Drives. Only, the target on these victims are tied to the killer's motive—their conflict—it's clear even now that our killer is making a statement, proving a point, perhaps. That can help narrow the victim pool as well. Whoever fits that narrative."*

"Do you think these are... Sexually driven?" Norman asked, surprised how quickly Henry had jumped in.

"There's something more. It's not just about getting a rush, or getting off from the act of killing... So we're not dealing with a primarily lust killer. Though there are shared elements. You know, this type of behavior most often mirrors the personality of the perpetrator, so, we're looking for something more... Subliminal. Between the lines. Sure there's sexual aggression, but why? That's what we want to know. That's our motive, the spark that leads to the fire."

"Alright."

"Next, we're going to want to go back over the reports you've piled together and Frank's autopsy, just to make sure we nailed everything. If you think of something—no

matter how wild, or seemingly impossible, you write it down. You hash it out. Nothing is off the table with these guys." Henry, almost having forgotten that he was carrying a cigarette, brought it back to his lips. *"From there, if we haven't caught the guy already, we can build a profile. It won't give us the identity of the guy, but it'll help us narrow the unique qualities of such a person."* He finally turned back to Norman, making eye contact. *"Did you get that list going? Any peeping-toms? Stalkers? We're going to want to look at anyone whose characteristics of crimes could relate to characteristics seen at the crime scenes."*

"Maybe a few guys, but again, not that serious of stuff. Not things I can remember off the top of my head, anyway."

"As well all know, the human information-processing system and memory is faulty, so don't beat yourself up about it too much. There's a reason witness testimonies land innocent people behind bars."

"That's reassuring." Norman commented, watching Henry turn back to the display of grotesque images of murdered teenage boys with his head tilting to the side before sighing, *"I should go make some more coffee."*

"That one's broken." Henry looked to the back counter. Norman—already making his way back to the door—rolled his eyes with a quick breath.

"There's another machine in the lounge."

When the handle turned, Abby poked her head in, giving a short-lived, small smile and saying, "sorry to

interrupt but, Mrs. Cooper is here and she says it's urgent."
As Norman bit back a short-fused, *oh thank god* that rang
through his ears and stood from his chair, leaving chunks of
oily, grilled slabs of cilantro and lime-drizzled salmon
caught over the weekend in a small glass bowl that his
wife, Stacy, had packed him alongside baked chickpeas,
sliced avocado and soft pita bread dipped into her
homemade hummus. He could still taste the lingering green
onion and garlic, shards of mashed almond against his teeth
while turning the corner to see Mrs. Cooper pacing
restlessly by the entrance.

"Norman—" She breathed out.

"Mrs. Cooper, is everything okay?"

She barely paid any attention to Henry, who hovered in
the hallway, overhearing the two's hurried conversation as
she explained that her son, Ethan, hadn't come home last
night. "I went to bed last night and thought maybe he was
just staying back with some friends, you know teenage
boys, they hardly tell you a thing until after the fact. Maybe
there was something that ran late with football practice,
right?"

"Absolutely." Norman nodded with his arms folded
over his chest. "And he still wasn't home this morning?"

"I called the school and he didn't show up for
homeroom. I got this gut wrenching feeling…" There was a
slight hiccup in her voice. She exhaled, trying to steady her
heart before continuing. "He never makes his bed, but when
I saw it had hardly been touched—that nothing was moved,

not even the pillows... I just felt there was something... *Wrong*. I know it. I can *feel it,* Norman." Her eyes wide, her posture leaned forward as if she was about to collapse to her knees. Pleading for Norman to offer reassurance. "I can't find him anywhere."

Henry interjected, "we'll go to the school and see if anyone's seen him, talk to his friends, anyone that may know." And looking over his shoulder for a moment before turning back to her, placing a comforting hand on the woman's shoulder, Norman agreed.

"Is there anywhere your son might try and run off to? Any immediate friends that he would be in contact with?"

"Any of the boys on the football team... I-I don't..." Clearly in distress, she shook her head, and Norman waved her off.

"We'll figure it out. You go home, try and relax, alright? I'll let you know if and *when* we find out anything. Everything is going to be okay. Just go home."

"With everything—With Andrew, and Luke—those poor boys—"

"There's no reason to think anything like that has happened to your son. He's probably just ditching school with some of the other guys, or with a girl. We'll find him. Just go home, take it easy, and trust me. Can you do that?"

Standing at five foot six, her eyes lingered to Norman's chest before she lifted her chin and gave a cloudy-eyed nod. Turning slowly and walking with a bruised tenderness to her gate. Once out of view from the entrance, Henry walked up next to Norman, who fought the urge to look at him.

"We find this boy *alive,* Henry."

"I didn't say anything." He responded gently before turning against his heel and going to grab his things.

Eight

Watching the student somberly pick himself from his seat, pushing his hands against the wooden armrests before closing the door behind him, Henry kicked his shoes up against the table and raised his brows toward Norman—who was seated in the corner—while leaning back with an open file in his lap. His eyes then going down the list of names that he and Norman had compiled throughout the previous set of interviews. "Nice kid." He dipped his head to the side in question. "Capable of murder?"

"That's not why we're here. We're looking for anything that could help us find Ethan."

"We're looking for a body, *sheriff*—A body that could very much lead us to the *killer.*"

"And you'd like that *so* much, wouldn't you?"

"You know each and every one of them so well to vouch for their innocence?" Henry pushed. "I'm just stating the obvious. Our killer isn't one to lengthen the process. They bite, they kill. They go for the throat, Norman, and they don't play with their food."

"Enough with the damn metaphors, alright? I've been working this case since that first boy showed up. I grew up in this town. I know these people and they aren't *bad*, Henry. Give them a chance."

Pulling back slightly, he gave Norman the benefit of the doubt. "Now, I'm not saying *all* of them are bad, but not all of them are good either. Prank gone bad, peer pressure, these kids will do just about anything to stay within the mold. To not jeopardize their *in-group* status. Practically everybody will. And pardon my expression, but one bad fucking apple and the whole lot goes rotten. All it takes is *one,* and that's what we're dealing with." He emphasized his words, looking back down at the file before his finger landed on the next name down from the last student's, and he furrowed his brows. "Blossom James." He muttered.

Norman pinched between his brows, sitting forward with his elbows on his knees. Then, Henry's voice lingering in the air, cooled by the buzzing of the A.C overhead, he glanced up after rubbing his palm over his face. "Yeah, she went out with Ethan for a little bit over last summer. About a month."

Henry frowned slightly, clearing his throat. "Mrs. Clemmington brought her up when I visited. Andrew hung around her."

"Yeah—" Norman blinked, lowering his hand. "Wait, when did you do that?"

Henry tossed the folder back to the table. "I went as soon as we left the hospital. Thought we wouldn't have any time to waste for me to spend it catching up, which, apparently we didn't, given our killer stuck to his schedule. So, I suppose we should go grab Ms. James?"

Nodding, Norman stood from his seat and slipped silently out the door. Venturing down the polished, locker-lined hallways with steady, sweeping steps toward the front office—where he grabbed Blossom's current hour—he filled his lungs with the scent of bleached tile, lingering cheap cologne alongside whatever was being sold in the cafeteria; a mix of onions and pizza, melted cheese and microwaved beef.

Back in the makeshift conference room the principle had facilitated for the two men to conduct their interviews with anyone they could think of—alongside whoever was mentioned that could have a part in Ethan's whereabouts—Henry's feet fell from the desk. He got up from the chair and, walking over to the window, where the greyed out streams of sunlight from the afternoon collection of puffy clouds shone hazy from open blinds, looked out across the trees toward the town center.

Pulling out a cigarette—quickly noticing that he was almost out—Henry lit it with the snap of his thumb. The soft tissue of his lungs stretching, filling with smoke before the next few minutes passed and Norman returned; the sound of the door opening causing Henry to look over his shoulder with the cool hue of the sun highlighting the streaked grey above his ears, contrasting the sharpness of his face and making the shadows run deeper.

Seeing that no one was behind him before the door closed, Henry turned the rest of his body away from the window so he was facing Norman and asked, "well, where's Blossom?"

Norman's expression that of a slight confusion and resentment, he showed a submission to the situation that Henry would not find himself. "She's not here."

"What do you *mean* she's not here? Where is she?"

Henry surged forward, an unknown rumbling of anger in his bones at the coating of mysteriousness this girl had apparently encased herself in. He put out his fresh cigarette against an ash tray at the corner of the desk before passing Norman and opening the door.

"I don't know-" Norman followed close as Henry made his way to the front of the school.

"Don't you guys keep a sign in and sign out sheet or something?" His gritted his teeth, frustration spilling from him. *Haven't they heard there was a god damn killer on the loose?* Stopping at the counter where two middle aged women sat, they looked up at him when he asked, "hi, ladies. Can you tell me if a Blossom James has passed through here? Checked out for the day? She's not in class and we need to speak to her regarding Ethan Cooper's disappearance."

Blinking from behind fingerprint smeared, round glasses that magnified her eyes and wearing a loose, blousy shirt left collecting dust as the years passed, the woman to Henry's right leaned close to her computer. "Oh my... Let me see." She said before leaning back and checking a clipboard that hung from the wall—the sign in and out sheet, which was littered by blotchy scribbles of black and blue pen—then shook her head. The woman to Henry's left chewed annoyingly loud on a piece of gum, looking at him with a slacken jaw and dazed eyes. "Uh, nothing here. Would you like me to call her home?"

"That would be great, thank you."

"Henry, it's *Blossom James.*" He crossed his arms over his chest and arched a brow.

Henry scowled slightly at him. "What do you mean? You're not surprised?"

"Not in the slightest. She's probably off with a boy, getting herself—and others—into trouble."

"Even more reason we should be pushing for her to come forward."

Norman smirked slightly, thinking, *if only he knew.* "Good luck with that."

Henry let out a forced breath, amusement lifting the edges of his tone. "You're acting like she's completely uncontrollable."

"Because she *is*."

Henry looked back with a tinted frantic look to his gaze at the woman who set the phone down. "Anything?"

"I'm sorry." She frowned.

Norman's hands then fell back to his side, where they rested habitually around his belt, thumb grazing the clip to his gun. "Let's finish with the other interviews, Henry. Just like you said before, we shouldn't be wasting any more time than we have." He said. A moment later, after Norman pushed, "let's *go,*" Henry thanked the two women and followed reluctantly, not willing to further argue with Norman in case he decided to suddenly ask why Henry was so bent on meeting this girl, when Henry couldn't even form a reason himself; the idea of Blossom so abstract he wondered, fleetingly as the two made their way back to the room, if she was even real.

Nine

The hotel's restaurant was just as busy as it was in the mornings, only, now with the lights dimmed and white vanilla scented candles lit along the walls as well as in the middle of cranberry red tablecloths, thick-cut meats were served on large plates paired with roasted, salted squares of medley potatoes and root vegetables.

Squishy, orange butternut squash, baked carrots, cut green beans and bright red bell peppers with caramel-glazed brussel sprouts and scoops of lavender-steamed, sticky white rice bunched on plates accented by an assortment of different colored, thick sauces; carmine yellows and blueberry reds, apple cider vinaigrettes dribbled over the bright yellow kale and spinach mixes of side salads dusted by pumpkin seeds and spiced tofu while wine glasses clicked with spidering strings of dry red blends.

Dressed in a taffy and periwinkle floral minidress that fell midway down her thighs, ruffled at the bottom with a peasant bodice and blousy sleeves cinched above her elbows, Blossom walked into the lobby where despite the nearing heat of summer, the flames of a grand, aged walnut fireplace licked the walls of dark, ash-stained brick; casting hues of flickering tangerine oranges alongside tints of candy apple red over the surrounding guests who huddled with iced bourbon in crystal glasses. Compared to the chic, done-up look to those around her who adorned shades of mulberry purples and midnight blues, with the smell of the afternoon rain still clinging to the loose curls of white hair brushing the pointedness of her shoulders, Blossom brought the freshness of springtime into the Evergreen Hotel, and with it, the allure of innocence.

Henry sat alone at a table in the far left corner, by one of the windows that sloped upward into the tall trees from a landscaped garden and outside lounge area, stone steps leading into a pit filled with logs eaten away by blue flames. His fork scraping against the inside of a bowl filled with seared and stripped steak that bled with pink-tinted myoglobin into crisp, golden potatoes and crunchy cloves of garlic glazed by butter sauce, he shoved some into his mouth. Chewing slowly, his brows stitched together with a deepened crease between them, taking note of the flavors coating his tongue as his hunger was finally satiated.

The sharp edge of his Adam's apple lifting, he swallowed and reached over, grabbing the white mug his coffee had been served in. Blotched by stains of brown splatters, the sides tinted a slight, paper-white from years of being poorly cleaned, when Henry glanced over the rim, his eyes suddenly came into focus on a girl—the girl he saw back in the Diner when he first met with Norman —Blossom James. He lowered the coffee from his lips, setting down his mug while swallowing the bitterness with a forced exhale.

The flame in the middle of the table flickering and bouncing, puffing with a thin trail of smoke dissipating above it, Henry leaned back, flattening his tie after taking notice to the pink candle.

"You must be Blossom James." He spoke up. "You weren't at school today."

"I was there." She batted her lashes, taking a seat in front of him. Henry felt his throat begin to tighten and cleared it. "I saw you and Norman were interviewing kids."

"Pity you couldn't stick around then."

She shrugged, lifting her shoulders softly before dropping them back down. She had her hands in her lap, twisting the fabric of her dainty dress between blushed knuckles."You guys are looking for Ethan?"

"Heard you knew him."

"Everyone did, he was the Town's little *golden* boy." Henry caught the sarcastic twinge to her words.

"You say it like he's already dead."

"We have a killer on the loose. I'm simply speaking as it is."

"And what is that?"

"Are you interrogating me?"

"Simply following your lead."

Blossom crossed her arms over her chest. "You don't strike me as someone who follows other's leads or takes orders so easily, a man like *you*."

"You don't know me." Henry shook his head.

"I know men like you, Special Agent."

"I'm sure you do." Even from where he sat he could smell the floral aroma of her perfume filling his skin with a buzzing warmth. There was something fragmented in her eyes. Her manicured brows softened, they reflected a certain romanticism, sparking a swirling dizziness in his head. "But please," he waved his hand. "Henry."

"*Henry.*" She repeated. Henry pulled his lips up, smiling with the glint of coffee stained teeth.

After a small pause, Henry set his elbows onto the table, straightening his shoulders. "So, why did the two of you split up?"

"Lost interest, I guess."

"Hm." He nodded. "With anyone now?"

The corner of her lips twitched into a smirk. "Fortunately, no."

He in the middle of taking another sip of coffee when he raised his brows. "Oh? I saw some banners at the school. Isn't the end of year formal coming up? Surprised no one's asked you yet."

"They have." She paused, lingering eyes sending Henry almost spiraling. He reached to his right, taking another gulp of coffee with shaky fingers. "Just haven't found the right one."

"Picky with your food."

"If you'd call it that."

"What made you lose interest?"

"He didn't satisfy me anymore. Got all soft."

"Soft? You mean... Emotional?"

"No, he just didn't *fuck* me anymore." She leaned forward. "Does that make you uncomfortable?" Henry narrowed his gaze before swallowing, but didn't say anything, so Blossom squinted gently and forgave him with as much cutesy acquiescence as someone who already knew the answer and simply asked out of vindictive, *I'm not angry, I'm just disappointed*-ness. "It's fine if it does. Every man seems uncomfortable by that stuff."

"Who said I was uncomfortable? I just didn't answer your question." He wouldn't call it that, but something was happening. He shifted in his seat and fought against it, feeling the prickling of a cold sweat against his temple.

Silence transpiring between the two, her finger trailed down the napkin that still held untouched utensils, unwrapping it with a pinch of her polished nails before grabbing the fork.

"May I?" She then asked.

Henry cocked a brow and pushed his bowl slightly forward. "Help yourself."

She went for one of the thick strips of meat, quickly biting into the tough steak and sitting back down after reaching over the table. Working her jaw and humming in satisfaction with a certain morbidity to the way she released a teasing moan, a pleasured sigh, a tantalizing breath, when she swallowed Henry couldn't help but picture the shredded flesh, sticky with mucous and indented by her teeth, moving down the peristaltic waves of her esophagus. He tore his eyes away.

Blossom set her fork down, looking at the man with her elbows propped up and her finger sliding against the dip below her bottom lip from the corner of her mouth, wiping free any remaining sweetness of the buttery sauce that coated the food. Beneath the table, her legs crossed, she then began to carefully kick her heel free from her shoe, slowly lifting her toes to graze the inside of the Agent's knee before he snapped his eyes back up at her. Widening them, his jaw clenched, still, he neglected to move.

He was paralyzed there, feeling her rub her foot up his thigh and back down, dangerously close to where the fabric of his trousers tightened. Nearly convinced he was simply hallucinating the interaction.

"Ms. *James*—" He warned, a slight choking of his voice making it weaker. His chest rose and fell heavily.

"Do *you* like me, Henry?" Blossom tugged at the inner lining of his pants with her toes.

His eyes fluttering closed, he licked his lips, feeling her retract her foot before hushing, "I-I don't know you."

However, when Henry opened his eyes again, Blossom had disappeared back into the crowd. Leaving merely a lipstick smear on a fork and the burning in his core.

A resigned exhale leaving him, his brows pulled together in confusion, he quickly reached down, grasping the serviette from his lap and crumpled the sage-colored napkin onto the table. His eyes lingering at the barely dented bowl of food for a few seconds.

It almost resembled a soup: drenched in the oil and fat and blood, the yellow potatoes tinted a slight red. And with the aftertaste of iron on his breath, Henry suddenly felt sick to his stomach.

Moving from the dining area through the lobby to the elevator until he safely hid himself within the confines of his hotel room, he proceeded to pace at the entrance, clenching his fists by his sides and shaking his head. Then, walking over to the bed, sitting restlessly on the edge, he cursed the dull throb he could feel deep in his pelvis. Falling with a huff onto his back.

His eyes closed, his fingers crawled to the stiffened bulge at the front of his trousers and he slowly unclasped his belt, the pressure releasing as a low whine escaped him. Meanwhile, he couldn't help but think of Blossom.

The smell of her perfume intoxicating him, his mind swam with the picture of her, this girl he heard so much of, yet hardly knew, had *just* met, walking up to his room in that tiny floral dress.

Fitting himself in his hand sloppily, hurriedly tugging and pulling as if to draw out something deep inside him, a thick ropey string that coiled in his belly, soon, with each harsh yank of his palm and squeeze of his fingers under the rim of his slick, drooling head, his jaw squeezed and a tight, animalistic groan escaped his chest. Impatient, disgusted, choking on his breath and feeling his heart thumping in his ears, his mind flashing with depraved, destructive and crude, all-consuming, fleeting images of the girl, this pleasure wasn't leisurely. It was a release of pent up greed and impulse, of unwanted desires and gross fantasy that had slowly begun to wrap itself around Henry since he first saw Blossom in the Diner. Like a thick root burying itself deep inside him, as if he was made of rotten, wet soil.

It was the raw heat that itched under the calloused patches of his rough paws and the aching emptiness of his chest since he first caught the scent of her. "F-Fuck-" Henry gulped. His limbs shaking, his open lips glistened just as his cheeks and forehead did with sweat.

Satisfaction at bay, yet not nearly as close as he would have liked, his toes curled and his knees lifted slightly. Legs splayed out in front of him like butterfly wings and his trousers caught just below the crease of his hips.

With the next stroke of his thumb across the overstimulated bundle of nerves, his eyes rolled back as he attempted to reach for his climax. He *hated* this.

The image of Blossom burning at the back of his mind and throat even stronger than the booze he managed to down just moments before his tingling fingers found their way to the thin fabric of his boxers, with the cool air streaming in from outside, the sounds of owls and crickets washing through his numbed mind, he gritted his teeth until his jaw ached, seething, pumping himself free of every foul thought that had crossed his mind. And as if tearing, clawing its way from his lungs, Henry then groaned, loud and desperate, "B-Blossom-" The taste of her name as sweet as the frost-glazing of strawberry filled cake, flowering in his chest until it choked him. He repeated it in such ways he wished had been stroked by *her* touch instead of his, finally letting out a harsh growl as his fingers achieved the relief he long sought for, thick droplets of cum milking from the contracting muscles of his shaft and soaking into the sheets beneath him.

Staring up at the ceiling in a daze, Henry thought, just for a moment, by the slight glint of the light shining down through the shadows, that he could see Blossom above him. A trick of the light, of his imagination, still, he felt his heart squeeze and whispered her name once more. Closing his eyes to the picture of her above him, her blonde hair falling in thick bounds over his face, her cheeks blushed and her moans wetting his ear.

Ten

If you were to head toward town center, toward the Diner and the sheriff's station, the entertainment center—which held the skating rink, arcade and bowling alley—attached to the shopping mall that held maximum fifty shops to its name, then took a left and followed the white, chipped wooden fences alongside narrow, winding roads, you would find yourself at the house Blossom James lived in; nestled in the back of the town, snug between fine lines of hazy monetary differences and hidden by the larger and more grandeur, doll-like houses in front of it, painted by shades of prettier blues and greens, whites that somehow stayed pristine through the whole year.

Green vines wrapping around the walls and encasing it with blooming flowers, if ever spoken of, the house would be described as a rather plain, boxy townhome with baby blue accenting white banisters, the type you'd imagine Little Red Riding Hood stumbling upon, an apricot pie still warm from the oven sitting on the ledge of a cracked window with trails of steam swirling above it.

Cutting across the lawn, stepping across the grass and moving up the cement path lined by potted plants and chipped, soil-crusted garden gnomes toward the white porch, Blossom dipped her hand into the skirt pocket of her dress. Her fingers grazing the surface of a smooth, flimsy polaroid before pulling a jagged silver key out so she could unlock the front door.

Inside, stiff curtains were drawn over dust-lined windows and the hardwood floors creaked as she made her way to the kitchen. With Sophie still at the Diner until well past midnight and into the early morning, having taken up (another) night shift, Blossom prepared herself dinner by dumping clumps of cold, leftover meatloaf with spears of broccoli and steamed white rice into a bowl. Drowning the contents in pizza sauce before sticking the food in the microwave for two minutes.

While waiting, she plucked a small clementine from the fruit bowl alongside a packet of peanut butter from the pantry.

Seeing the Agent made her hungry.

After squirting the oily substance onto the flat of her tongue, she swallowed down the leftover clumps from behind her gums with the swipe of her tongue over her teeth, scraping every drop from the plastic packet by biting down before—leaning against the coffee dusted countertops—plopping the separated slices of clementine into her mouth. The microwave going off, she then tossed the torn peels onto the counter and quickly licked her fingers before absent-mindedly drying them against the front of her dress skirt.

Lifting the steaming contents into her bare hands—the heat that radiated from the bowl burning into her palms—she took a seat at the empty kitchen table and finally stabbed her fork into the mushy loaf, breaking it apart into smaller chunks with the grains of rice turned spongey, stickier from the sauce. Scooping them into her mouth, chewing through the gummy texture while the outside of the meat burnt the inside of her cheeks, still the middle was cold and she redirected her attention to the window, where, visible through half-shaded blinds, the moonlight covered the trees in cool blue tones, making the shadows stretch over them in a swirling black abyss that seemed to engulf the Town.

The bowl cleaned by unsatisfied fingers scooping up the remnants of smeared pizza sauce and crumbled meat, after she finished, Blossom went to grab an oversized t-shirt from her drawer alongside fresh panties, locking herself in the bathroom and letting the delicate fabric of her dress fall around her ankles before sweeping it, alongside her pink, lace panties, to the side while unclasping the hooks of her bra.

Stepping into the tub, she twisted the faucet to the left, allowing the ice cold water to fall down the curve of her back. Then, leaning her head back, Blossom closed her eyes. Wetting her hair until her teeth chattered and her scalp went numb.

Her skin stripped raw, goosebumps covering her belly, arms, thighs, her nipples hardened and her temples tingling, adrenaline coursing through her veins, after finishing her shower Blossom stood in front of the mirror. Resting her weight into her arms with white knuckles and a clenched jaw, her t-shirt clinging to her wet frame while she gripped the edges of the pink porcelain sink. Tears threatening to break, stinging her eyes, she squeezed her jaw tighter and shook her head. Breathing out with the softness of a flowering bruise, tender and hesitant.

Huffing, her shoulders falling, she then lifted her hands from the sink and held them—palms exposed—out in front of her. Looking down at them for a moment before closing her eyes.

Feeling the buzzing under her skin, the itch that somehow, she couldn't ever quite reach, Blossom thought about how it must feel to watch red splatter over the pink porcelain, how it must feel to scrub clots from between her blushed knuckles—the warmth—the release, and took another deep breath. The images in her head dissipating back into reality when she finally reopened her eyes and lowered her hands, with the scent of honey-lemon from the air freshener, her cheeks blotched red, she stared into the mirror.

These images, violent, harsh, grotesque, lingering at the back of her mind and flickering on at random points in the day, had taken hold of her ever since the age of fourteen when she learned what men want when they touched the small of her back and allowed their warm, rum-stained breath to hit the soft skin of her cheek.

Sometimes, lost so deep in their grip, she could still feel the stickiness of the man's seed that smeared against her belly and taste his drunkenness against her lips as he kissed her slowly. She could still feel the heat of him filling her insides, stretching her muscles open for him as if he was breaking into the locks of a gate, inviting himself inside her walls.

The man, one of her father's colleagues from the hotel, the first of them, had followed Blossom upstairs, pinned her down onto the squealing springs of her bed, and had thrust his hips into her frail body with loud grunts. She recalled that his touch was angry, impatient, and that he had told her to shut up; not listening to her cries of protest, all the while her mother sat downstairs talking to his wife. A dizzying amount of white wine melting down the sides of her glass. That's all she could remember, really. His voice in her head, telling her those things. Telling her how bad he had wanted her for all those years, watching, waiting.

He had hunted her, preyed on her. But from then on, she developed a sense of how to use her body to manipulate the minds of men into thinking they could pollinate her flowers, take her honey, and drink her sugar as if they owned her. She learned to use the gentleness of her fingertips for grazing the scruff of overaged men who quivered at the sight of her and wished they were forty years younger and the fluttering of her eyes, the sweetness of her kiss, the shape of her breasts and the inner of her thighs to then make them submit to the hatred she felt for them.

From then on, *she* allowed *them* to bury themselves in her body, and while they thought they were in control, that they could *take* from her, she was really consuming them. Taking everything they had, gulping them up, eating them alive.

Baring her teeth and lifting, then softening her brow, Blossom twisted her lips into a glaring smile. Putting on different expressions until her cheeks went numb and her mouth fell into a deep, upside down U, such as a party clown. Unable to smile anymore, she let out a shaky exhale. Reaching down into the drawer to her right and squeezing a droplet of concealer onto the back of her palm.

Smearing the makeup over marble skin designed to reflect others' emotions like a mirror, hiding the lavender streaks under her eyes as well as any evidence of the tightness in her chest and the way her throat felt as if someone had poured hot cement into it, preventing her from screaming as it solidified into stone—screaming so loud the mountains would weep for her and blood would spray onto the dirty mirror and the goddamn world would know her pain—instead, her eyes a vast, empty void, she blended the concealer into her jaw and pulled her lips into another smile, this time, though, it was gentle. Subliminal.

Eleven

Streams of mustard yellow sunlight seeping over him, Henry woke late the next morning as a bruising exhale left his dry lips, the craving for a cigarette making his fingers itch and the lack of caffeine in his system making a headache bloom at the base of his skull.

Squinted eyes looking down at the aftermath of last night, left untouched, he grimaced from repulsion and cursed himself, gruffly pushing himself up with stiff joints and muscles taut from the uncomfortable position he had unconsciously pulled himself into before making his way to the bathroom. Stripping of the wrinkled clothes he failed to discard the night before then proceeding to scrub away the rehydrated, viscous liquid that crusted over his stomach and thighs with oat milk and blackberry soap, he wished at the same time to scrub away the shame and guilt that accompanied the prodding memory of what he had done. What had *made* him do it.

To wash it down the drain with the splattering, steaming hot water that fell around his feet.

Beads of sweat and water sliding down the sides of his temples while strands of dripping hair fell before his eyes, with exhaustion clinging to him like wet rags, weighing down the movements of his limbs, Henry leaned his forehead against the wet tile. Rubbing away the sleep in his eyes while the temperature of the water blistered his red-blotched skin and distracted him from his thoughts; suddenly craving the Diner's staple banana bread French toast with caramel sauce, candied pecans, and whipped Mascarpone cheese, as well as a much needed cup of coffee.

The clock striking near 12:30 p.m when he entered the Diner with the chime of the bell, Henry's stomach growled again with the fact that he failed to finish his dinner the night before.

He first spotted a middle aged woman with a book pressed open under her palm, picking at a piece of crumbled avocado toast to her left, a half-filled iced latte melting down to her right while behind her, an older man —Mr. Jones, the same man who had walked into the Diner upon Henry's first day in the Town—filled out the day's word puzzle with black ink bleeding through the thin pages of the newspaper. Henry's gaze slowly turning to the counter, with the skip of his heart and nauseating sensation of butterflies in his stomach, a sudden striking of nervousness then pinched his nerves when he saw Blossom.

Wearing a macaron-pink, frothy dress that puffed with delicate fabric from thin straps, the length frilling out to her ankles where lime green socks had been pulled up from white sneakers, she sat cross legged with her hair held back by pink metal clips. Cheeks pinched with a blotched rosiness that also tinted her pointed nose; resembling a girl's play doll with porcelain smooth skin.

The look offered a glaring contrast against of how she looked just the night before, or how Henry had consequently imagined her following their meeting. The errant, reprehensible memory making goosebumps melt down his arms as he walked over to her, knowing it was fruitless to try to avoid their next encounter, even when he felt himself flush with heat and a hesitance toward the idea of her possibly being able to tell how he had satisfied himself toward the thought of her, especially when she had so brazenly approached him, Henry's eyes shifted over to the immense amount of food surrounding her: golden, fluffy pancakes dusted with powdered sugar and topped by pink discolored whipped cream, a spoonful of homemade, canned strawberries contrasting bright red and trickling down the sides, soaking at the bottom of the plate; roasted sweet potato hash browns with smeared splatters of thick ketchup melting from the heat, green slices of fresh avocado mashed to the top of the patty, the oil glistening beneath the overhead lighting; poached eggs over toasted rye bread with tomato paste and basil sprinkled over the oozing yellow yolks that dripped from stems of arugula; and an almond chocolate croissant, the middle seeping from a flaky, soft exterior.

Arriving at her side, Henry stopped and subsequently widened his eyes, seeing directly in front of her was a thick-cut of grilled steak next to a milky scoop of buttered white, mashed potatoes. Before looking up at him, Blossom carved her knife into the loin, cutting with small, precise sawing motions, the silver blade falling through a juicy piece of fat that bubbled like a sponge, hitting the plate before she lifted the meat to her mouth and ground it up between her teeth.

She consumed it, as if it wasn't meat at all.

A droplet of the juice catching her bottom lip, wiping the back of her hand across her mouth, Henry could hear the alarmingly crude sounds of her back molars working the tissue apart with an almost bloodthirsty characteristic to the way she already tore another piece from the whole, raising it halfway to her mouth while she made eye contact. "Special Agent." Flashing pearl-white teeth, bits of meat stuck between them, pink to the gums, she took the next bite while still looking at him, surprisingly unforgiving in her appetite, or in the way she gulped down the food and without hesitation, reached for more.

Satisfying herself in front of him.

Henry motioned to the stool next to hers, asking, "may I?"

And a harsh swallow later, she responded. But he had already begun to lower himself, smoothing out his tie in the process. "It *is* a public space."

"Just being polite."

Using the same knife to take apart the pancakes, she washed down the salty umami taste of the meat with the sweetness of rich strawberry syrup. "You don't fool me as someone too concerned with politeness, Special Age-" Blossom caught herself just as he had done the night before. "*Henry.*"

His stomach knotted at the sound of her saying his name as a woman—not Sophie—walked over to him. However, he forgot about his craving for actual food as he was then filled with a nauseating sense of dread and simply ordered coffee, watching Blossom dip two fingers into the gravy that pooled around the steak and coated the mashed white potatoes.

Sucking lightly around her knuckles, when she released them, a popping sound emitted from her pursed lips and they glistened as if he had just caught her in the act of licking up the remnants of glossy cum from her chin. Consequently, his cheeks burned with a slackened jaw and he felt as if he needed to apologize, turn away, get up and leave.

Despite having insinuated himself into her morning, Blossom seemed to remain in control over him, a power he didn't remember giving.

Henry lowered his eyes toward the coffee that had been slid in front of him, pulling his brows together with confusion, creating a deep crease above the prominent, thin bridge of his nose as he attempted to recollect when in fact it was poured. Nonetheless, staring into the black liquid, he couldn't.

"I'm sorry, I'm famished." Blossom spoke shyly, running her tongue over her gums.

But you're not sorry. Why would you be?

"Have you not eaten?"

"Here and there." She shrugged back at him, cutting the last bit of steak before setting the knife to the counter, causing a wave of relief to shoot down Henry's spine. Reaching into his pocket, he then fetched a cigarette. It was the only thing he could think of that would calm him. There was a few moments of droning silence filled with the background noise of the Diner before she spoke up again. "Do you have any suspects?"

His nose scrunching for a moment while his lungs tensed and burned, they then went numb from the rush of nicotine. "I'm not sure I can tell you that."

"Can. or won't?"

"Well, we really don't know all that much information yet, he—"

"The killer."

"Yes."

"How do you know it's a he? A man?"

"Most killers of this nature are." Henry leaned forward, as if teasing her. His lips twitching into a slight smile, it amused him. She amused him. And she *knew*.

"Shouldn't you look at all possibilities, though? The killer could very well be a woman." She fed herself a few bites of the creamy, soggy poached eggs, licking the yolk from the corners of her indulgent lips before it dripped even further, as the myoglobin from the steak had done. Henry's eyes fell to her bare back, trailing the space between her shoulder blades and imagining running his fingers down the curve of her spine, seeing where it led him. The word *deviant* flashed across his mind, but he shook it off.

"Unlikely."

"Why?"

"The injuries simply don't match anything I've ever seen to be at the hands of a woman."

Blossom's smile dropped. She turned back to her coffee, pushing the plate of eggs and toast away as if having *just* lost her appetite and stared into the reflection of the lights overhead from black tar liquid. "Don't underestimate the rage of a woman, Special Agent." She muttered. Then, with a flicker of her eyes toward his direction, he caught a shift in the atmosphere

"Is that a threat?"

"That's up to you to decide."

"What are you saying? Do you know more than I do?" Henry asked from beneath narrowed brows. He was challenging her.

"Oh… *So* much more."

"There's a search party for Ethan." He changed the subject, no longer wishing to push her in that direction due to the acerbic edge to her words, which immediately softened.

"Are you asking me if I'll be there?"

"We could use all the eyes we can get." He deflected his answer from the real reason he asked, and that was, he couldn't get her out of his head. Thinking perhaps it would be less painful if she wasn't just in his head, but tangible.

"Of course." Blossom lifted a brow, then redirected her gaze to the food in front of her. "When is it?"

"I'm on my way to where some volunteers are meeting with Norman, after I leave here."

She nodded.

Her appetite soon returning, Henry continued to watch her, entranced, fixated, the belt around his black trousers tightening again as she suckled, bit and tore through her food.

Twelve

Large, overgrown branches of green pine swaying overhead with trunks reaching deep into the ground, bulging roots broke through cracked soil and, tangled cobwebs roping around the shrub the two overstepped while they tried to find clear pathways, delving further into the woods in their search for the missing boy, Ethan Cooper.

"So, Henry, tell me about yourself." Norman glanced toward the man as he waved away the buzzing of an invisible fly. The sweat that stuck to his skin was sticky and humid, hot. It was the heat of a nearing summer that would be sweltering that pierced the cool shadows stretching from where the sun couldn't reach through the trees that creaked with the rogue breath of wind, massive.

"Well, there's not much to tell."

"Come on, you *must* have some wild stories," Norman rubbed the back of his neck. His shirt clung to his shoulders with darkened stains of the perspiration dripping down his spine. "Being an FBI agent and all."

"If you're talking about the job, then sure."

"So?" Norman trailed off, tilting his head.

Henry sighed, feeling a fly land on his forearm, the sleeves of his button up shirt rolled to his elbows. Having left his jacket in the car, he swatted it away. "Uh... I attended school, got my bachelors, applied to the academy, attended Quantico, then got selected and passed the background check. Landed the job by the time I was twenty-four."

"Damn."

"Not all that exciting, considering it was what I had always wanted to do."

"Got anyone back home?"

His heart skipped a beat. "Not anymore."

"I'm sorry."

Despite his heartfelt apology, as always, the FBI agent was ruthlessly cold. "It's fine, really." Henry cleared his throat, offering more explanation. "Her name was Cindy. We met in college, dated for three years, got married after we graduated... And everything was perfect. Until I applied to Quantico." He paused, the lie tasting like spoiled tomato, acidic and fuzzy with mold. "Then, one night she was gone. A week later, she called me for a divorce. It was always about the work." He spoke through the rehearsed details, superficial and detached.

Still, it did the job and when he looked back at Norman, his expression had softened with sympathy toward the man, who was more or less still a stranger.

"I'm sorry, Henry."

"It's okay, turns out she was right, in a way." He muttered.

"That doesn't mean it doesn't hurt, though."

"Not anymore." Henry smiled again, but it was weaker, less forced before changing the subject. "What about you?"

Norman shook his head, then sighed. "I'm the one who never left, you know... I uh, my dad was with the police, so he took me under his wing. My wife, Stacy, we met in high school, the same high school my kids go to now—Jonathan and Maggie, who I mentioned to Frank —"

"Yeah."

"This town is my whole life. I was born here, raised here, I work here, and honestly, I'm planning on dying here too. If I have any say in it." He sucked in an audible breath through clenched teeth in an attempt to laugh, but it just came out in a forced breath, and Henry looked over at him.

"Did you ever want to leave?"

"Sometimes, mostly in my younger years, but... Not so much now. Now I'm glad I stayed. Or, I thought I would be. It's safe. It *was* safe, dammit."

"We'll find him."

"What if we don't?" Norman snapped.

"We will. That's why you called, right?"

"A god damn wolf in a sheep's pin. He could be here, right now, and we wouldn't have a clue. How many other boys are gonna have to die before we do?"

Henry was about to respond when, veering off from the group ahead, an older man with a wool sweater, as if he hadn't seen the weather report and khakis, brown leather shoes polished with rolled down white socks showing bony ankles, walked toward the two. He held one of the stick-poke poles in his left hand with closed fist and a flashlight in the other. It was turned off.

"Sheriff?" He called out.

"Mr. Whitmore. Is everything alright?" Norman and Henry both slowed.

"Uh—yes—quite, I just thought I'd introduce myself to..." Extending his hand toward Henry, he cocked a brow, but took it.

"Special Agent Henry Williamson. FBI."

"Fascinating. Never met one of you before."

Henry took back his hand. "How does it feel?"

"Relieved." Mr. Whitmore nodded. "It's good Sheriff Green called you, these poor boys. And uh-well, I heard of that Cooper boy's disappearance and... After discovering Andrew I thought it'd be best to come forward. Meet you in person. Considering I wasn't able to do so before."

"News always did travel quickly in small towns. You found Andrew Clemmington's body?" They three began walking again, Mr. Whitmore falling to Henry's right.

He looked to Norman, hesitating before answering the question. "I thought that would have been relayed?"

"It was." Henry nodded. "I watched the tape. Your interview."

He blinked. "Oh, okay."

There was a few moments of silence before Henry asked, "what were you doing beneath the bleachers?" To which Mr. Whitmore gave a nervous laugh, eyeing the stranger before his voice hardened.

"I teach photography. I was showing the students to look in places for possible shots that others wouldn't think to look. I didn't realize I was going to stumble on the corpse of a student of mine—hold on, are you insinuating—"

"Just wondering." Henry cut him off. Stepping through a bush that rose to his shins, the stems snapped against his pant leg and he motioned toward the search party up ahead with the slight of his hand. "You should go back with the group, we need eyes like yours Mr. Whitmore. Thank you for coming out." Recalling that

Andrew's body had been found close to 8:00p.m. And if Henry wasn't too off, that was long after-school hours.

Once Mr. Whitmore left them, Norman let out a heavy breath. "You know, you got a real way of making friends."

"He lied."

"He wasn't showing students where to take photos, that was a lie. Also, I'm not here to make friends. I'm here to help you with this case. And believe it or not, insinuating himself with me, that points him out like a sore thumb."

Norman took the rag he had stuffed in his back pocket and wiped the sweat from his brow. "He sometimes hosts after-school get togethers for the kids to be able to wander around and take photos. Gets them dinner from the Diner and everything. He wasn't lying."

"So you double-checked with the other witnesses?"

"I didn't think Whitmore was a suspect."

"Everybody is, Norman."

The hot sun beating down on them, around noon, most of the group of volunteers had split up and veered toward the Diner for lunch—Norman included—while Henry reached into his pocket and suppressed his hunger through the calming effects of nicotine, continuing to walk through the woods until the heat began to make his stomach turn and his temples throb.

Pausing under a shaded area, he loosened his tie, pulling it off and shoving it into his pocket, then reached up to undo the top two buttons of his white shirt when a twig snapped behind his right shoulder.

Whipping his head around, coughing slightly into the back of his hand due to being caught off guard, his gaze met Blossom's and his shoulders relaxed once more.

"Sorry." She apologized with a sharp exhale. "Didn't mean to startle you."

Pink glitter eyeshadow making her cheeks sparkle slightly, she had changed into a cropped, Barbie style t-shirt, paired with 70's style—solid bubblegum pink—and high waisted bell bottoms. It was the most casual he suspected to ever see Blossom.

"You came." A look of astonishment plastered over his face, Henry took another long drag from his cigarette. Holding it in his chest for a few seconds.

"Like you said. You can use all the eyes you can get." Blossom walked up to him, carefully stepping through the dark hues of green. The two stood there for a moment before Henry turned softly against his heel and motioned for her to walk with him.

"So, who are you?" Henry felt her shoulder brush against his arm.

"That's a complex question, Special Agent. I'm afraid I don't necessarily know how to answer that. But I can tell you my favorite color."

"So, what's your favorite color?"

Blossom smiled, shaking her head. "Black."

"Bullshit." Henry shot out, feeling almost a disgust slosh up the back of his throat. "Seriously?"

"I have an admiration for black but no. Pink."

"What do you mean admiration?"

"Well, black has always represented darkness and evil, shadows. But—what people don't see—is that pink holds the same capacity for darkness. You have shades of red and purple, but you also have beiges and whites. Pink can just as easily as black be dangerous. But it's more versatile. Because you either have black or don't. Pink is alluring and deceiving."

"You've clearly put some thought into it."

She shrugged, then batted her lashes up at him. "It's also really cute, and goes with just about everything."

"Of course." He paused. "And what do you want to do after you graduate?"

"Are you asking if I'm going to college?"

"Are you?"

"Never thought it was that important."

"Don't you have anything you want to pursue?"

"Maybe I'll become an FBI agent."

He laughed, the two of them walking through the trees. Henry rolled his cigarette between his fingers, staring down at it before taking another puff. "If you really wanted to, you'd need to go to college."

"That's a shame."

"You really have no interest in getting out of this town?"

"I never said that."

"So, where do you want to go?"

"You're *awfully* interested in me."

"You're an interesting person."

"You just met me." She paused. "And I sense there's more to you than you're letting on."

"What do you want to know?"

Blossom pretended to think for a moment, tilting her head to the side. "What's *your* favorite color?"

"Black."

"Too easy."

"Grey."

"Cliche."

"Brown?"

"God…" Leaning her head back, blonde slipped down her spine from her shoulders and she rolled her eyes. "Boring."

"I'm sorry, I've just never thought about it." But when she met his gaze again, having walked up ahead of him, turning her head over her shoulder, Henry licked his lips and sucked in a breath. "Blue."

"Blue?" There was a shift in her expression and she paused for a second. "Why blue?"

He looked away, noticing that she was almost leading him toward the side of a hunting shack—nestled by the creek and most likely abandoned, overtaken by the foliage around it—then noticed that there was a path stretching from the town's cemetery. "I guess it's the color of the ocean."

"It's *also* the color of my eyes."

"I'm not surprised, you *are* a blonde."

"I sure am." Biting her bottom lip, Blossom glanced down, then sidestepped so her shoulder hit the rough wall of the wooden shack; splinters rubbing against her shoulder blades. From afar, Henry watched as she reached out, motioning for him to give her the cigarette and cocked a brow.

With slightly curled green leaves tickling the back of her knees, Blossom smirked back at him when reluctantly, he obliged, turning the heels of his polished black shoes into the loose dirt, uprooting the delicate, thin tangles of weeds that wove their way up from the unkept blades of grass and walking over to where she leaned her hips forward just enough to make a point of it.

Handing her his cigarette, she wrapped her lips around the end and took a long inhale. Mimicking what Henry had done with a fleeting, lingering brush of her lipstick over the white paper. He could only imagine what it would taste like when she handed it back to him. Then, allowing the smoke to trail from her next breath, a soft hum escaped her at the rush of nicotine flooding her mind and soaking into her muscles. When she finally did lower the cigarette from her mouth, going to hand it back to Henry, his fingers grazed hers and with her other hand Blossom wrapped his tie around her knuckles.

Enamored by her presence, by the sudden floral aroma encasing him with butterflies in his stomach, Henry looked down at her, his brows pulling together as she seemed to also be wrapping *him* around her finger.

"How old are you, Blossom?" He whispered.

"Eighteen." She responded, proud and flippant, as if she knew exactly what that meant, the power it held. How utterly, beautifully destructive that was. She was *dangerously* young, disgustingly so, and Henry could feel the sweat perspiring from his pores, salty and slick, sticking the fabric of his collared shirt to his chest; his heart throbbing heavily—painfully—up against his ribs while he began to lean closer; a warm breeze hitting his face and allowing for the scent of blooming lilies, jasmine and honeysuckle mixing with the red berry spice of her perfume to fill his lungs.

However, sucking the air deep into his chest and holding it there, it then turned sour. Spoiled. His next breath was that of the sweet, metallic bitterness of blood, causing him to pull away from her.

Walking around the corner of the shack, taking the rusted metal handle under his hands and yanking the door open, Henry was abruptly hit with the pungent, thick aroma of a bloody butchers shop without A.C. The musk of an outhouse left to ferment in high heat. The cold, harsh smell reminded him of boiled cabbage and onion, of rotten eggs and pickled vegetables—Kimchi—coming down on him all at once, like all the air had been sucked from his lungs with a vacuum, only to be replaced with that... Stench. Gagging, his stomach turned and his hand flew up to pinch his nose, taking slow breaths.

Stepping into the enclosed and moist space, the wooden walls slightly damp, finally, his hand fell from his face as he looked down at the body of one Ethan Cooper—his decomposition accelerated by the summer heat—with his face twisting into a scowl as he pulled his phone out and rang Norman.

"I think I just found your missing boy, Norman."

"Wait-what?" Henry could hear the bustle of the Diner behind him, Sophie's voice cutting through the line with a fuzzled, *what's going on? Did they find anything?* "What do you mean? Is he okay? Where?"

"Get Frank and his team down here." He said, his voice strained. "To the shack a little ways down from the cemetery."

Norman's voice cracked. "Is he—"

"No question about it."

When the line went dead, Henry shoved his phone back into his pocket, his shoulders slumping with a heavy exhale before looking back to see that Blossom was standing at the doorway; her attention fixated on Ethan's rotting corpse. With softened brows, but otherwise, a numbed look of satisfaction glossed over her eyes, she studied him.

Slowly, with careful steps and his head tilted slightly toward his shoulder, *cautiously,* Henry moved back toward her and asked, softly, "What do you feel, Blossom?" Not particularly understanding himself where that question had come from, given the fact that he hardly knew what he felt himself, having blocked out those feelings such a long time ago. Because of this, he recognized the look in her eyes. Yet, at the same time, there was something behind that… Something he couldn't place his finger on.

"Are you asking because I let him fuck me a few times?"

Her gaze snapped back to him with a single blink, like a rubber band breaking, and Henry shrugged. "Usually that means something to people."

Then, Blossom's voice dipped, and there was a twinge of vulnerability to it. "Can I be honest with you?"

Henry nodded, his hand coming to her shoulder. Glancing down at it, despite the slight weakness he caught in her gaze just as he heard it in her voice, it was once again numbed and when she looked back up at him, her blue eyes became as sharp, as stinging as ice to bare skin. "You can tell me anything."

Letting out a sigh from her slightly agape lips, Blossom looked back to Ethan. "I don't... Feel... *Anything.*"

Thirteen

A thick, crawling swarm of hungry maggots already lay waste to Ethan's bloating corpse by the time he was found. Inflicted with rigor mortis, the summer heat created a pressure cooker within the capacities of his stiff limbs, accelerating the breakdown of organic materials alongside the rate of which bacteria was able to eat away at his internal organs—turning them to a sloshing glob of pink paste—and like a blanket of white that resembled the thick yellow of puss oozing from the crevices where the flies had laid their eggs, the maggots also bathed in the soupy, viscous mix of red and brown fluids pooling beneath him, soaking into the floral patterned mattress he had been tied to, where greenish yellow and tinted pale pink, spongey tissue had already marbled. Beginning to separate from the striated muscle fibers beneath the subcutaneous fatty layer.

"Fourteen stab wounds, all done with a carving knife while he was tied up with the rope—he fought, by the looks of the tears and the bruises around his wrists, which were then replaced with the pink ribbon post mortem." Frank pointed with a black pen.

"So what killed him?"

"The killer began stabbing, you can tell by the amount of blood that his heart was still pumping, then slit his throat to finish him off." Crouched low, Frank propped his forearms against his knees with a huff, then looked up at Norman.

"How long has he been here?"

"Because of the heat, I'm gonna have to get him back to the hospital to say for sure, but... I know he wasn't here long before being killed. There aren't any signs of torture, starvation, or mutilation. Whoever did this most likely lured Ethan out here, then killed him that night."

"So there was no hope."

A gloom hanging over Frank, he shook his head. "I'm sorry, Norman."

"Good work, Frank. Thank you." His voice hardened by the dull ache in his chest, he then looked to the door. The shutters of Frank's camera going off with a quick, white flash out of the corner of his eye when he walked away with careful steps, making note to move around anything that could be deemed evidence. Stepping from the shack and back onto the grass, the door closed behind him with a twisted squeal of rusted hinges and the thudding of wood. To his left, he found Henry and Blossom talking to one of his officers, who was collecting her statement.

"Special Agent Williamson and I were walking together when... We came across the shack and—upon nearing it—that's when he caught the smell. I stayed outside while he went inside to check it out." She clasped her hands in front of her, glancing periodically to Henry, who gnawed on the end of the cigarette.

Approaching them, Norman noticed that when he drew his lips back, there were lipstick stains against the white. His stomach turned. "Did you go in after him?" The officer—Anthony—asked, and Henry looked to Blossom before she responded.

"No. I stayed outside. You know, in case..." She trailed off.

Anthony nodded, scribbling in the rectangular, leather-bound journal he brought with him, saying, "no, no, that was the right thing to do." Before glancing up from beneath straight, brown brows. He had tightly wound curls wrapping around his ears of the same shade of hickory, the ends lightened during the summertime to a peanut. With soft features and a round nose, he was just shy of forty, and still carried himself like a twenty year old. "And how do you feel, Ms. James? This must have been... Shocking... If I'm not mistaken you knew Ethan?"

"We were close last summer, and it's just—" She let out a sharp breath with the quick slump of her shoulders and pressed her lips together. "Thinking that someone could do something like this horrific... Especially to someone as caring and selfless, as Ethan... It makes me wonder what kinds of other things people—you *think* you know—are capable of."

"I'm so sorry to keep you, but would you be willing to fill this out?" He took out a folded, white paper from his back pocket and handed it to her alongside a pen from his breastpocket, which was running out of ink. "Just start from the beginning when you arrived at the search party."

Blossom's voice just above a whisper, she took the items from him with a small, "of course." But then, looking around for somewhere to write on, Anthony sucked in a small gasp as to what was happening and lifted his brows, motioning toward his back.

"Here, sorry I forgot a clipboard."

"Oh, it's no problem." She smiled, a light chuckle escaping her as she stepped forward and laid the paper along his spine. Anthony curved his shoulders slightly to ensure the flattest surface he could, and with her smile lingering, Blossom met Henry's eyes, beginning to relay exactly what she told Anthony before scribbling her signature with small, cursive lettering.

Norman cleared his throat, and Anthony looked to him over his shoulder, his hands planted on his thighs.

"Anthony, didn't I remind you to grab a clipboard before we left?"

"Huh?"

"I thought I told you to grab a clipboard."

"Oh—"

"Done!" Blossom stepped back, snapping the paper back and holding it front of her for Anthony to grab once he straightened his back, swallowing a nervous lump in his throat.

He didn't say anything before turning and making his way to the patrol car he had ridden in, cursing as soon as he opened the door to see that he indeed, had not forgotten to grab a clipboard, as there was one on the floor of the passenger seat.

"Do you have a ride home, Blossom?" Norman redirected his attention back to her from watching Anthony. Before she was able to respond, however, Henry stepped forward. A twig snapping beneath his heel.

"I tried to contact Sophie, but she's at the Diner, so I told Blossom I could take her."

Looking to him with a slight frown tugging at the corners of his lips, registering what he said, there was a moment of silence. Then, Norman—knowing he wouldn't be able to fight against it—resigned, "alright, just be quick."

And, stepping backward with a twinge of playfulness in his tone, Henry grinned. "You really think I'd miss a chance with a fresh body?" Earning a scoff from Norman, who then shook his head and began making his way back toward the shack.

Fourteen

Norman insisted on allowing the Cooper family a few days to deal with their grief. So, becoming engulfed by the smell of nearly burnt, cheese-filled crusts to greasy pizza alongside the twinge of salty, fattened, soggy fries melting in sugary, bright red squirts of ketchup, the lingering aroma of chemical cleaning sprays and lemon-scented wood polish burned into their olfactory receptors while Norman followed Henry across the dark purple, space themed carpet inside the Entertainment Center. Flashing neon lights pulsating to the beat of cheap, radio-pop eighties music put on repeat, they passed groups of bell-dismissed, Coco-Cola drunken teens whose voices—high-pitched squeals of flirtatious laughter—seemed to drone out the music and Henry took note of how they acted as if nothing was wrong; skinny pubescent boys slinging their lanky arms over pudgy girls whose Moms buttered them up with breadsticks, casseroles and sugary sweets and still told them they looked beautiful (even when they went from a size two to a size six) as well as how the seniors at the high school leaned over to girls three years their junior, whispering small promises of affection they'd forget as soon as the next preppy little school girl came along and stroked their ego.

"What exactly are we looking for?"

"Ethan's friends come here almost every night." Norman caught up to him with three, exact strides. He was taller than Henry—not by a lot—but it always seemed as if he was catching up to him.

"Mhm." Henry nodded, slowing to a stop. "And I don't doubt they would have stopped. Seems like every person eighteen years and younger is here." *The perfect hunting ground.*

"I'll go see if any of the names she gave us are registered at the front counter." Norman waited for a second, then rolled his eyes when Henry didn't respond, dipping behind the Agent, not bothering to ask what had caught his attention, when, up ahead, leaning with his elbow propped against the counter of where the shoes were held, was Mr. Whitmore.

His other arm crossed over his chest and his hands clasped together, thumbs grazing the buttons of the mustard yellow polo he had tucked into a pair of black jeans, next to where he stood, her feet heavy from the weight of glossy, ankle-high booties that reached under the hem of her bell-cut pants, Blossom leaned forward against her palms and let out a laugh, bouncing strands of blonde falling forward before she swept them back.

Blossom noticed him first, a bright smile growing on her cheeks as her eyes flashed with excitement. "Special Agent!" She bit her bottom lip, resting her chin against her shoulder with a kiddish excitement exuding from her when Henry began making his way over to them. Mr. Whitmore looked over his shoulder at him. Instinctively taking a nervous step away from Blossom and clearing his throat.

"What do we owe the honor?" He asked with a light smile.

"Here on business, is all."

"All work, no play… No pleasure?"

"Never said that." Henry lifted a single brow. Tipping back on his heel. "But you'd know that, wouldn't you, Mr. Whitmore?"

He chuckled. "I'm not sure what you mean."

Henry shifted his eyes downward and noticed the pinned, silver name tag. "You work here?"

"I just take up a few shifts on the weekends."

"Really?"

"You know, even in a small town like this, teachers…"

"Of course. Just a particular place to choose to work, considering how many teenagers spend their time here, and frankly, how many choose to work here as well." The corners of his lips twitched into a smug, closed-mouth smile. Whitmore didn't say anything, despite his mouth opening as if to refute what the Agent was alluding to. Nonetheless, caught in the lights and the music, the pressure of his overwhelming presence, Whitmore then backed away, sliding his hip against the counter and merely ducked his head. Leaving Blossom and Henry alone, at least for a few more moments before Norman caught up.

"Holding up alright?" Henry asked.

She tilted her head. "How are *you* holding up?"

"I've seen plenty of bodies. This is no different. What did Whitmore want with you?"

"Oh... I like that... *Ice cold.*" She looked him over. "What I meant, though, was new town, new people, new secrets to uncover. How are you holding up?"

"Thankfully it's my job to uncover secrets and to meet with new people. I've also been met with welcome, which makes my job easier." He sassed.

"Don't bullshit me, *Henry.* These people aren't welcoming you. They don't know you."

"It could be worse."

"Are you going to uncover *my* secrets?"

He frowned. "I'm surprised a girl like you has any."

"Then you're in for some... Shocking surprises." She giggled, pushing herself from the counter with a light jump. He almost reached out to help her, but squeezed his fist instead, holding himself back.

"Oh yeah? And what might those secrets include?"

Blossom responded just before Norman walked out from behind Henry with a look of bitter apprehension toward the girl. "I suppose you're just gonna have to figure them out yourself, huh."

Norman shoved the list of names into his pocket and gave Blossom a smile and courteous nod. "Ms. James."

"Hello, Norman." She blinked. Turning back to Henry with the flick of her tongue over her bottom lip before she tipped against her heel and began to walk away. "Pleasure seeing you, Henry."

"Pleasure's all mine." He watched her leave, the sway of her hips leading to the smooth, steady, confident steps of her feet over the pizza, beer and vomit-stained floors.

"You've got a funny way of looking at that girl, Henry."

"What's funny about it?" He turned his chin to his shoulder and peered at Norman. "Oh, come on. You can't deny that... You don't look at all these... Preppy, skimpy seventeen and eighteen year old girls and don't think about when you were that age with the impulse control of a twelve year old."

"No. I don't. Because I'm not seventeen, or eighteen anymore, Henry. And neither are you."

"Doesn't mean I can't still look."

"I'm gonna ignore the fact that you just said that, and —" He paused. "You would go out just to watch girls? You're joking."

"You didn't?"

"Again, no. I had friends. You didn't have friends?"

"Still don't."

"No fucking shit." Norman scoffed.

Henry squeezed his jaw slightly, then changed the subject. "Does Whitmore always make a habit of hanging around teenagers?"

Norman folded his arms over his chest. "There have been... Rumors, before. But nothing of substance or reason to think anything more. He's a teacher. He knows these kids. Why, did you see him?"

"Yeah, he was with Blossom before I walked over. Told me he works here."

"What do you want me to say? Shocker, he doesn't? No, he's been coming here on the weekends to pick up a few shifts and help with the bills. Plus, as you should know, it's apparently quite difficult to ignore Blossom James."

"It's just odd."

"It's odd because you're making it odd. And—"

"And what?"

Norman sighed. "Quite frankly, you're one to say what's fucking *odd*."

"Oh… Cause *I'm* odd?"

"Because you don't know him." Norman urged. "He doesn't mean any harm. Like I said, he knows these kids."

Henry blinked. "Alright, then. Fine." Breathing slowly and holding it in his chest, wanting a cigarette. But he instead asked, "did any of the names come up?" Referring to Norman's interaction with the middle aged woman at the front of the entertainment center.

"One. Kevin. He's slotted in for a 7:00 game with four other people. Aisle ten."

"Great." Henry smiled, waving for Norman to lead them over to the group of boys that leaned against the arctic blue-leather cushioned booths, metal trays with sloppily cut pizza in front of them with cheese and marinara sauce smearing against disposable plates. One of them having gotten fried pickles, hot sauce burned the corners of their mouth, calmed by the puss-yellow mayo that crusted around the thinned white paper of a .75 ounce condiment cup.

After purchasing a medium Diet Cola, cherry flavored, Blossom brought the straw between her lips and took a long, satisfying gulp that burned in her chest with the popping, sizzling and burping of perspiring foam around the edges of the plastic cup, walking back to the metal ramp that would have led her back to the main floor, where she proceeded to watch the FBI agent and

Sheriff Norman Green approach the group of Ethan's (old) friends.

Norman talked to them first, introducing Henry and stating he was with the Bureau before one of the kids rudely commented that they had heard he was in town. Henry took out his wallet, flipping it open to show the golden engraving of his badge and ID with the snap of his wrist while, behind him—her forearms propped over the top rail—Blossom leaned her hips back. Continuing to take occasional sips, her cheeks tugging upward in amusement at the boys' dismissal of such authority in name of their so-called 'grievances,' to which both men knew was really them saying *fuck off, we have a game to play and I don't have the interest in answering your questions.*

Blossom could practically taste the salt in their words that at the same time, dusted their jeans.

Henry and Norman then sat on the other side of the booth after a few boys made room. Leaning his shoulders forward with his fingers intertwined, knuckles blotching white when he ran his thumb over them, puffs of black hair curled upward at the ends of thick strands with salt-dusted roots smoothed back above Henry's ears as Norman, to his right, leaned back in a non-intimidating lowering of his chest with his hands resting in his lap. He mediated the intensity that exuded from the FBI agent, a mild, ashen sheen over the structure of his brown hair turning it to an iron that shone in steady waves under the dimmed lights. Tilting his head to his shoulder, the corners of his lips dropped with concentration.

It wasn't long until they wrapped up the conversation with the boys. Shaking each of their hands, Norman then walked Henry back to the entrance in silence, the two passing where Blossom had watched them from until growing restless and moving on; exiting from the Entertainment center into the night. Henry's eyes shifting across those who remained by the time they finished, he failed to locate her and wiped his fingers down the sides of his mouth. Inhaling deep, stretching his lungs full of the stuffy air until his chest tightened and he let it out forcefully. His next breath being that of the pristine, dampened night breeze, cooled by the lack of the sun's rays.

Norman placed his hands on his hips, unclipping the holster of his gun before snapping it back such as one clicks a pen while thinking. Turning to Henry, then looking past him back into the Entertainment center, he asked, "do you think they were telling us everything?"

"Of course not. But that doesn't matter." Henry lit a cigarette, letting out the first puff of smoke from pursed lips like the steam escaping the top of a train.

"Why?"

When Norman met Henry's squinted eyes, there was a snap of his holster, then a couple, agonizing seconds of silence between them.

"Because they don't know anything that would have helped us. He left practice, which ended later than usual because he said his mom wanted him home for dinner, which was a little odd—"

"When she didn't."

"So clearly Ethan had some different plans in mind. And that's when he... Vanished." *And ended up dead.* "He didn't tell them where he was going."

"So you think they're telling the truth."

"I think... They don't know enough to lie."

"Then this was a complete waste of our time." Norman turned away with a clench of his jaw. His hands falling from his belt.

"No, we got what we needed. A clearer picture of who Ethan was. You're gonna have to get used to running into dead ends with these types of things, Norman. Don't take it so hard." Looking out into the woods, Henry felt a burp building with a sharp, shooting acidity at the back of his throat, but swallowed it down. Lowering his cigarette from his lips and holding it out in front of him with one arm crossed over the middle of his torso. "With that in mind, we have three bodies now. We can start building a picture of what these boys had in common, including their friends, how they spent their time, which will then allow us to start looking into why the killer is targeting them. Frank will have the autopsy for us tomorrow morning that'll tell us what really went down."

Nodding, Norman smoothed back his hair, then let out a breathy laugh. He could feel the tightening coil of stress nestling beneath his ribs. "I don't understand why you're so god damn okay with all this." He shook his head, his eyes falling to his shoes.

Henry fought back a scowl. "I never said I was."

"Well," Norman snapped his head up. "You sure act like it."

"That's how you get the job done. You move on. You look at the evidence. You don't let your emotions get in the way of-"

"You could have shown a little more sympathy toward Mrs. Cooper's situation. You could at least start showing a little *more* emotion. Or do you not have any?"

"I wasn't there to hold her hand. You did that just fine on your own." Norman lifted his brows, his words as strong as the bourbon that laced his breath with a juxtaposing warmth. "Despite what you probably think, I don't enjoy young men being murdered. I'm here to help *stop* that. But I understand you're trying to figure me out, and by doing so you've observed some things that may make you question my decisions. That, I understand. But make no mistake." Turning his heels, Henry kept his words low. "I am just as effected by this as you are-"

"Bullshit. I knew these boys. I know their families. Having to tell Mrs. Cooper that her son was butchered? Mutilated? Just part of the job for you. You don't have to hold her hand. But for me? I'm going to have to live with these people's pain just as much as the absence of their sons. Sons *I* knew. While you just move on to your next case, your next adventure. You go back to the city and forget all about this. You have that luxury. What I'm asking is for you to... "

"You want me to crack open a beer? Grill a few steaks? Make small talk and butter up the pretty young Moms around town? Smile, laugh, kick my feet up and offer security to these people? Make them feel safe again? Lie to them and tell them everything is going to be okay? Offer a comforting hand? A shoulder to cry on? You asked for the Bureau's help. I am here to *help*. But you need to allow me to do my job. I know you may not agree with or understand some of the things I do, or what I say, but when I tell you that I'm here to *help,* you need to trust me. Or else this isn't going to work."

Norman eyes had gone cloudy. He lowered them to the ground, exhaling, "I know, I know. I'm sorry."

"You're not the one who needs to apologize, but you don't need to make it any more clear than it already is with everyone else in this god damn place treating me like a stranger." Henry flicked his cigarette to the ground, then walked toward his car as a breeze ruffled his hair and kissed his cheeks with an abnormal, summer warmth that contradicted the coldness of which seeped through his bones. Looking to where Norman still stood outside the front doors, he opened the driver's door, calling back, "we'll see if the Coopers are ready to talk and resume the

work tomorrow. I'm sure the *killer* will understand."
Before sliding behind the wheel and twisting the key into
the engine, the beams of bright, white LED headlights
illuminating a few feet in front of him while he passed
the Diner, where, nursing a black coffee, Blossom
watched from one of the booths by the window.

Wearing a plain white shirt and a pair of loose
underwear, Henry sat with a pillow propped behind his
shoulders and paperwork sprawled over the stiff mattress,
a tray full of cigarette butts placed next to two coffees,
one a quarter-full on the side table. Unable to sleep.

Smoke trailing from his lips, dissipating into the
stuffy air when he exhaled, he reached over with a slight
grunt and grabbed the coffee. The cold black liquid filling
his mouth with a bitter aftertaste before setting it back
down and glancing at the blinking clock. It was nearly
12:45 a.m. Clenching his jaw against the feeling of grain-
sized grounds grinding between his teeth, he swallowed,
goosebumps covering his arms. Then, tearing his
attention toward the door, three sharp knocks cut through
the room.

Wondering with a watchful eye who would come by
at such a time, Henry hesitated to get up. Still, before he
could arrive at a conclusion, three more knocks cut off
his thoughts, quickly bringing him to his feet. Pushing the
messy papers from his lap and taking one last inhale from
the cigarette between his fingers before putting it out and

grabbing the gun from his desk, Henry snatched back on the pants he previously kicked off for what he anticipated being the rest of the night, leaving them low around his hips—unzipped and unbuckled—while making his way across the cold tile of the kitchenette, his bare feet sticking slightly to the surface as he lifted them with light, careful steps. His heart beating heavily against his ribs, holding the gun to the small of his back and pressing his shoulder to the door, Henry took a single moment to glance out of the peephole before yanking the door open.

Fifteen

Entering the Evergreen Hotel, the scent of dust, cigarette smoke and lingering cleaning chemicals filled Blossom's lungs while she looked around the lobby, peering into the lounge where the bar was, where three men still lingered under the smokey haze of dimmed red lights, then walked up to the front counter with bouncy, light steps. Maneuvering herself toward where a younger man—the name tag of *Jeffrey* pinned against his uniform's dress jacket—stood behind the cool glow of an over-heated computer. She had seen him around school before, a year above her. He had since graduated.

Her arms crossing over the hardened, polish-coated and stained countertop, she then leaned her weight into it and kicked her heel up. Running her tongue along the corner of her upper lip and grinning at him when he glanced up at her over the lowered lids of focused, olive green eyes and under unkept, nearly black brows. "*Damn,*

Jeffrey… You got… *Hot*…" She teased, earning a hesitant smile from him when she playfully winced before continuing. "Listen…" Blossom leaned forward, raising of her shoulders. "I need you to do something for me. Something a little… *Shameless.*"

Lifting his chin and looking her over, he questioned, "what's in it for me?"

"Well, I'm sure you're gonna wanna find out…" She raised her brows. Pulling back the front of the soft, light wool coat she had covered herself with and revealing, beneath it, a pink velvet dress that hugged her slim form, standing on barbie-doll, plastic block heels, Jeffrey glanced down at the shape of her breasts, eyeing the dip between her breasts and how the dress's spaghetti straps hardly left anything to the imagination, before Blossom hid herself away again. "But first, you gotta tell me what room the FBI agent is staying in."

Blossom's fist remaining raised in the air when the lock finally slipped from its place and the door swung open, Henry stood there, staring at her as if attempting to figure out whether she was actually real before asking, "is everything okay?" A hesitant curiosity evident in his tone.

More disheveled and… Unkept than usual—than any of the other few times she had seen him since he arrived —Blossom's heart skipped a beat and goosebumps covered her skin. She looked down at the carpet, her hands clasping in front of her, when Henry stepped back. Opening the door wider for her to walk through.

"I'm sorry for bothering you so late…" She spoke quietly.

Bringing his gaze to meet hers when silently, a deep sigh escaping him, Henry closed the door behind her before walking to the opposite side of the room. Replacing the gun in his hand for a cigarette while Blossom hovered in front of the door. "It's alright." He took a puff. "But you never answered my question." She still didn't respond. So, Henry took a few steps forward. She could smell the cologne that hung to his clothes, to his skin, and breathed it in. "Is everything okay?"

"You're asking why I'm here…" She released her hands to her sides.

"I am."

"I wanted to see you." She spoke clearly, her words as sharp and blunt as the edge of a knife.

Henry didn't say anything, watching closely as she moved to the bed. A slight bounce to her hair when she sat, the springs squealed gently and he could see the way she pressed her fingers into the stiff, crinkling sheets, twisting them around shiny white polish before reaching her hands to the buttons of her coat and shrugging it from her shoulders. Throwing it behind her, planting her hands behind her in the next moment, Henry was sure a blush had crept onto his cheeks.

"You changed."

"Very perceptive of you…"

"Did you change for me? Just to come see me?"

"Would you have liked that?"

"I don't care what you wear."

"No… Of course you don't. You're a *professional.*"

She said it mockingly, before he waved his hand, asking, "So is that all? You wanted to talk?"

"Well, yesterday we didn't see each other, and our last interaction *had* been we *so* rudely cut short."

"You call finding the body of a missing boy a rude interruption?" Lifting the cigarette to his lips, something pulled at him to walk up to her and a moment later, when he loomed over her, smoke trailing from his lips, his heart slammed heavy up against his chest. Blossom lifted her chin and tilted her head to the side with the softening of her brow. *Is this what she really wanted?*

"Well that, and the way Norman inturrupted us back at the Bowling alley."

"Isn't it really an Entertainment center?"

"Same difference. I only wish I wouldn't have had to make the trouble of waking you at—" She glanced over her shoulder at the clock "—Nearly 1:00 in the morning. Yet, here we are."

Stitching his thick brows together with thought, he contemplated that perhaps she was merely a dream, of course, with that being said he then took to mind just how *dreamy* she looked, her white hair pushed behind her ears and her eyes locked with his, a slight blemish on her cheeks and her jaw relaxed, her posture almost inviting him to press himself between the empty spaces of her flesh. There was something so *tempting* about Blossom. Henry had noticed it from the first time he met her. But now, the temptation was... Different. This time, it was directed *at him,* with the faint scent of her perfume lingering in his lungs and poking at the back of his mind.

"You're persistent." He noted.

"Is that a bad thing?"

"I've dealt with worse." She smiled at his words, and Henry shook his head. "But don't worry. You didn't wake me."

"Have trouble sleeping?"

"Occasionally."

"Something on your mind?"

"Why do you care?"

"Just making conversation."

"You wanted to talk, makes sense."

"Good."

"Thing is, though, I don't do small talk."

"You seem to be doing it just fine right now, as well as having done it just fine all the other times we've spoken."

"Well, that's because I find you... Of interest."

"You've already told me that."

"Speaking of talking, you lied today."

"Oh?"

"You told Anthony you didn't enter the shack."

"Less paperwork for you, less need for explanations."

Henry turned away from her, muttering, "you know, it's late."

"I noticed."

"I've got work to do and I'm sure your Mom wants you home."

"She's working all night. I've got time before she even notices I'm gone. Plus, when she comes home she usually just heads straight to bed or drowns herself in the comfort of shitty white wine."

"Your mom sure works a lot."

"Better than being stuck around me, I suppose."

"You and your mom don't have a good relationship?" He asked, not knowing why he would but letting it hang in the air.

"I thought you didn't do small talk."

"Didn't we just go over this?"

"Well, no. In simple terms I don't suppose my mom and I have a good relationship. You have a good relationship with your mom?"

"She died five years ago."

"That doesn't answer the question."

"She put up with me."

"Oh…" She bit her lip, teasing a brow up. "So you're a trouble maker."

"*Was.*"

"I'd beg to disagree."

Realizing that they were utterly, painfully alone, with an instinctive step back, Henry looked down. "Why don't you like white wine?"

"I've always preferred something stronger. Something that bites." She pushed forward with a furrow of her brows and the sharpening on her tone. Observing him. "Also, I think you want me here. I don't think you really want me to leave."

Amusement curling his lips upward, Henry looked at her through the dissipating smoke that shot from his next breath. "I never said I did. But that doesn't mean this is appropriate."

Goosebumps covering her arms, her heart leaping in her chest, Blossom suddenly pushed herself off the bed. Advancing toward him.

Henry noticed her movements and took another step back, then another, until his shoulders hit the wall. Warning,*"Blossom-"* Her name choking in his throat as it closed, making it difficult for him to breathe. Adrenaline crashing through him.

"I didn't know you *wanted* appropriate, Special Agent. You shouldn't lead a girl on like that."

"I've done nothing of the sort—now, *please—"*

Neglecting to listen to him, her hands lifted to Henry's waist. It was a bold move, and tugging him forward, one step closer, his entire body tensed. He lifted his hands away from her, palms exposed, the cigarette threatening to fall from his knuckles and looked up toward the ceiling. Blossom saw his Adam's apple rise and fall with a heavy gulp, and smiled.

He was afraid to touch her, and prayed someone else would knock on his door, interrupt them. Because if he let himself go, if he lowered his guard, Henry knew he wouldn't be able to stop himself. Then, her fingers began working at the buckle of his belt.

For a few seconds, his knees weakening, warmth began to ease him into submission and he discarded his cigarette, tossing it as best he could onto the desk without making mess. However, ash still smeared against the top of the folder it landed on, flecks of burning paper went dim. Becoming dizzy with want, every molecule of his being screaming at him, his thoughts began to wash away and he couldn't remember what he *wanted*. He could only feel her, pressing herself against him, touching him. But then, as if receiving an electric shock, Blossom managed to undo the button and tug down his zipper, and Henry reached his fingers around her wrist. Snatching her hand from the depths of his underwear before she could do any real damage. "Don't."

His palm sweaty against her skin and his nails digging into her knuckles, his voice was groggy and thick. It was weak of him to try to talk, to try and deny that she could *feel* how much he wanted her, and she curled her hand into his. But didn't pull away. Her voice dipping into a whisper, almost a whine. "I thought you wanted me? I've seen the way you look at me... I can hear it in your voice." She pushed herself to her toes, grazing her lips against his, her breath melting against the slight stubble of his chin. He had forgotten to shave since he arrived. "I can see your *hunger,* Special Agent. You haven't done such a very good job of hiding it. I'm simply resuming what we had in store for us back in those *woods.*"

Henry closed his eyes as he exhaled, conflict buzzing through his veins. With her other hand, Blossom then caught the hollow of his cheekbone under her palm. She was gentle with him, and he noticed himself leaning his face into her fingers. But with a dip of her chin, Blossom suddenly caught his lips against hers and without warning, they were kissing. And *he* was *kissing her,* too.

Just like he had fantasized about, she tasted *sweet.*

"We..." He pushed his words into her mouth. "We can't be doing this…. Blossom…"

"Shh..." She kissed the corner of his lips. "Just let go."

Despite his words lingering in the air, he continued to what he wanted with his teeth nipping at her bottom lip and her tongue warm against his lips. Henry lowered his shoulders into her, a certain calm coming over him before his nerves pinched again and he hitched his breath.

"Fu-Fuck..." He choked, turning his head. Suddenly his hands found her shoulders, and she looked up at him with wide eyes when he managed to push her back for the second time. "Blossom, I'm investigating a murder that may very fucking well have something to do with you, which makes you a liability. Do you understand that?" He was out of breath, disheveled hair sticking up. "I can't do this. If anything happens, or—" He blinked down at her, catching himself from saying anything more and saw that tears had begun to sting the corners of her eyes. "I can't do this." He hushed. Still, he didn't pull away. Blinking, Henry glanced down at her mouth, then back up to her eyes, just as she did the same. "You don't want to do this, Blossom. You should be with someone your own age." His voice now a mere whisper, she turned her cheek. "I'll drive you home." He sighed, finally beginning to slip from her, untangle himself from her hands. Yet, like a fish slipping from a bear's jaw, Blossom just yanked on him harder.

He ended up only two inches from his original position, his back against the wall and his eyes on the ceiling. She was stronger than he imagined. Without another word, she grabbed his wrist, guiding his hand up her thigh, then beneath the soft velvet hemming of her dress.

She wasn't wearing any panties.

"I don't *want* someone my own age... I want *you.*"

Henry's eyes widened and he retracted his hand as if he had just put it to a fire. Blossom's nails dug into his skin, and he winced slightly. Nonetheless, feeling the heat in his face flood his groin in a sweeping wave of dizzying arousal, after a brief moment of hesitation, Henry squeezed his jaw slightly, slowly relaxing into her, and followed the trail back to between the heat of her thighs. His thumb brushing the swollen flesh before he dipped into her slick depths.

Blossom nearly collapsed in shudders against him. Mewling. He watched her, with almost an expression of horror while she began to grind herself into his palm and rested her forehead to his chest. Lowering his head to press his mouth to the top of her head, feeling her walls contract around his knuckles until she moaned his name as poisonous and alluring as venom before with a shake of his head, closing his eyes again, Henry's other hand then found its way around her throat—his knuckles pushing under her jaw—and forcing her to lift her face.

With a deepened, desperate kiss, Blossom stumbled over her heels. Her knees hitting the edge of the mattress and causing her to fall against the springs, her dress bunching around her hips when he pushed her back. Climbing over her, Henry then began to make up for all the times he wanted to kiss her, dreamt of it, fantasized taking her in his arms and having her all to himself. Now he did. And lost in the impatience of finality, he almost ripped the clothes from her body, restless, hungry, throwing the fabric to the floor before pushing her higher up to the pillows.

Bent papers crumpling under their bodies until he pushed them to the side as well, her legs wrapped tight around his hips. Causing the achingly painful erection that began to bulge at his waistline push against the inside of her naked thigh as Henry's face buried into Blossom's neck.

Small noises escaping her mouth, just as sweet as she tasted, with his whole body shaking, hot with sweat, he then bit his tongue to keep himself from crying out when he finally buried himself in her heat.

Squeezing his eyes shut, Henry shuddered and twitched, moving his hips slowly in order to ease himself into the feeling; his hands planted on her body and holding her still while she wrapped her arms around his shoulders, her fingers burying themselves in the thick locks of his slightly damp hair. Tugging at it and making a tight growl rumble deep in his chest. Having quickly pushed his undone pants down to his legs, the belt catching at his knees, at that moment, he truly understood how badly the body yearns to be touched.

Craving the sensation of flesh on flesh, bone grinding up against bone such as the gears of a machine, just as it desires, feeds, responds, and nourishes, it acts as a monster. And in their appetite for flesh, for belonging, for *control*, they threatened to consume another with an unforgiving grip and raw intensity.

The small whines and gasps that filtered through the air, the curses she let out fueling his confidence, when Henry lifted himself over her, placing one hand on her hip with bruises trailing his touch as he fucked her harder, clawing at her, his aching joints yearned for warmth, for pressure, for the gratification of relief. He let out a pained breath, but didn't falter. Possessing a strength he once forgot.

Sweet and tender such as the metallic aftertaste of thick-cut tenderloin, as he buried himself deeper into her heat and felt her squirm beneath him, Henry began to imagine her blood flowing under the surface of her skin. Filling her limbs, circulating from her beating heart, flushing her cheeks the gentle rosiness that contoured the tip of her nose. And when he opened his eyes again, leaning up to kiss her, her lips—glossy and pink—readily opened for him, allowing his tongue to run over her gums, tasting her teeth as he held her face in his hand, taking her in; all of her.

Dragging his nose down her neck and burying it in the softness and warmth of her breast, letting her fill his lungs with hints of lavender and freshly cut grass in the springtime, she smelled of raspberries, flowers, honey and innocence. A garden. *His* garden. Its roots wrapping around his muscles, his bones, it washed away the ash that had begun to suffocate him. Tying him to her—her, who lay beneath him and clung to him, desperately kissing his shoulder, neck and jaw, tasting the sweat against his skin—her fingers buried in his hair and her thighs squeezing around his hips, a single, desperate moan escaping her parted lips as he finally planted his seed under the dusty, heaviness of the smoke-filled room. And just like that, it felt as if Henry was taking a breath of fresh air for the first time in years.

Blossom melted into the cool, damp sheets, and into the buttery, sweet release that followed his physicality. Turning her head toward the window, she could see the outline of the trees outside the hotel, sloping up the mountain beneath the cool moonlight.

Imagining crawling inside them, she fantasized the feeling of the bugs that would cover her arms and legs, burrow inside of her, and how the tree, strong and thick, would embrace her inside its darkness. Weeds and vines and flowers sprouting from her flesh as she pushed her fingers outward toward the warmth of the sun, becoming one with the tree, ancient, beautiful, mysterious.

There was a hollowness in Blossom's chest. As if someone had dug a hole into her sternum in preparation to plant something where her heart was supposed to be before getting distracted, allowing for worms to dig deeper into the soil, for spiders to lay eggs into the crevices of her flesh, and for rot to take place. Nonetheless, as she pulled her lips into an exhausted smile, breathing from her nose, running her fingers through Henry's hair, combing it back while he buried his face under her jaw and his arms wrapped around her waist, that emptiness within her, sticky with his seed, like heartburn, had suddenly become remedied by blooming bruises, sweet destruction. Temporarily filled. And the rot inside her, temporarily remedied.

She closed her eyes, listening to the buzzing of the lamp Henry had turned on. The imaginary flies swarming around her until the sweet relief of darkness coaxed her into the next morning, while Henry, lost in the darkness of sleep, envisioned his own kind of beautiful nightmare.

In this dream, he was sat slouched in the chair by the desk, the sun warm against his shoulder as the morning dawned. Looming over him, stretching over the raspberry stained-worn carpet, as if yelling to him: RISE AND SHINE, ASSHOLE, NEW DAY! AND LOOK AT WHAT YOU'VE DONE NOW. With the heat of a blue-lipped fire consuming him, he rubbed the back of his neck and let his head bow, a headache blooming at his temples. Moving his hand up beneath his view, he checked the watch around his right wrist, reading 7:30 on the dot, and closed his eyes. His chest falling with an aching sigh.

Then, he inhaled the burnt rubber taste of simmering paper from his freshly lit cigarette and looked over to the bed, where the shape of Blossom pulled the sheets to her form.

She lay half on her chest, half on her side, one arm tucked under the stiff pillow she had taken from Henry's side, her bright, crystal blonde hair disheveled, yet perfectly spread over her shoulders and the pillow. A few loose strands had fallen over her forehead.

Imagining himself walking over to her, sitting on the edge and running his fingers between the bridge of her nose to just above the slight curve in her brows and pushing the hair away from her face, tucking the strands behind her ears until she stirred and opened her blue eyes to the sight of him—still glossed over with sleep—half-unknowing of where she was until a gentle smile twitched at the corner of her pink lips... Lips he so badly wanted to kiss again, the memory of the night before was crude and sour, causing Henry's shoulders to tense. He took another drag of his cigarette, letting her be.

A simple mercy.

Instead, he admired her beauty, and such innocence as her sleeping— from afar. Taking in how... Delicate, she looked.

Her pale skin blushed pink against her cheeks, elbows, collarbones, she looked like a porcelain doll. Handle her too rough, and she'd break.

What he wouldn't admit, was that he wanted to break her. Splinter her into a thousand tiny pieces under his touch and mold her under his fingertips. He wanted to see the effects of him on her. And he knew it was cruel, but everyone is cruel. Henry then wondered how she may be cruel, and felt his heart twinge with the slightest bit of unease.

As if she could hear his thoughts, Blossom lifted her head and looked over at him, her head turning with a gentle snap. She stared at him for a moment with a set jaw before smiling.

It wasn't the natural, silly smile she gave him in his fantasy, no... This was... Something else. The unease didn't go away, but he smiled back, and she pushed the hair away from her face.

"Is everything okay?" Blossom observed the slight sickness in the way his breath hitched.

Henry shook his head and got up from his chair, leaning over to put out his cigarette before making way over to where she appealed to him with open arms, falling back onto the pillows from having propped herself onto her elbows. Pulling Henry into her with a slip of her palm around the back of his neck, he planted a firm kiss on her mouth.

However, lingering, when he opened his eyes, his now pounding and a cold sweat having perspired over the back of his neck, suddenly the captivating, tempting facade made of alluring features, gentle batting of her lashes and plump lips had pulled into a terrifying smile. And the memory of when she had looked so pleasant faded into a terrible, twisted fantasy.

As soon as she had woken, it was as if she was no longer a blank canvas for Henry to project his fantasies upon her, but instead a living, breathing, conscious creature. Staring back at him as if she could see the want pouring from his veins, written all over his face. Stumbling away, the heel of Henry's shoe somehow missed the carpeted floor and in the next moment, he found himself falling.

Darkness swallowing him whole.

Suspended, shadows wove their way through the fibers of his muscle and tissue, soaking the marrow of his bone and tugging at the particles of his being. About to tear him apart when Henry looked forward and saw that in front of him—no longer in his hotel room, but standing in the pitch black that stuck to his shoes like black goo— was Blossom.

Staring down at her, she wore the macaron-pink, frothy dress she had been wearing back in the diner with her white hair pulled into a high ponytail using a pink ribbon and Henry swallowed the lump in his throat, tears stinging his eyes as his his dropped into his belly like the rotten seed to a flower that had long wilted, shallow breaths making him lightheaded.

With no words coming from the slight opening of his lips, he blinked. All the while his pain was hardly reflected in her gaze. Instead, her eyes glossed over with a numbness he couldn't understand, she looked up at him with a softened, sympathetic, yet empty expression.

Reaching out to slip his palm against the softness of her rosy cheeks, feeling her skin under his like how he held her face to his the night before—tasting such sweetness for the first time, seemingly finding something he hadn't even been aware he was missing, searching for all these years—Henry's eyes fell down to his abdomen.

His white shirt clinging to his hips and ribs, vibrant red contrasted against the darkness around them and with white knuckles gripping the handle to a long, silver blade, Blossom twisted the knife into Henry's muscles, earning a groan to escape him as he was then enveloped by the explosion of pain bursting through his limbs, a weakness overtaking him. He slumped forward; falling to his knees while his face buried in the softness of her dress, pinching and twisting the length between his fingers, bunching it into his fist, breathing in the scent of delicate white flowers, vanilla and tender fruit, apricot and citrus orange.

When the next tender, bruised breath left Henry's lungs, that all dissipated from his mind and he was left empty handed. His palms extended in front of him. The shadows having swallowed Blossom, pulling her away from him.

With the taste of blood and dirt lingering against his tongue, his blood pounding in his temples, he proceeded to hurriedly check himself for any indication he was dying. Still, his shirt remained dry and the only pain Henry felt was that of his sore joints. But then, laughter began to rip through the seams of the darkness like the claws of an animal tearing through the soft flesh of man, not giving him a moment of relief before his veins filled with ice and his hand wound tight around his tie.

Slowly looking over his shoulder with wobbly knees, holding his breath, strands of hair wiped over the lines in his forehead while his whole body went cold, dread pulling the strings of his already cracked composure.

Curled over herself, as if a spotlight shone through the black, harsh laughter spilled from Blossom's glossy pink lips. It looked like she was sobbing, only, her shoulders heaving, her laughter continued to ring through Henry's ears. Loud and spiteful, bursting sets of forced cackles that caused his muscles to tense ever worse until they ached with the horror that glinted in his widened eyes.

The color drained from his face, Henry watched Blossom's whole body snapped up, inhuman, the crack of bone harsh and the sound of her cut off yelp turning to a swallowed gurgle as if someone had woven their hand at the back of her head and tugged on the thick strands of white hair,

Exposing her strained throat with her spine curved, her eyes, as crystal blue as the pale sky, met Henry's and the laughter stopped abruptly. Wrapping him in a deep, pulsating silence.

Slowly, however, her lips curled again, her jaw locking open. Baring her teeth with too much gum in a wrenching scream. The bloodcurdling sound ringing through his ears while her nails clawed at her chest, hands violently digging through the soft connective tissue and tearing it to ribbons, blood gushed thick and black over the pink of her dress, painting it red. It was then that Henry saw that there was something terrible inside her attempting to break its way out.

It shattered the marrow of her ribs and slithered from her belly, melting away her, into a grotesque creature with razor-sharp canines and claws drenched in blood. Her screaming becoming louder, until Henry was sure his eardrums were about to burst, he was caught in a state of paralysis, stuck watching her tear herself apart.

Sixteen

Gripped by white knuckles as droplets of pulp-infused, bitter liquid smeared against the wooden cutting board, the knife slipped against the thick skin of the grapefruit and Henry peeled back the outer coat with the tearing of white sheets to reveal the frayed pink interior while warm sunlight shone through dirty windows and dust swirled across the carpet. Then, his fingers dipping into the center of the fruit, tearing apart veins and cracking open the slices from the thin layer of skin that kept them apart, after placing the pieces on the plate he pulled from one of the cabinets, he grabbed the spatula from the countertop. Continuing to push yellow and white eggs around, pulling up around the bubbled, crisp brown edges and shaking the handle just ever so slightly to flip them, cracked black pepper spotting the bleeding yolk while salt soaked up the oil-coated bottom.

Standing there in a pair of his red and yellow plaid boxers and a black t-shirt, his hair pushed from his eyes with a boldness to its untamed shape that was lost when he combed his air back, wetting it down with a thin layer of gel, his eyes shifted to the bed while nutmeg-dusted pancakes steamed to his right; the white, creamy batter spotted with swollen blueberries that stained the expanding surface in blotches of deep purples and pinks.

Most of his lovers were gone before the sunlight broke through the rooftops or shone through the thick branches of the trees, exposing the cruel needs of the night before. But with Blossom so gently grasping the pillow beneath her chest, her hair strewn in waves of blonde around her head, Henry furrowed his brows. Feeling as if she had been there all his life. Not understanding how so quickly she had gotten underneath his skin, or what would happen, how this girl would... Affect him. He bit the inside of his lip, turning back to the food and shuffling the pancakes next to the grapefruit two at a time when they were ready.

As usual, he woke shortly past 6:30. Wanting to do something nice for Blossom, partially because he couldn't stand the idea of being there with her without some sort of distraction, he had decided to drive down to the store and purchase food; knowing it would soon go rotten in the mini fridge of his hotel room, as on most—if not all—of the time he been there, he simply went for a cup of coffee and breakfast at The Diner. However, he was beginning to suspect he'd have breakfast, lunch, or any sort of meal anywhere, if only that meant he could have it with her.

After the eggs were done cooking, he piled them next to the pancakes and drizzled maple syrup over both. Taking a moment to taste the creamy, savory mix of flavors with a large bite and washing it down with the black coffee he brewed thirty minutes after getting back.

Pouring a second cup of coffee for Blossom, he then carried the mugs over to the bedside table, circling back to grab the food before sitting on the edge of the mattress.

The springs squealing gently under his weight, Blossom began to stir. Seeing this, his brows curved and a soft, slight smile pressed to his lips and when she turned to face him, he nodded to the plate in his hands. "I made breakfast." While she eased herself up against the headboard. Shifting himself closer to her so he sat against her hip, one arm slinging over her, the plate stung her thigh through the sheets as steam rose between them.

Looking down at the globs of Tuscany yellows and oozing yolk mixing with the egg whites, discoloring it a cream color, the golden brown pancakes stacked sloppily with beads of syrup clinging to the round edges, her fingers then wrapped around the fork that buried into the eggs, proceeding to take one bite after another before licking her lips free of the wet, oaky, savory tastes. "Thank you." She mumbled, still tired, her eyelids hanging low.

"Of course."

"Were you watching me sleep earlier?" Blossom asked, Causing Henry to tear his gaze from hers.

"I didn't realize you were awake." She giggled, digging into the pancakes. "I like the way you look when you sleep." He continued.

She fought back a smile, then cleared her throat and inquired, "where did you learn to cook like this?"

"You mean pancakes and eggs?"

Setting the fork down, Blossom sat back, motioning toward the coffee with a slight of her hand. Henry nodded, confirming that she could have it, and she brought the black mug to her lips. It was bitter coffee, a dark, cheap house blend, but it jolted her nerves and was good enough that it made her shoulders relax.

"Considering you didn't just put a breakfast burrito in the microwave for me, color me impressed."

"Somebody microwaved a burrito for you? How *romantic*."

His chest warm as the sun hit his back, it stretched over the strewn bedsheets and he glanced back up when she shook her head. "Nobody's made anything for me before, actually."

She was wearing the collared shirt he had thrown to the floor the previous night, the fabric unbuttoned down her naval, the sleeves loose and left undone around her wrists. He hadn't even noticed she put it on, thinking of her getting up in the middle of the night, lurking over the bed in the dark before using the bathroom and staring into the mirror, wondering what she was doing in his hotel room, in his bed, in *his* shirt. Perhaps beginning to get ready to leave when she decided to stay.

"Well." Testing the waters, he spoke quiet, hesitantly. "I'm happy to be the first."

"Don't get *too* confident." Blossom put the coffee back onto the bedside table.

Scoffing sarcastically, Henry dipped the plate to the floor next to the bed, slinking further against Blossom while his words melted against her throat. "Don't get too confident, huh?"

Shivers running down her spine, with a yelp when he yanked her by the hips beneath him, she buried her fingers in his hair while he began nipping and sucking at the skin leading to her collarbone, the mattress dipping when he crawled over her, his hunger still not satiated even as pancakes and eggs melted back into batter in his stomach and the lingering taste against her lips made his heart beat faster. Reminding him of when he was young and he'd stuff packets of gummies into his pockets, sucking on sweet licorice candy until his jaw ached. Yet, there was still never anything as tooth-rotting as Blossom James.

Seventeen

She left that afternoon.

Tipping herself over the edge of the mattress with a slight kick of her heel and a bounce while Henry laid propped against the pillows, one arm propped behind his head and ash staining his teeth—mixing with the coffee on the bedside table that went cold—Blossom left him with the lingering taste of her applied lip gloss that made her bottom lip stick to his when she went to pull away from their last, gleeful, cheerleader jumping onto the metal fence to steal a firm, go-get em' smooch from her footballer boyfriend type kiss, preppy and sickening. It made Henry's cheeks burn and a certain unease, slick and fat in his belly, turn over.

"I have to go to school." She whispered against the hollow of his cheek while Henry wrapped his fingers around the back of her neck, trying to steal another kiss before allowing her to pop back up from his hold.

Watching her, he puffed a quick, half-joking, "you don't seem like the type to be in such a hurry for your first hour."

—When she smirked at him from across the room. "Oh... I'm not. This is just part of my elaborate plan."

Henry pushed himself up slightly and blinked with superficial surprise. "Your plan?"

She then playfully leaned her shoulders forward and whispered, as if revealing a secret, "in leaving you wanting more." And just like that, Henry stared at the closed door.

Butterflies filling his stomach, seeping into his lungs and making his whole body feel high on adrenaline, he scoffed toward himself before turning his head to look at the clock. Noticing just what time it was when his phone, faced-down by the lamp, buzzed agitatedly.

He supposed it would be Norman asking him where he was with some messages more or less irritated by the fact he hadn't heard a word from him since the previous night and the fact that they had work to do. Still, melting back into the sheets and bitterly smoking the rest of his cigarette, neglecting to look at it, Henry felt this clawing desperation, an anxiety, make its way through his being. Like an animal had mistakenly burrowed in the warmth of the spongey make up of fatty tissue that supported his worn skeleton, now attempting to escape, all he could think about was to distract himself from these feelings.

Henry lit another cigarette, going to the mini fridge in the kitchenette and reaching for the bottle to calm his internal strife when—with an abrupt flash of disheartening memory to how he had previously meant to pick up more liquor from the gas station—his hand retracted, empty, and he looked to the trash. Seeing the discarded, empty bottles that also scattered sporadically through the room—three or four lined neatly along the edge of his desk after he had found boredom during his free time—with a scowl pulling at the corners of his mouth, he took long strides toward the bag he had brought his clothes in (and neglected to unpack) yanking a fresh shirt and pants from the unfolded mess of fabric before snatching his discarded belt from the carpet and making his way to the mirror by the entryway. His unkept brows pulled together, the bridge of his nose scrunched, he then swiped his hands over the sides of his hair, quickly flattening the disheveled ends while cursing at the lightening sheen of grey that diluted the black.

The jagged silver of his keys digging into the pads of his palm as he following the wishful lingering of floral perfume into the hallway, polished black shoes proceeded to thud against the musty raspberry red that seemed to pool against the floor from cream-tinted walls as he walked with the slinking movements of a wolf through carnage; not too hurried, not lingering, purposeful and stalking.

Sticking out like a harsh bruise while passing by those whose eyes trailed over his narrow figure and felt the tension of his presence nearly pulsating through the hotel, he was as noticeable as a twitching organ about to burst, as a gaping wound revealing the innards of a dying man. Except, if anyone were to tear him open, claw through the calloused, ivory flesh that hugged ropey muscle in an attempt to reveal—expose—what makes the FBI agent tick, they would be met with nothing.

As if he was a cadaver whose organs had been long removed, the vessel of his being left to wilt and rot, sometimes he would even wonder if he was already dead. A corpse who went through the day out of pure habit and nothing more than brittle bone and a cold, rough touch to show for his existence. If everyday, he was becoming less tangible than the last, and he would be reduced to a simple memory, perhaps a feeling, a reminiscence of who he *used* to be.

Before.

Henry didn't know how much time had passed, only that the sun still soaked through the bar with hues of dimmed, mustard yellows and he was running low on his third bourbon. He stared into the glass, head spinning, shoulders slumped forward and his lips forming a slight frown. Despite his original intentions, the sound of her moans, dainty, tantalizing, like the fine webbing of a spider's intricate designs bouncing against fat droplets of rain that reflected the cruel reality of how he hadn't resisted his impulses—how he had instead given into them greedily, hungrily—plagued his thoughts just as bad as her perfume lingered against his tongue.

Throwing his head back and succumbing to the last gulp of the barrel aged, eighty-proof and rich amber, almost an almond-gold liquid, he attempted to wash these thoughts away, or at least into submission, but all the same, the harsh sting that coated the back of his throat fading into notes of chocolate liqueur and dark, ripe cherry and blackberry, as if she had infected him into a state of perpetual necrosis, he couldn't forget. He couldn't flush her out of his system.

Henry's lips twisted upward into a sneer and he brought the glass back down to the polished mahogany counter. His breath hinting of vanilla and spice until the aftertaste of tobacco washed through him, closing his eyes, his fingers slid down to pinch the space between his brows and he brought his palm to cup his forehead. Then, just as one would do when suddenly remember something long forgotten, he abruptly lifted his face again. Looking to the bartender in a daze of expectance while dangling his cup out in front of him. The edge tapping the surface of the table just as Norman walked through the doors.

"He-hey…" He gulped. The intoxication slowing the rate of which he seemed able to produce his words before he managed to push them from the raw cords of his cold and disdainful voice, "can-can I have another... I need another drink."

The sleeves of his crisp white shirt rolled up to his elbows, his jacket slung over the stool beneath him— shortly after his question hung in the air, failing to get a response, Henry noticed the hesitation of the bartender and snapped at him. "I asked for another. Fucking. *Drink."* Successfully getting him to walk over and pull the spirit from under the counter.

However, as soon as Henry began his attempt to persuade the man to leave the whole bottle, Norman walked up to his side; grabbing his shoulder with a rough squeeze of his long fingers while making eye contact with the bartender, whose name was Don (short for Donald) and nodding. "Hey, no, actually he's good. He's had enough." Tuffs of black hair still sicking up from one of his previous attempts to keep himself from face-planting, his hand fell from his face and Henry was quick to protest, glaring in disbelief toward the sudden restriction being placed on his alcohol intake. Nonetheless, at the same time he attempted to formulate an excuse or some inkling of reason, Norman snapped his head toward him and sharpened his words into that of a tone used when scolding a child. Pointing, "you've had *enough.*" Which successfully cut Henry off before he got even three words in.

Not a minute later, shoving his wallet away after attempting to pay Don a twenty—money that was refused out of sympathy for his apparent troubles—like peeling gum from the sole of his shoe, Norman then pulled the dead weight of Henry's figure from his seat. Proceeding to drag him from the darkness of the bar into the light of the bare sun shining down from a clear blue sky.

Unable to stand upright, there was a newfound disheveled-ness to Henry while he slumped against Norman, clinging his arm loose around his shoulder before slamming into the side of the car with a grunt, nearly falling to the ground in a heap of limbs as a result.

After swinging the back door open and wrapping his hand around Henry's arm, Norman swiftly shoved him inside. The tensing indentations of lean muscle against his forearm showing the strength of a man who had picked up countless other drunks throughout the Town, since drunks were consistently the only problem the Town had faced before suddenly everyone had *murder* on their mind.

Even when the side of his face smacked against the padded leather seats and Norman was forced to shove his legs in after him, saying, "yep, in you go. That's it," before finally slamming the door against his shoes, he felt an inkling of hope toward Henry: the FBI Agent he naively held high expectations of from the beginning. Standing there, sweat beading along the collar of his forest green, short sleeve shirt, the first couple buttons undone to show the white t-shirt he wore underneath his uniform and tucked into the matching, cropped trousers, he could hear him groan while attempting to situate himself into a position conducive of making his head stop spinning—the sound muffled, but discernible through the slightly cracked windows—and Norman simply looked up toward the sky, not understanding what was going on and feeling as if he had no other place to go. Stuck.

Spotting a single, rouge bird flying overhead with steady flaps of its wings and the cool breeze ruffling its feathers, freedom in the way it swooped and spun and rose higher toward a single, hazy white cloud that formed with the nearing of an afternoon storm, he placed his hands on his hips and drew in a deep breath. Closing his eyes.

By the time Norman managed to park in the lot of the Evergreen Hotel, Henry had sat up against the seat with his head hanging back, exposing the hard edge of his Adam's apple that bobbed when he swallowed. The muscle of his jaw clenching, wound tight, his chest rose and fell with slow breaths while his lips fell slightly agape and his eyes remained half-lidded, a thin layer of perspiration on his forehead. Looking him up and down with a scrutinizing gaze, he asked, "what room are you staying in?" But Henry merely pulled his brows together, not responding. "Henry which room do I dump your shit-faced ass in so I can go home?" Norman then snapped. "Jesus Christ, Henry if you don't give me a room number I'm gonna just leave you in the parking lot."

"F-four-" He finally huffed.

Norman widened his eyes, repeating, "four…"

"Twelve."

Sitting forward, shaking his head with the utterance of, "oh thank god." Norman then opened his door.

After a struggle to get Henry out of the car, to his feet, all the way into the building, then to the elevator—during which he thought about grabbing one of the luggage carts and hauling him to his room that way—Norman went to grab his key, quickly realizing he had neglected to go back and grab his coat. Stopping in the middle of the hallway, he cursed under his breath and guided Henry to the nearest wall, allowing him to slide down it—the idea of just leaving him *there* coming to mind—nonetheless, Norman leaned his hands against his thighs and spoke low, understanding at the same time that the chance of Henry processing what he was saying was extremely low.

"I need to go grab a room key. Alright?"

"My… Jacket. It's in my jacket." Henry looked up at him. His eyes glazed over.

"Yeah, well, you'll need to pick that up later. I'll call the bar and let them know not to tow you either." He muttered back, straightening his spine and looking back toward the elevator. "Just—don't move. Okay?"

Henry hummed in response, already hovering over the edge between consciousness and unconsciousness, risking the latter at any moment.

Norman glanced back at him with unease before making his way back downstairs to the front counter, a relatively painless trip as the older woman swiftly gave him a spare key, having seen him trekking the distance of the lobby but also knowing him, just as everyone else did, before he hurried upstairs again.

Finally making it inside Henry's room, Norman dropped him to the bed, for a moment thinking Henry would slump off the edge to the floor as he clumsily turned from his back to lay on his stomach; something he wouldn't have necessarily tried to prevent as he stepped back. However, his hands gripping the stiff sheets, Henry managed to keep himself afloat.

Norman ran his hand back through his hair, about to turn around and leave Henry when he mumbled something incoherent. Smacking his lips together, sweat beading against the curve between his collar bones, it was muffled against the sheets.

"What?"

"Blo-" Henry swallowed, letting out a deep breath. "Blossom. I wa-want Blossom." He finally pushed, as crystal clear as the blue sky in the peak of the current season. "I... I need to talk to her can you... Can you go get her?"

The color from Norman's face dissipated into an ashen, sickly color and he opened his mouth, then closed it, then opened it again. "Excuse me?"

Henry then groaned, curling to his side in agony. "I need to talk to her." He repeated. But then, letting out a muffled, heavy breath that warmed his lips, he heard the door close behind Norman and he let himself melt into the dizzying waves of alcohol that numbed his veins until consciousness fell away such as the fading memory of a dream.

Eighteen

The alarm clock on the bedside table glowing a lime green, when Henry finally woke, it blinked at him ten till 5:00 a.m. He slowly pushed himself up against the mattress into a seated position, his head pounding and his mouth dry, unable to think of how he ended up in his hotel room. Instead only remembering with harsh vividness what occurred before. The events leading up to it. Still, just as soon as he found himself craving a cigarette, sitting there, staring forward with his eyes glossed over and hair disheveled, his shirt yanked halfway from his pants and collar tugged toward his shoulder, his skin buzzing, he found himself craving *her.* Like an addict after the first hit when the rush comes down. When they'd give everything, anything, just to back to that level of euphoria for even another second.

Just the same, Henry knew he *couldn't* stop.

And frankly, he found himself not wanting to.

It didn't take long for him to realize that he had left his jacket, which contained his room key and car keys—alongside his actual car—at the bar. Confirmed by a hand-written note Norman had left by his spare pack of cigarettes that said he spoke with the employee working and they had his belongings in the back, after reading the message, Henry crumpled the paper into a ball and tossed it into the trash. Shortly thereafter calling a cab, arriving at the station just before sunrise; knowing he wouldn't be able to collect his belongings until earliest 10:00 a.m.

When he walked in, he noticed that Abby was already at the front. Dressed in beige, high waisted, cropped pants buckled over a powder blouse, she sat at her desk with the phone tucked between her ear and shoulder, nodding in silence while scribbling notes to a yellow pad.

Having seen her only a handful of other times—all in passing since she was most often answering calls or dispelling concerns throughout the Town—other times coming to the conference room to tell them something or accompanying them to help with the workload, Henry figured she was a nice, quiet girl who got the work done without question, old-school in her interactions as she showed him respect but held little curiosity toward him, which, he appreciated.

Though, when Norman was out, leaving Henry alone at the station, he did admit to himself that he enjoyed the company she would sparingly offer. An example of which was her knocking on the conference room door and bringing in her lunch to join him, with a hint of hesitance toward the way she hugged the plastic container of a sun-dried tomato pasta salad she made for dinner the previous night to her chest; the blend of zesty tomatoes, capers, garlic, olive oil and red wine dusted by parmesan cheese and basil coating the squishy Conchiglie in a pollen gloss.

Of course, Henry had allowed her to sit about five seats down from where he had scattered paperwork and had been compiling notecards made, sorting them into categories and attempting to find clear patterns that could link the behaviors to traits the killer may possess, proceeding in pouring himself another cup of coffee before asking her a series of questions, finding out she actually moved out of the Town for some time before returning to care for her father when he got sick, due to her mom having already passed away.

Norman was right. She would have been a great lawyer, from the way she spoke with clear verbiage and seemed unapologetic in her mannerisms. When she began talking about something she was passionate about, her work, the station—which she was very passionate about —her eyes lit up a little more and she tucked a loosened strand of brunette hair back behind her ear. Her hands moving with her strong, confident words until she realized she had been talking for too long, waving the next thought away with a shrug.

Glancing up toward Henry with the flash of an acknowledging smile, he simply nodded back at her, turning right around the corner and disappearing into the conference room where he'd reside until the sun rose over the tree tops, eliminating the need for the florescent lights lining the ceiling and until Norman opened the door half past 8:00 a.m.

Before arriving, however, Norman opened the door to the Diner. Feeling the cool relief of the AC as opposed to the heat of the sun that already bore down on the back of his neck as it washed away the nipping breeze of nighttime, peaking up from the trees while soaking into the sky with the frightening promise of a new day, filled with new surprises and new disappointments.

The muffled background noise of those who occupied the countertops and booths calming the already pulsating, bothersome amount of thoughts running through his mind, creating a sense of dread at the idea of going to the station, where undoubtedly, Henry would arrive soon after—if he wasn't there already, Norman attempted to process the events of the last night. Turns out, it wasn't that hard to locate an FBI agent in a small town if you asked around enough. Having called his cell four times, all sent to the inbox, he was then directed to the bar following the sentiment of, *chances are, when you can't find a man, check the booze aisle.* Which, hardly surprised him. What *did* surprise him, though, was the words that came pouring from his mouth when he got him back to the Evergreen Hotel.

Norman's thoughts trickling down from the last hundred or so that crossed his mind in trying to justify what possessed the Agent to ask for such a thing as Blossom like water would overflow from the top of a worn down, cracked fountain, sputtering from mold-ridden holes, these holes were the same he could feel drilling through the neural pathways of his brain. Worms wriggling through wet, rotting soil and disconnecting his thoughts until the only thing he could think about doing was to go to the Diner, get a fresh cup of coffee, and see Sophie. So, he moved around the rectangular countertop toward one of the booths located on his right, slid onto the leather cushions and clasped his hands on the table, waiting for the steady clacking of two inch heels behind him.

A glass pot of coffee in hand, Sophie reached over his shoulder. Sliding a mug next this hands before pouring.

"Well, you look like shit." She said.

He looked up at her, listening to the sound of coffee splashing up the sides until the liquid lapped into silence and she pulled the pot away. A small smile tugging at the corners of his mouth, indenting the thin lines that led to his jaw. "You, on the other hand…" Norman responded as Sophie moved to the opposite side of the table. Pushing forward the small silver bell creamer she had filled with a delicate mix of his vanilla syrup and whole milk.

"I heard about what happened." She sighed.

He shrugged, tipping the creamer and watching the black swirl with white before it diluted into a light brown. Taking the first sip of coffee, the sound of the milk frother from the coffee machine behind them suddenly screeched and gurgled, steam puffing from the rubber knob as the smooth medium roast warmed his chest. "I got him back to his hotel room before he could do any real harm."

"Uhu."

"Don't give me that."

"I'm not *giving* you anything." Sophie reached forward, grabbing the mug from his palms as he let it hover in front of his mouth. He shook his head, fighting back a smile. "But you know exactly what I mean."

"He's *particular.* Alright? But what I can tell is that doesn't mean—"

"He's an asshole." Sophie shot back. "And now, apparently, a drunk." *You should have seen him last night. You should have heard what he said. Then you'd really have a bone to pick with the man.* Norman laughed, hearty and full while Sophie took a long gulp of his coffee, her eyes widened as if to say, *am I wrong? Look at me and tell me I'm wrong.*

"Yeah, but you know this town talks... So, he got a *little* drunk—"

"You had to drag his ass out of the bar and shove him into the backseat of your patrol car, Norman."

"I'm just saying—" Norman scratched his jaw. "That doesn't make him a bad guy. He's weird, sure, but they wouldn't have sent someone who wasn't going to get the job done. I'm sure he's the best. Plus, all Special Agents a little weird."

"You've never met a special agent in your life, Norman."

"You've seen the shows! He probably just didn't have enough to eat—I mean, I've only seen him *peck* at food, he hardly ever finishes anything, Sophie,—so you really can't... You can't box him in. Not yet."

Sophie leaned forward. "Then *when?* I've seen the way he looks at my daughter. That's reason enough for me to have some suspicion."

"Sophie, Blossom goes after anyone that'll *bite.* I'm pretty sure Henry isn't off the menu. And I know you want to make assumptions, but he'll probably just... Brush her off. He's with the FBI for Christ's sake. Then she'll get bored, realize she can't fuck around with his head, and move onto the next guy. Again, he really hasn't been here long enough for anything to have happened, and as far as I can tell he really hasn't even had time to get himself into that much trouble," the words tasted sour in his mouth as he found them leaving his lips too quick for even himself to believe. "Don't be so quick to worry."

"Then why was she there with him when he found the body?"

"Is it really so bad that he's asking for people to help?"

"You know Blossom."

"That doesn't mean *he's* going to—"

"Oh come on. Come *on*. You're really defending him like this?"

"We don't know him, Sophie." Norman's chest fell with a heavy breath of defeat. "I don't know."

"Exactly, we *don't*." She paused, observing him. "And something tells me, despite all this effort to make him seem... Tolerable, in the least, you know exactly what I'm talking about. You feel the same way."

"Don't pull me into this—"

"I've known you far too long to not know what that look means."

"Just because I don't *like* him doesn't mean I don't think he can do the job. He's *doing* the job. I mean, maybe he thinks Blossom knows something about the murders, so he's letting her think she can get close to him."

"This isn't a spy movie, Norman." Leaning forward, his hand wound tight around the mug, his brows softened and Sophie knew the answer to her question before she even got a chance to ask him. "You really trust him?"

"I *have* to. We all do."

Three coffees deep into his work, Henry reached over smudged and crinkled papers with bent staples and splatters of coffee soaking the edges, tapping the ash from the end of a cigarette while his eyes trailed the length of the table, finally settling on Norman, who stood for a moment at the door, looking at him.

"You know, I'm surprised you're even alive right now." He kicked the door shut. Henry leaned back in his seat, a flooding, cool sense of relief easing the tension in his shoulders when Norman cracked a bewildered smile.

"Unfortunately." He then sighed.

"You do that often? Drink your sorrows away?" Norman walked over to the seat diagonal from Henry, who, wrapping his lips around his cigarette, took another drag. Holding the smoke in his lungs, letting the nicotine melt through him before responding.

"Occasionally."

Occasionally was putting it lightly.

"Mind if I ask what the hell happened?"

"I just went out for a couple of drinks to ease… Well, seeing that kid in the shed." Henry lied, again. "I suppose I didn't have enough to eat, or something." *Or something.*

See Sophie? I told you. Nothing to worry about, just a jaded man whose seen a little too much in his day and needed a drink, Norman thought before responding with a small, "alright, no worries," under his breath. Thinking also back to the unprecedented rage he felt toward Henry in that moment and how he had been so quick to twist his perception of him. *Confirmation bias, you jackass.* Still, just as the two men began their work, two light taps at the door redirected their attention.

Norman stood from his seat first.

"Ms. James?" He asked, paying Henry a short glance from the side of his eye and seeing his eyes had fixated on her while she stepped into the conference room, pushing the door open with her shoulder. Wearing a long, cotton pink dress with big, round buttons down the middle, the straps thin and bosom hugging her figure, the skirt fell just below her knees, swaying around her.

"Sorry to interrupt, it's just—"

Norman's voice was stern, to the point. He looked at her questioningly. "Is something we can do for you? Did you have an appointment?" *Did Abby forget to tell me about this? No—she wouldn't have. This is just Blossom being Blossom.*

"Blossom?" Henry whispered under his breath, the taste of honeysuckle lavender prodding his mind.

"I just brought coffee." She smiled, lifting a clear plastic cup with the Diner's logo on the front. It was black. The other one in her hand was milky, a light, walnut brown.

"That's—" Norman cracked a smile and rested his hands on his belt. "Very kind of you." His tone laced with surprise and superficial kindness while she walked from the door, moving around the table to where Henry pulled his shoulders back and straightened his posture. A slight bounce in her gate, when she handed the coffee over, the FBI agent gave a fleeting, closed-mouth smile, though his eyes were less than forgiving. They pointedly snapped up to her gaze as her fingers grazed his and she pulled her hand back, turning to Norman, who observed the two, the words, *don't bite. Don't bite. Don't bite...* Echoing through his mind.

"I just wanted to give a thank you for everything and how hard you boys have been working." She said. Sliding the other coffee onto the table for Norman to retrieve. She had gotten his order from Sophie. "I can't imagine the amount of stress you're under with such a case." She batted her lashes. Henry's top lip twitched and he clenched his fist by his side.

Norman gave a small nod. "Well, it's our job."

After a pause, Blossom just gave a shy—goody-goody—smile and walked back to the door such as a child told to leave the room so the adults could have a private conversation, hesitance evident in the way her hand lingered at the knob before twisting it and slipping from the room, leaving Henry feeling as if the wind had been knocked from his lungs.

Grabbing the coffee she brought him and taking a sip from the plastic straw, letting the fleeting unease and superstition caused by her appearance to wash away with the creamy, vanilla-flavored syrup Sophie so diligently put in for him, a sigh left Norman's lips and he supposed, in the same thought, that she had also been the one to send the two coffees. The way she told him, *don't let him get to you* before he departed ringing in his ears, now diluted in the specialty of Blossom James to make herself to center of attention; just as the undertones of fresh milk delivered from the Jefferson's Farm early in the week carried the reminiscent taste of his morning cup and how they were now diluted from the ice that had been filled to the top, he reassured himself with, *there's nothing to worry about. He didn't bite* while setting the plastic cup down to his left and sitting. Grabbing one of the yellow folders from Ethan's pristine, new cardboard box that was labeled with fresh sharpie and pulling the autopsy report Frank completed for them earlier that morning out, meanwhile, Henry glanced toward him, wearily. The knowledge that he'd have to deal with Blossom later making his heart flutter.

Nineteen

That night, white bulbs surrounding a pink vanity mirror, leaning forward, Blossom ran the soft, coated tip of a matte, pink cream over the curves of her pursed lips; the color similar to that of the slight blush on the tip of her nose alongside her angled cheeks. Wearing a pink furry off-shoulder knit top, cropped just below her ribcage with a silver zipper that exposed the dip between her breasts, a pink ribbon choker with the small, diamond-accented bow sitting above her collar bones as well as a purple lined tartan print, mini pencil skirt with a slit that reached the middle of the top of her thigh, she tucked a strand of her tightly curled blonde hair behind her ear before standing from the seashell-shaped seat that swiveled in front of the small white desk and turning against the block heel of her white plastic shoes, the metal belt of her ankle strap pinching just ever so slightly the skin of her ankle.

Music muffling through the walls, reverberating with harsh throbs of heavy-set beats, there was *party* taking place just outside her door—her mother having reserved herself to a shared girls night made up of three other moms huddled on the back patios in cushioned lounge chairs with glasses of Pinot Blanc and the lemon acidity, bitter almond of Verdicchio shared over blush inducing and poorly written erotica—while Blossom smoothed the front of her skirt of any wrinkles and opened her door, letting the hues of bright mulberry, amethyst, bubblegum pink and sapphire blue saturate her pale gaze.

Not an hour later, numbing her thoughts with the kiss of lavender vodka, the rate she refilled her cup with liquor and strawberry, pineapple, and raspberry juices to help with the subsequent shots of booze cleaned through her system, causing time to blur into a mere, distant memory while she sat against the countertop. Legs dangling over the edge, the music pounding in her ears and mixing with the muffled voices of those who swayed around her—bodies bumping into one another within the closed space between the living room and hallway—she looked through the crowd with a narrowed, unwavering gaze despite the alcohol that coursed through her veins; almost predatory, she held herself slouched with a softened spine and pouty, agape lips. Her knees spread and her arms hanging between her thighs.

It was then that a young man in a grey t-shirt decorated by the High School's initials with large red letters matching the signature colors, wearing an engraved dog leg necklace with his brother's initials and a beer in his hand caught her attention, sliding past his friends and readily approaching her such as a fish taking the bait. Licking his lips the way a wolf would lap its tongue around the polished point of its canines when preparing to go in for the kill.

After locking the door of the guest bathroom with a flick of his wrist, Kyle Madison slid his red solo cup next to the tooth brush holder, meeting Blossom's watchful gaze as she hovered ahead of him with a small smirk before closing the distance between them.

Allowing him to cage her in with his arms, the small of her back pressed to the edge of the counter, though the heavy beat of the music continued to muffle through her ears, it was eerily silent while Kyle moved his salmon pink lips to form the statements "god, you're beautiful…" Alongside, "do you know how long I've been waiting for this?" While he looked over her, as if gauging what he was in for with high-arching, unkept eyebrows that curved down into olive green eyes rolling over her lips, then her cleavage; glinting with an all familiar hunger that made Blossom's stomach flutter.

Sand-colored skin pale beneath the bright, white lights that burned from round bulbs above them, highlighting the taught curls of brown-rooted hair, fidgety fingers inched closer to her and he showcased an impatience for even pretending he was there for anything else while finally pressing his body to hers so close she could feel the growing stiffness between his hips. His heartbeat throbbing against his chest as if it were her own. The spritzed ocean-scented cologne he wore filling her lungs, swirling with the sickening grease that shimmered against his bottom lip and the heaviness of the beer on his breath, Blossom suddenly felt dizzy. Woozy. However, before she could make sense of the nearing sense of discomfort, Kyle dipped his head. Lips latching to hers and stealing her next breath.

Helping prop her onto the counter so he could then fit himself between her legs, wet moans soon filtered against her teeth with his tongue slipping against her gums, opening her mouth wider. Still, the taste of lingering fruity vodka and cream soda wasn't the same as the taste of warm bourbon, and his cheap drug store cologne was not the same as that of the honey, amber, musk, rosemary and oak moss base of Henry's 1973 bottle of Paco Rabanne Pour Homme. Not to mention the feeling of his lips was no where near Henry's roughness, ash-stained skill at making warmth pool in her core with a coiling arousal, and the dizziness Blossom felt worsened, a certain coldness rushing through her body she hadn't felt since that stuffy afternoon, locked in the confines of her parent's room.

Dismay evident in the way she pushed his hands away from where they began tugging at the metal clip of her belt, she turned her head so his sloppy kisses left her mouth and she no longer had to feel the scraps of chicken left between his teeth from his lunch and the vinegar of his fried pickles, beginning to slip down from the countertop, muttering, "I changed my mind—" When Kyle suddenly put his full weight into her and wrapped his hand around her wrist, pushing her shoulder back from where she turned it against his chest with a sharpness to his touch that took her by surprise; his other hand coming up to her hair and twisting the cornsilk strands around his knuckles with a gentleness she knew could change in an instant.

Blossom flinched as his knuckles brushed her jaw, but spoke again, this time louder louder—wondering if the words were even leaving her vodka stained lips. "Kyle, I changed my mind. Let me go. Come on."

Yet, with acidity sticking to his mead-stained lips, Kyle shook his head, leaning in closer to her with his nose pressing to her cheekbone as he suddenly breathed her in. "You know, for someone who apparently fucks around so much, I wasn't expected so much... Apprehension." His eyes flitted over hers and he chuckled. She could practically taste the alcohol on his breath. "Don't worry so much though, babe. I'll be easy on you."

"Let. Me. Go." Blossom pushed.

"I'm *sorry,* babe! But you're the one that got in the *fucking* bathroom with me. You, of all people, should know you can't go around leading guys on, being such a tease, then leave them hard as a god damn *rock* and say," he forced his voice into a higher pitch, the words cutting into Blossom's skin like the edge of a knife. Trembling, she squeezed her jaw, swallowing the sticky lump in her throat and stared back at him with wide eyes. Hoping he'd truly look at her, truly *hear* her, and step away. Or perhaps the alcohol would twist in his belly and the greasy, deep-fried chicken wings doused in hot sauce and packaged, glazed marinara would spew from his lips and fill the bottom of the toilet in red. Closing her eyes, Blossom pictured red, but didn't fight back, even as he tugged on the strands of hair wound around his fingers such as a ten year old boy would reach in front of his desk and yank on the pretty girl's polished pigtails, even as he mocked her with, "oh... I'm so sorry Kyle, I-I changed my mind. It's not you, it's me. I'm just not in the mood anymore, oops!" A grin peeling his lips back like the thick skin of a tangerine. "Don't be such a prude, Blossom. I know you've given it to just about every other guy in school. Why not me?"

I don't know. I don't know.

Reopening her eyes, Blossom thought of snapping her head forward and making those pretty teeth his mom spent so much money on *bleed.* To chip them. She wanted to twist the roots from the gums as he watched with horror. Nonetheless, pressing his less than impressive erection against the inside of her thigh, she simply slouched back against the counter. Gripping the edge with yellowed knuckles.

He was right. Why not? *What is happening to me?*

She was used to men thinking they could protest her decisions as if she could possibly be persuaded, as if she was simply playing with them, toying with their minds. As if *no* meant *try harder.* And to a certain extent, usually she'd be amused by his insistence, perhaps let him think he was winning for a moment longer. But now, with her mind fogged by the swirling, nauseating buzz of being more than just tipsy, all she wanted to do was get out of the cramped space of the bathroom, the walls caving in on her as her mind immediately went to the thought of finding Henry, as if he could ensure her safety. As if he could protect her from the spidering cruelness in her bones or the venomous, cruel memories that plagued her mind; sparking a growing rage in her belly that seeped through her veins and made her cling to Kyle for support while her knees weakened and her chest heaved with labored breaths and she felt him unbuckle his belt and tug her shorts down her hips, the sides of her thighs burning against the jean material.

Slick and irritated, Kyle filled her with a single snap of his hips and she twisted her nails against the sleeve of his shirt, keeping her eyes locked with the pattern of the exposed tile behind the shower curtain. There was something more terrible, more vulnerable to the way she felt right now than any other time this had happened, than any other time she had willingly stepped into the wolf's den and let them do what they did best: consume, use, tear, shred, shatter. White and black squares blurring, she chanted softly to herself, following the rhythm of the way her vision bobbed up and down by the gruff, wavering and weak thrusts of him fucking himself up into her, *"I'm in control. I am in. Control."*

When Norman called it a night—late for dinner, again—Henry walked to the bar, collected his things after putting it off nearly all day, then, with yellow street lights helping illuminate the narrow, winding streets, made his way toward Blossom's house with white knuckles sliding down the leather-stitched steering wheel when he made the final left and was suddenly greeted by groups of teens scattered houses down from where the majority clustered on her lawn; spilling from the front door like blood oozing from an open wound.

The sight making his heart lodge in his throat as if the spark of rage in his core had sent the throbbing organ fleeting into his esophagus, cutting across the road and pulling up in front of the driveway, Henry twisted the keys from the ignition with an aggravated sneer then stepped out against the paved sidewalk.

Her hips aching and bruises flowering along the small of her back from being pushed against the counter so unforgivingly, Blossom felt Kyle slip from her warmth, softened, raw and sensitive, *fulfilled,* and finally pushed herself from his hold. Stumbling away while quickly pulling up her shorts, her heart lodged in her throat and her knees wobbly, threatening to no longer be able to hold her upright while she attempted to stabilize herself with a palm to the wall, her other hand finding the doorknob.

She knew she didn't have time to collect herself in fear of being stuck in the bathroom for even a second longer—she *had* to leave—and she wanted, desperately, more than anything at that moment to find Henry as he was all she could think about, unearthing her roots and claiming them as his own. Yet, ripping her from the fleeting sense of safety she found in the thought of possibly opening the door to find him waiting out there in the sea of great whites sniffing for the honey of her pollen, Kyle grinned, looking at her hunched, shaking figure and asked, "did you... Did you cum?" Before she yanked the door from its hinges, making her escape.

Knowing she'd have to drink a lot more in order to wash away the lingering rage and the overwhelming disgust that crawled beneath her skin like ants scurrying over her arms and legs, regardless, like a beaming, pink target, a flame to a moth, as soon as Blossom entered the hall, someone called her name.

Striding up to the door, which remained open for people to come and go, Henry saw that the living room crowd had grown to the point of pushing up against the walls, clotting the hallway and seeping into the kitchen. Wondering at the same time if Sophie knew what talking place, or if Blossom even bothered to ask her for just a *few* people to come over, then again, his lungs becoming filled by the stench of alcohol and cheese from the pizzas scattered over the coffee table, he remembered who he was dealing with and breathed out the undertones heavily sprayed cologne; standing amongst the youth of a small town who danced and bumped into one another, dizzily spinning until their minds escaped the confines of reality.

Aware that he was completely invisible, that if he took one more step into the house he would disappear... Become engulfed, even then, before continuing his search toward the back of the house and pulling him from his mind, two teenage girls—one sixteen and the other eighteen from the looks of it—dressed in colorful, fitted fabrics that rode up their thighs as they took bouncy steps, brushed past him with giddy, blushed smiles beneath bright eyes and an allure of innocence that wasn't as pointed, or harnessed as Blossom's. Causing a slight smirk to hint at the corner of his pressed lips.

Beginning to follow them, Henry felt as if he had been caught in a dream where he was standing amidst a herd of baby lambs and peered between sardined shoulders, tracking the girls during a slight moment of distraction before spotting the perfectly oval-shaped back of a head fluffed by shiny blonde hair—Blossom's head —stained with the blue lights that soaked up the shadows of the hallway until they turned pink, seeping into an almost blood, coagulated red. And just like that, dodging the mindless sway of hips alongside the catching of heels against rigged frays of beer-stained carpet, his stomach twisted with something more dangerous than rage. His true appetite taking hold.

Wearing an earth-toned green and yellow plaid shirt tucked into beige khakis, Mr. Whitmore pushed through the crowd toward Blossom, motioning toward his drink, then the lack of hers when he came to a stop. "Hi! Can I get you one?" He yelled over the music. However, noticing the lights glinting against the swelling of tears around the edges of her globbed mascara, he reached a hand out. His fingertips grazing the goosebumps of her arms. "Is everything okay? Did something happen?" He pinched her elbow. "Do you want to go somewhere? You look like you need a moment."

"That's… Um… I'm good. Thank you, though."

She wanted Henry.

"Come on, I'll take you somewhere quiet—" When Whitmore began to pull on her, Blossom tugged herself back and her back collided against someone's chest. As if on cue, Henry's voice suddenly shot through the slurred mix of music and booze, having walked up behind her just a second before.

"She said she was good."

Blossom took another step back, pressing to his side and keeping herself close to him. Refusing to look at Whitmore, who greeted Henry with a strained, "Mr. Williamson." While squeezing his cup so hard the plastic nearly snapped.

Henry didn't return such courtesy, his fingers brushing her knuckles as he glanced down at the top of her head. "You are aware the vast majority of tonight's crowd are your students." He then redirected his attention with a lift of his brows.

"I'm aware. Just looking out for them."

"With a pink vodka lemonade cocktail?"

He laughed nervously, "I don't know what's going on, but I can assure you... Everything is quite alright." And nodded.

"Oh yes, it absolutely is." Henry finally smiled. Dominance exuding from his stance and the way he peered at Whitmore with the lift of his chin. If it weren't for Blossom clinging to him, her fingers having found his sleeve, he would take a step forward, furthering the intimidation. "Perhaps though, you should leave before I have any reason to think it *isn't*."

Finding no words to say that wouldn't have worsened the situation, Mr. Whitmore clenched his jaw, grumbling under his breath before pushing his way past them.

"Thank you—" Blossom stepped away, a sudden embarrassment and harsh realization that she'd have to explain herself making her avoid Henry's gaze and attempt to move away from him. Nonetheless, he reached out and snatched her arm.

"What the fuck are you doing?" He hushed, pulling her back.

"Nice to see you, too." Her words harder than she meant them to be, she locked eyes with him. His cologne filling her lungs and the tightening of his hand around her arm till his knuckles turned white making her knees go weak. Just that alone was more than any boy she was with before could ever do. Still, compared to how she had been handled not even five minutes ago, this was different. This wasn't thievery, this was ownership. He didn't expect her to try and pull away again, so he didn't dig his fingers into her skin, nor did he squeeze until he could feel the hardness of her bone. Rather, there was a tenderness to his bruising touch.

"What is this? What are you doing?"

"Having some fun, is that a crime?" Blossom sassed.

"Underage drinking *is*, the last time I checked—"

This wasn't the reason he was there.

"And what are you going to do about it? Arrest everyone here? Handcuff me?"

This wasn't what she wanted.

"*Stop.*" Henry tugged at her again, gritting his teeth. "Just stop acting like a damn *child*. This isn't a joke, Blossom. And it's no fucking time for games."

"Why are you here?" At this point Blossom wasn't sure why she was doing this. "What do you want from me?" His grip releasing from her arm with a pull of his arm back as if retracting it from an open flame, Henry blinked. "I'm just trying to enjoy the party. We *all* are." She then emphasized.

"Blossom for fucks sake this *isn't about the party.*" He took an exasperated breath. "Can we can go back to the hotel and talk about this?"

"What do we have to talk about?"

Defeat evident in the slump of his shoulders, Henry noticed the puffiness of her eyes and the pout in her bottom lip, a heaviness settling in his chest that masked, temporarily, over his anger. "Don't do this."

Blossom studied him through a blank expression, not understanding why she wasn't just going with him. "Don't make me." She finally responded.

Instead of pushing further, Henry simply straightened his shoulders again with a nod alongside the sandpiper-rough utterance of, "I understand." Making Blossom's stomach drop as he turned to leave.

Paralyzed in the grips of a panic that tore away at the seams of her composure, making her eyes sting with fresh tears that threatened to break and expanded in her chest, bloated, throbbing and fat, Blossom choked on her next breath. She couldn't understand why he was *leaving.* Why he didn't see that it was never just about going with him. Instead, it was like a rift through the ocean. And she was caught under the tide. She didn't mean for this to happen, not this soon.

Pushing against the foot traffic of couples trying to find a place to drunkenly consummate whatever shallow promises they made over beer pong, sour-cream dipped potato chips and mixed, lightly roasted nuts—promises soon to be forgotten with the upheaval of the booze that coursed through their veins—Blossom went after Henry with hurried steps; thinking of all the things she wanted to say to him while running across the lawn, the heels of her shoes digging up the roots of grass, sinking into the freshly watered soil. Nonetheless, her palms slapping the surface of the driver side window when she finally skidded to a stop, she didn't say any of the things she had thought of. Instead, she simply looked at him with wide, pleading eyes. Bouncing lightly, her voice thick and quiet as she pushed, "H-Henry? I'm sorry—*please*... Just... Don't go. I'm sorry."

Staring forward, slowly rolling down the window, all he did was mutter, "get in the car." Then, his gaze meeting hers, this time it was filled with something darker, more cruel, than Blossom had seen before. She brought her bottom lip between her teeth, nervously biting down.

He could see she was weak, her knees threatening to buckle under her, and a part of him wished they would, so she would need him, and he wouldn't be able to reach the end of this, if there was one. "If you don't get in the car, then I'm leaving, and *this* is *done*."

Before.

Henry put his coat up in the hallway, falling against the door with his breath laced heavily in a mix of chocolate liquor and vodka, whiskey and sour lime before stumbling into the kitchen; setting his briefcase down on the countertop and opening the fridge, the cool, blue light saturating his features while he grabbed another beer.

Popping the cap off, when he turned, he saw that Cindy—woken from the door slamming shut—was hovering in the hallway. Wearing a pair of matching, satin and peach-decorated pajamas, her short-cut black hair waving around a square jaw, round lips pressed together with disapproval, she crossed her arms over her chest and lifted a single brow at him. "I was beginning to think you finally drank yourself to death."

Henry snorted, lifting the rim of the bottle to his lips —his teeth clinking against the glass—and took a spiteful swig of the alcohol, which didn't nearly hold the same amount of potency compared to that of which already ran through his veins, causing his dutiful, loving wife to then scoff at him before turning and disappearing back down the hallway to their shared bedroom.

By the time he followed, Cindy had already crawled beneath the sheets, the only light left on being that of the hallway. Kicking his shoes off, Henry dragged himself across the bed toward his wife in an army crawl, his face falling into the crook of her neck with a heavy sigh. Despite the alcohol numbing his limbs, he was still able to feel the desire to be touched, the desire *to* touch settling in, and wrapped his arm over her. However, she tried to shrug him off, her voice heavy with distaste.

"Please, Henry, not tonight."

Yet, Henry continued trailing sloppy kisses to the corner of her jaw, propping himself at her side and mumbled, "but I *want* you… *I need you*…"

"You're drunk, and I'm tired. So please, just go to bed—" Still, her words did nothing to dull the sharp shooting throbs of arousal that had already tightened the muscles of Henry's core, sending his hand to her arm. She was small, small enough for him to maneuver her where he wanted, and he quickly pinned her beneath him. "Jesus christ—HENRY—" His mouth coming to hers, for a moment his kissed her heavily, then shoved his hands down to her belly. His teeth grazing the strained muscle of her neck as she squirmed and fought back against him, but with his drunken weight, knees pushing apart her legs, to no avail, Henry didn't budge.

That's when, in a state of panic and horror at the thought of what he was about to do, feeling his hands dip beneath the hem of her bottoms, Cindy Williamson, catholic-raised, barren, resentful, but honest and caring, dutiful, had smacked her palm upward of Henry's jaw when he lifted his head, about to lower his face to hers and try to give her another kiss that would have tried to tell her, 'I love you. I'm trying to love you. Love me back.' — And Henry bit his tongue with the snap of his teeth, falling to his elbows. Caging her in even worse than before with a pained groan. Then, rage boiling as intense and hot, as uncontrollable as his needs, his fingers found their way around her throat. And perhaps then she realized the mistake she had made. Nonetheless, that didn't matter, not anymore, because in the next second, pushing himself up with locked elbows and his pelvis digging into hers, friction building between the rubbing fabric of his now soaked boxers and belted trousers, his knuckles white, blood pounding in his head and the darkness so much worse, Henry was unable to see his wife's lips turning a bluish grey and her face as red as beets until her eyes rolled back with the onset of unconsciousness and sparks of a quick release followed the slumping of her hands, her body going limp.

The autopsy report revealed scleral and conjunctival petechiae, a broken Hyoid bone and multiple bruises that had flowered even when Henry frantically attempted to wake her in trembling desperation. Yet, no matter how many tears were spilled and how many apologies were given, Cindy's eyes remained glossed over with death, her lips open in an eternal struggle for air.

And, with the forgiveness of her death being ruled an accident, a misunderstanding, Henry Williamson was sent to the lecture hall.

Twenty One

Attempting to distract her mind from replaying what happened in the bathroom, Blossom looked outside and watched the trees blur into hazy shades of black turning to spruce green where the moon shone down on the thick, intertwining branches. Her thumbs twiddling in her lab, she felt like a child about to be scolded, only, sitting next to Henry, not knowing what she was doing there, why she had agreed to get in, what was *happening* to her, much less... What was *about* to happen, this was worse. This was *so much worse.*

Fear trickled down her spine.

Had he managed to calm the storm?

No.

Still, she bit her lip, closing her eyes for a moment and allowed herself to melt into the seat, squeezing her fists together to combat the tremble in her fingertips while, gripping the steering wheel, harsh, the muscle of his jaw flexing as he gritted his teeth so hard his teeth ached, Henry drove aimlessly through the Town. Knowing he didn't want to go back to the hotel. If he could keep this isolated, it would be easier to recover from. *Like a forest fire.* So, seeing from the road that the lot to the park was empty, he made the turn, pulling into an empty space before twisting the keys from the ignition with a deep breath as Blossom opened her eyes, slowly turning her gaze to meet his.

"I don't know why you think it's okay to play these games with me." He let his attention fall to the darkness of the swaying trees and the empty field.

"I'm *not*—"

"You throw yourself—continually—at me, then in my hotel room, after I explicitly express that it's not appropriate for me to involve myself with someone tied to a case, not including the fact you're *eighteen*—then you pull that *stunt.*"

"It was just coffee."

"Like how you just wanted to *talk* back at the hotel? I'm arrogant, sure, but I'm not a fucking idiot."

"I never said you were, but I didn't get to see you last night, so of course, with the thought that you could use a coffee, I expected it would be alright."

He laughed. It was sharp, mocking her. "Don't *bullshit* me, *Blossom.* I haven't been here long, I get that

—But one thing I'm sure of is that you did that shit in front of Norman on purpose."

"And what was I *doing* exactly?"

"Inserting yourself, because you're the type of girl who thinks herself so *important* that you just need to be the center of attention all the time." Turning his head, Henry smirked. "Am I wrong? Or should I continue?"

"Oh, come on… You're really going to act like you *don't* like this? That you *didn't* like me showing up to the Station? In front of Norman?"

"What's that supposed to mean?" He snapped.

"I've been watching you, just as you've been watching me and I know you find pleasure from me being so young and that the idea of me being so… *Palatable*… so innocent, makes you feel like this hot shot FBI agent again. Despite being so fucked up from all the horrors you've seen… From what you've *done*."

"You know nothing about me."

"I knew the moment you stepped into the Diner that you were like me. I also know that was the moment you wanted to fuck me."

"Is that right?" He was seething, his breath shaky. *She was making him lose control,* he could feel it.

"But, like you said, I'm *eighteen*. So, it's not *my* fault you got a hard-on and didn't know how to keep your head on straight—" Blossom's voice quickly rose into a bruising acidic flick of her tongue and Henry's hand suddenly crossed the space between them.

The back of her head smacking against the glass of the passenger window, strands of blonde hair fell into her face.

Looking at her with a wolf's gaze, with a hunger satiated only by violence and destruction, he pulled back only slightly with the sight of blood trickling from her nose. When she smiled at him, her teeth stained red, her tongue running over her gums, Blossom's entire body juxtaposed the idea between sweet and innocent to malicious and coarse. She was as sharp as a blade, yet as sweet as a flowering bruise. And his affection for her was as equally a perfect mixture—balance—between the desire to destroy her, tear her limb from limb, devour her, and protect, nurture, save her from all the evil in the world, including himself. But what he didn't realize, as she batted her lashes back up at him, her body molding under his fingertips so easily he for a minute was convinced she had been created for the sole purpose of *him,* was that she was a wolf, too. A wolf in sheep's clothing, a false prey. A predator of equal conviction. Henry's hand remaining around the slimness of her throat, feeling the material of her collar beneath his fingers, *she made him* want *to lose control.* And he wanted to hurt her even more, like an addict after rebounding.

"Oh no, did I strike a *nerve?*"

"I don't want to fight with you." Henry's voice cracked slightly. Yet, he still didn't release her from his grip, only further imagining what blood would look like in the whiteness of her hair, smeared over her cheeks and oozing from her perfect teeth, cracked, chipped and worn with bite marks on her skin, her flesh tattered and bruised. He looked at her beauty and felt his stomach rumble.

She pushed up against his palm, allowing him to feel the heavy throb of her pulse beneath his touch, the back of her head tingling as if someone had stuck needles into her skull. In the next moment, however, after meeting her unforgiving gaze, scowling, Henry shoved her once more before gruffly letting her go and falling back to his seat. Frustratedly taking out the crumpled pack of Marlboros from his coat with a red smeared hand that stained the white pack as he lit the cigarette between his teeth then breathed out a lungful of smoke.

Catching herself before she hit the back of her head again, a shaky exhale left Blossom's lungs and she slowly, hesitantly leaned forward, reaching out so her fingers grazed the fabric over Henry's thigh; the darkness in his eyes exciting her just as it had the first time he looked at her. His violence toward her in that moment a comfort in replacement of the void she could feel eating her alive from where the other boy had forced his way in.

After a small glance to the way she played with the pant leg of his trousers, Henry saw that a few droplets of blood had splattered over the curve of her breasts and his stomach rumbled again. "You don't know what I've done." He took another puff before pushing his hair back, tugging gently on its length as his chin lifted, exposing the strained tendons of his frustration while, slipping her palm further toward the inside of his thigh, Blossom shook her head. Then, she began climbing out of her seat, situating herself against him with a swing of her leg; immediately going to his throat like a predator going for the kill. Lifting his hands and quickly putting out his fresh cigarette before placing his palms at the crook of her hips out of instinct, Henry sighed tiredly, "don't— Blossom—stop," but with her teeth coming down around the harshness of his Adam's apple, he didn't do much else to prevent her from continuing.

"I didn't mean to upset you." Blossom whispered, holding Henry's face in her hands. "I don't want you to be angry with me."

"I know…" He muttered back, nearly suffocating against the stickiness of her lip gloss, becoming lost in the haze of want and desire as she unbuttoned his shirt.

Slipping her left hand to his groin, palming him between her thighs and feeling the length of his need while wrapping her right hand below the cut of his jaw and shoving the back of his head against the seat with a satisfied smile, Blossom then proceeded to take him from the restriction of his tightening trousers. Allowing him to bury himself inside her warmth with the arch of her spine and a desperate whimper; her hand falling from his throat as she then gripped his arms for support and closed her eyes against the sensation. Her head falling back, Henry sat forward, brushing his nose and lips against her pulse before finally giving into the emptiness of his stomach and the ravenous hunger that throbbed deep inside his marrow, his teeth sinking into her flesh, indenting the soft ivory.

Seated in the back seat of his car where they had impatiently moved to in the process of shedding the rest of their clothes, now, with his shirt half buttoned up Blossom's chest, her panties pulled low over her hips, she rested her head in Henry's lap with her knees resting crooked against the leather cushions while he wore his trousers with the belt and zipper still undone and the leather straps hanging from the loops; his bare chest blemished pink from the hickies she laid against his pecs and abdomen, lipstick smears and scratch marks blooming against his muscles. Taking sporadic, easy puffs of the cigarette that hung from her lips, smoke trailed above her and Henry scrunched his nose, peering down at her, muttering, "those things will kill you." While plucking the cigarette from her teeth. After which, she glared up at him and pouted such as a child would.

"That doesn't stop *you*."

"Yeah, well," he wrapped his lips where hers had been and breathed out, "I'm old."

"Clearly, you've got a bit of grey in your hair, *daddy*." Blossom continued to sass, teasing him with the lift of the corners of her lips into a look of smugness before Henry wrapped his fingers around her jaw, squeezing just enough for her mouth to open.

"You're disgusting." He whispered. Lowering his head down so his lips barely grazed hers when he removed the cigarette, he then gently blew smoke into Blossom's mouth. She breathed it in willingly, her eyes rolling back with a pleasured hum.

"And you *love* it." She smiled, running her nails down his chest before turning her head and planting her mouth against the tensed muscles of his belly. Kissing up his abdomen, her arm crossed over his lap so she could push herself up the scope of his lean figure and Henry caught her in another kiss when she reached his jaw, his lips tasting of ash and the salt from the sweat that perspired against his collar bones, stinging the tip of her tongue from where she trailed up to his Adam's apple. "Are you going to the dance?" She then asked, causing Henry to pull away from her.

"What?" He stitched his brows together.

"I got a new dress... I thought you'd like it. It's a little different—"

"Wait—you're asking me to go to the dance with you? You mean, a high school dance."

"Yeah."

Their first conversation echoed in the back of Henry's mind, when he offered his surprise at the fact she had yet to solidify a date for the event and she expressed just not having found the right person. The *right* person, Henry was *not*. Yet, there she was. Batting her lashes at him, her body pressed to his in the seclusion and darkness of the back seat of his borrowed, Bureau-issued car, wanting *him* to go with *her* to a *fucking high school dance.*

"You know I can't do that…" He whispered.

"Why?" She murmured back at him, like a kicked puppy. His fingers began to shake and a nervousness seeped into the marrow of his bones.

"I shouldn't have to explain that to you, Blossom." His tone stern, Henry then lifted his thumb to her bottom lip, wiping the smeared gloss and blood that crusted from the dip of her chin. Her saliva wet against his skin as he asked, "you really think it'd be a good idea for me, an old man, to show up to a high school event?"

"You crashed the party tonight."

"Yeah. Because I needed to talk to you, not to hang out."

"You're *fucking* a high schooler." Blossom lifted her brows. "And anyway, what, would you want me to go find someone else to go with? A boy my own age?"

His voice hardening with a quick, "no," Henry squeezed the muscle of his jaw.

"You want me to get all prettied up in this new dress, for another boy? Let him—" Blossom bit her bottom lip, fighting back a grin as she continued teasing him.

Nonetheless, Henry wouldn't have it, and catching her lips in his, he pushed Blossom back beneath him with a grunt. Their legs tangling as his fingers knotted in her blonde hair, tugging gently at the tender spot from where the back of her head had smacked against the window. She fought back laughter, and Henry hiked her leg up his hip. Digging his pelvis against hers, feeling her tense under him and the laughter choke into something much more scandalous. "Don't play games with me, Blossom."

"Oh…" She exhaled. "But it's *so fun.*"

Twenty Two

A swirling blend of bright colors, with the zest of summer as stinging as lemon to a cut lip, the following weeks were almost... Blissful, if that was the correct term; as if caged behind the sharp, rusted and twisted barbed wire of a dream extracting pink from his veins, Henry didn't know how else to describe it. The engine dying beneath him with the slight hint of gasoline mixing with the scent of leather polish, he dangled his fingers out of the open window, breathing out lungfuls of smoke and attempted to process such feelings while sitting outside Blossom's house.

A few minutes after he had twisted the keys from the ignition, the front door shut with the slap of the screen door and he tapped the ash from his cigarette, flecks of grey fluttering down to the asphalt, then redirected his gaze from the windshield—from the lines of houses bordering his eyesight that looked as if they had been

copied and pasted, molded from the same cookie-cutter—
to Blossom. She walked with wide, excited steps, nearly
running before jumping into the passenger seat and
throwing her arms around his shoulders, the door
slamming behind her.

Still sitting forward, he laughed in response to her
impatient enthusiasm, mouthfuls of smoke puffing from
his lungs when he coughed gently, the back of his hand
coming to cover his mouth while she began peppering his
cheek. "Wait, wait—calm down—hey," he choked. When
her right hand pushed his face toward hers, Henry then
grabbed her wrist. Finally turning to face her. "*Hey.*"

"Hello…" Blossom smiled, giddy, her breath hitting
his skin as she pushed toward him again and sighed, "I
missed you…" Still, he merely glanced down at her
mouth, then back to her eyes, feeling her wind her fingers
in the ends of his hair.

"You always miss me." He muttered back, taking a
final, long drag and allowing smoke to dissipate between
them, leading her to pout toward his hesitance to kiss her.

Nonetheless, with a smirk, flicking the cigarette out
the window so he could wrap his hand around her waist,
after deciding he had made her wait long enough, Henry
kissed her until the two of them were out of breath, their
cheeks hot and he was ready to pull her the rest of the
way into his lap, his hands covering her back, fingers
pressing to her spine and grazing her scapulas.

When she pulled away—something he didn't know if he could have done—and let her head fall to the side, she looked up at him and asked, "can we go somewhere?" While his right hand fell to her thigh and he began to tease the hemming of her mini, red jean skirt between his fingers. The taste of fresh bubblegum still hinting against his tongue.

"I can't."

"Why?" She stroked his hair, sweeping the strands back from his hairline like a mother does when comforting a child. Then, when he responded, her palm cupped his cheekbone and she stroked her thumb over the slope of the bridge of his nose, grazing the evidence of tiredness beneath his shadowed eye, which she couldn't tell the color of, if it was black or grey or brown, as barely any light was reflected from its depths. The intensity of his gaze never failing to entrap her.

"Norman and I are going back to the crime scenes. To see if we can find anything we may have missed before." Henry reached up and brushed back loose strands of blonde from Blossom's face, reciprocating the movements of her own hand, as if she had intended it to be nurturing. When he pulled back, she took his hand.

"And do you know what you're looking for?" Shaking his head, Henry rubbed his thumb over her knuckles. "Well, why don't we go look?"

"That's what me and Norman are going to do."

"That's not what I mean."

He pulled back further, narrowing of his gaze. "I'm not taking you with us."

"Thats not what I mean *either.*"

"Then what—"

The realization coming over him of what she was alluding to, Blossom sensed this and pushed forward once more, kissing his cheek, then stole back her hand and reached behind her. Pushing open the door so she could slip from her seat.

"Meet me there tonight?" She asked in the process before he could say anything, her words curling upward with a lightness that was so *Blossom* that Henry fought the urge to grab her; catching out of the corner of her eye the shifting of the curtains in the living room as a sign toward the fact that Sophie, who was working another night shift from 9:00 p.m until nearly 6:00 a.m, had come to the window to see whoever her daughter was visiting.

"Blossom—" He redirected his attention with the beginning of a protest, squeezing his jaw, but cut himself off with a sigh when she raised her brows. Reluctantly giving in with a grumbled, "fine," before she closed the door, running back up to the house.

An exasperated breath turning to a groan, after watching Blossom disappear back inside, he reached forward, feeling the engine kick back on with a jolt. Then, releasing the break and stepping on the accelerator, he drove back down the winding neighborhood in order to stop by the Diner and get Norman the lunch he requested before he had left, using the excuse that he was going to grab them a bite to eat and be back in just fifteen minutes. Even though it wasn't until almost thirty minutes later that he walked back into the conference room, smelling of a candy store.

After night had veiled over the Town, the darkness overtaking the trees and occasional, powerful breezes sweeping through the crisp pine, Henry followed the same path he and Blossom had taken the day of the search party with careful steps, the silver glint of the moonlight shining between mangled branches giving him a mere idea of where he was going before her voice rang through his ears, causing the hair to stand on the back of his neck and his heart to skip a beat.

"I'm surprised you didn't trip and break your neck on the way here." She called out.

Picking his eyes up from where he was diligently trying *not* to trip, having waited for him by the shack, the sound of a distant owl and clicking crickets carried through her voice under the wash of the wind and creaking of the earth around them. "Yeah, well, I'm not as clumsy as you think." He sighed just as an unrooted, half-buried branch caught the toe of his shoe. Tripping forward, Henry caught himself with the yank of his hip and a harsh curse, but by the time he managed to collect himself with a swipe of his palm down the front of his chest, Blossom had already burst into a series of high-pitched giggles that soon turned to laughter. "You have a sick sense of humor." He said, bitterly, staring at her with sternness exuding from his presence while passing the torn strips of caution tape that still hung from waving branches and lay over the soil, the only obvious indicator of what happened just a few feet ahead since everything within the walls of the shack had been cleared out, either locked away as evidence or disposed of, the floors scrubbed and the mattress burned to ash after being stripped of its blood-soaked fabric, the flesh that had peeled like wet tissue paper from Ethan's back when they removed his body still caught between the fibers.

"Tell me about it." Blossom began stepping backward when he neared, just as she had done the first time. When her shoulders hit the wall, she tipped her head back and Henry's eyes trailed down her body; stalking her, before finally closing the space between them and planting his hand to the side of her head, caging her in.

"So…" He whispered as she reached up, wrapping his tie around her knuckles. "What are we actually doing here?" He paused, tilting his head. "Other than looking for clues to help with the investigation, of course."

Blossom bit her bottom lip, her chest falling heavily as she reached her other hand to his hip, the leather sliding against her knuckles while Henry lifted his brows and allowed her to press the length of his body against hers with the tug of his belt loops. Under the moonlight, the blue soaked through her hair, saturating it like how the lights of the party had done, and pinning her between his body and where the stench of rot lingered, Henry dipped his chin. Not having the patience to wait any longer, about to kiss her when her words hit his mouth, dangerous and beguiling. "I want you to do to me exactly what you wanted to do the day we found Ethan." She whispered, her voice shaking gently as adrenaline buzzed through her veins and she suffocated on the scent of his cologne, the feeling of *him* making her heart beat heavy.

Their eyes locking, she watched Henry squeeze the muscle of his jaw as he searched her face through the darkness, looking for clues to tell him whether or not she was joking.

"Who said I wanted to do anything then?"

"Well," Blossom glanced down slyly and smirked, "I could think of *one* right now." Causing Henry's cheeks to burn. She tugged at him again. "Oh, come on... It's just us, Henry."

"Somebody could see."

"I bet you'd like that."

"It's *risky*..." Despite the warning in his tone, there was an underlying tease, as if he wasn't really protesting, and she could practically taste it. So, she hardened her tone enough to push him over the edge.

"And? I mean... *Henry.* We've never been particularly *reserved* to the confines of privacy, given how many times we've... In your car... The bathroom of the Diner... My backyard... So for a man so worried about being seen, the woods should be just *easy peasy* fucking *lemon squeezy.* If you really wanna get risky, catch me on my lunch break during school, then we can discuss possibly getting *caught.*"

Henry licked his lips, a chuckle perspiring from his next breath in the place of words as his stomach rumbled slightly, a result of her perfume swirling heavily around him like a cloud of vanilla and strawberry... Toxic, yet addictive, something he could only relate to the harsh bitterness of ash that made his throat raw and his mind hazy, choking him—cold—in contrast to the warm air stretching the elastic alongside collagen fibers of his lungs that laced with the scent of soggy leaves and soil.

Maintaining eye contact, after trailing his fingertips along the rough edges of the wood and slowly curving his palm around the back of her thigh, hiking up her skirt, Blossom wrapped her arms around his shoulders. Grunting when Henry hauled her legs around his waist and slammed her against the wall again, clumsily unbuckling his belt with shallow breaths cutting into more carnal sounds while he took her, rough and agitated, leaving flowering bruises under his wake.

Twenty Three

Sitting on his bed and leaning back against the headboard, holding in her lap a white box of udon noodles, honey-glazed tofu dusted in chopped green onion and broccoli sprouts clumping against syrupy peanut sauce, speckling dots of green against the gooey, amber coloration, Blossom twisted the noodles around the spears of her plastic fork, a wet sound emitting from the way she then lifted the food to her mouth. Chewing slowly while watching the tv flicker and not realizing Henry—sitting at his desk, one ankle crossed over his knee, his elbow against the corner of his desk with his own white box of takeout from the Diner in hand—had begun to speak.

"Did I tell you about the time when the elevator of the apartment complex I live in trapped me inside for over an hour?"

"What?" She asked.

"When the firefighters finally arrived, at that point, I was just sitting up against the back wall. Thinking about if suddenly, I just dropped hundreds of feet." When Blossom finally turned her head, replaying what he said in her mind, it looked as if he wasn't even there, living a dream. "In all that chaos, in the sounds of voices suddenly yelling at me to do things, everything was so... Clear. But now, I feel like sometimes I'm just going through the motions... One thing after another happens, they tell me where to go, what to do, who to talk to, who I can be with, and I listen. I do my job. I'm fucking good at it, too."

"I know you are."

"But then it was like... Even though I did exactly what they wanted, when they wanted, no questions asked, things just started to get... Too fast. I stopped being able to keep up."

Blossom shrugged, wondering where all this had come from. "You got old. Happens to the best of us."

Henry had previously been working, but now it was near 11:00 p.m., the hotel room filled with a dim yellow light overhead that swirled with smoke, and he was tired. "That's not the point." He took a bite of the white rice and Mongolian beef, the thin slices simmered in a soy, brown sugar, garlic and ginger sauce. "What I'm saying is," he chewed quickly. "I turned to booze to help slow things down. I got prescribed pills and got deferred off the front lines. Just because I couldn't seem to keep things straight in my head."

"And what happened in the first place to cause things to stop being so straight?"

His expression going numb and his eyes cold, he swallowed the memory of *that* night like a dry pill and met her eyes after looking down into his food with a scrunch of his nose. To the left of his elbow, and cigarette burned steadily, smearing ash at the bottom of the tray. "Like you said. I got old."

"But not *that* old." Mocking him, she set her food on the bedside table while swinging her legs over the side of the mattress and made her way over to Henry as he leaned his temple to his lifted fingers, rubbing the memories that had come flooding back to him away.

"What I mean is that I'm with you, I don't feel like I'm constantly trying to catch up with everything so much. It's like. Everything almost stops. Everything slows." He said, gruff, dismissive.

Stopping right in front of him, Blossom's hand then reached to his ankle. She pulled his foot from where it was propped and his heel hit the carpet with a thud. "Nothing has slowed, Henry." She began, teasing her fingertips up the lines in his trousers, created by where the tension around his thighs pulled at the fabric, leading to where the waistline cut into the space above his hips with a tight, leather belt. "You're just too dumbfounded to see it." After dropping to her knees, allowing him to bury his fingers in her hair and have her, she gave herself to him.

Except, with Henry leaning forward, hunching his shoulders over himself, he caught her chin. Pulling her head back so she looked up at him with a sympathetic look—something even she couldn't tell if it was authentic or not—a softened curve of his brow making her stomach flutter. "You don't need to do this Blossom. Not for me." He hushed.

And with his caressing, gentle words ringing in her ears, she realized Henry Williamson had a hold on her— control over her—that she didn't remember giving. Sparking fear in her: fear for what this man was doing to her, but most terrifyingly, what she *wanted* him to do.

"I know." She muttered back to him, her fingers hooking into his belt. Still, as soon as she began to unclasp it, he grabbed her hands. Pulling them away with a shake of his head. Standing, then guiding her over to the bed, he sat her down on the edge. Hesitating between her legs before easing her down to her back with nimble fingers pressing into the indention of her shoulder. Her eyes locking with his, Henry lowered himself to the carpet and carefully undressed her, lifting her legs over his shoulders.

Not ten minutes later, resurfacing while licking his fingers and sucking lightly on them, watching the blood that flushed through her cheeks fade into an almost fearful, pasty white, Henry pushed himself on top of

Blossom as she lifted herself to meet him in a sloppy kiss before placing his hand around her throat.

Leaning her weight into him, nearly slipping off the bed and into his arms when he quickly pulled away, she then whined, "choke me…" Her nails digging desperately into his boney knuckles. "Choke me—" But Henry turned his face away from her, closing his eyes from the unsettling display before staring at her with a curious kind of terror toward the flashing desire to tighten his fingers and watch the color bleed from her lips.

"*I can't.*" He hushed.

Sweat making strands of white hair stick across her forehead, she pushed his palm against her esophagus again, this time harder. "Come on… Please." He tried to pull back, but she caged him in. "You don't need to be afraid anymore, Henry… You can't hurt me."

His chest still rising and falling with heavy breaths, he could still taste her against his tongue. "I don't—" He exhaled. "I'm not afraid."

"Then choke me. Hit me—do anything—just…" Tears began to sting the corners of her eyes. "Make me *feel* something."

His stern eyes meeting hers, he then noticed the glossiness and how they had rimmed with a slight blush pink. He hadn't ever seen her like this. Suddenly, the anger came bubbling up. Feeling himself falling deeper into the same rage he had felt in the car, when it burst from the seams of his composure, Henry finally tightened his hold around Blossom's neck until she croaked a barely audible, "thank you."

Recognizing this rage as the one growing inside herself, blooming, just as his touch, she then pulled back her lips over pearl-white teeth with a wide smile and because of this, Henry knew in that moment she took pleasure from seeing the violence exude from him, seeing him fall apart. It fueled her like gasoline to a fire sacrifice to an old god.

This is what she wanted.

After Henry had fallen asleep, the sheets wrapped around their legs, the muscles of her neck still tender with the blemish of light, easily concealable bruises, Blossom pressed her ear to his chest. Listening to his heartbeat, the smell of his cigarettes making her stomach turn while laying there nestled against him and soaking in the same feeling she had experienced when she was sixteen, when she was being ushered away into one of the hotel rooms just two floors down from the one she was in now, where she had experienced her first kiss—the first one that made shivers run down her spine and goosebumps lay eggs on her arms as her skin soaked in the summer sun, the first one that made her honey turn thick like nectar, bumblebee sweet—and she allowed the boy, Adam, to press his hips into hers, extracting such trust that had been implanted inside her through ripped movie tickets, empty coffee cups, melted icees and smears of ketchup wiped clean by hungry fingers. The feeling of warmth and contentment, ease.

Nonetheless, just as everyone soon after had done, it was also there that, as soon as he filled her with his milk and took her honey, he sold it and tore the last petal from her flower, using it as a bookmark in his story of lies. And she learned that it would never be different. It never *could* be different.

The next morning, first becoming aware of the sheets twisting around his waist, the stiffness of the fabric and the smell of the chemical cleaner that had been used, Henry let out a soft exhale. Then, his ears became filled with the steady sizzling and popping of something being cooked on high heat and he knitted his brows together, slowly opening his eyes to see that the blinds had been closed, keeping the sunlight from the room. Thinking about the amount of messages he would most likely have waiting for him from Norman by the time he finally checked his phone, he didn't know what hour it was, much less what day it was, only that it was the end of the week and he was hungry; but perhaps that was only due to the consuming scent of burning sausage and buttered eggs filling his chest.

A low rumble tightening into a groan while he turned to his back, his chin then fell to his right shoulder and he spotted Blossom.

Standing in the kitchenette, barefoot, wearing one of his collared shirts, the length hung just above her knees. With the sleeves rolled loose below her elbows, flipping thin cuts of sausage patties over with a fork that scraped the bottom of the pan, clinking against the blackened metal, grease pooled beneath the ones she had already finished—piled on a white plate to her right—and she dropped another slice of softened yellow butter into the pan.

Following with a nearly translucent scramble of eggs and chopped green onion, which didn't take long to cook, she bit back a smile when Henry finally spoke up, his words still groggy with sleep. "Well... Would you look at that..."

Glancing toward him with a raise of her brows and smile, she asked, teasingly, "like what you see?" While continuing to push around the globs of solidifying whites. After adding salt and pepper, she scooped the eggs onto the slices of toast she had popped into the silver toaster earlier—something Henry didn't even realize he had—the white turned to a crisp, caramel brown with rusted burn streaks from where the red hot wires had touched and squirted packets of artificially sweetened ketchup in messy zig-zags over the yellow. Then, she poured two mugs full of recently brewed coffee before balancing the plate of food in the crook of her arm—something her mom had taught her with the expectation of having her work at the Diner as soon as she was old enough—and carrying the coffees over to the side table, where she

carefully set each item down. "I'm sorry it's not a lot...
Or maybe it's not that great—you don't really have that
much here. Plus I really don't cook." She dismissed, but
Henry just shook his head.

"No, I love it. Thank you."

Waiting until he pushed himself into a seated
position, Blossom then climbed back onto the bed,
propping herself on her knees, then fell forward to her
palms, kissing him with the turn of her head. It took
Henry a moment to catch up, but when he did, he weaved
his fingers through the softness of the hair that fell in
waves at the back of her head, cupping her skull in his
palm while his other arm wrapped around her, pulling her
to lay diagonal across him, where he dipped his fingers
beneath her jaw and grazed over the marks he had made
the night before, almost taking a pride in them.

Twenty Four

Still left without any new leads, Norman reached up, clipping another photo to the white board. This time a photo of a middle aged man named John; the magnet snapping against the glossy, black and white finish and narrowly missing the scribbled marker streaks that pointed locations to names to dates to times to victims, so on so forth, creating a knotted web of information they had yet to untangle.

John had a record of voyeuristic capacities when he was younger, repeat offenses that spanned from when he was twenty to twenty-five, his desire for peeping at girls in lockers and two incidents of breaking and entering into dorms dwindling, however, by the time he arrived back in the Town at the age of thirty after leaving when he was nineteen for such collegial reasons that landed him with the inability to do anything more than work at the small library in the first place.

His hands slowly falling to his hips, Norman's eyes scanned over the growing collection of suspects when he fell back on his heels with a huff. Feeling as if they were reaching for something they couldn't even identify. Completely in the dark. "You know, John came to Maggie's thirteenth birthday party? And every one since then." He commented, more so to himself.

Still, Henry—sitting behind him, propped on the top of one of the chairs (not sitting in it, but perched on the back with his feet resting against the stiff padding)—caught a whiff of his words, like a vulture perking up toward the sound of a distant prey, and holding a folder in his lap, knuckles resting under his chin while he looked through the papers, attempting to figure out which of the suspects they had begun compiling fit the general idea he had formulated on who could be responsible for the deaths of three boys—and possibly more—he looked at Norman from beneath the weight of his brows. Lifting them just enough to ease the pressure from the folds that had formed as a result of his concentration. "And how old is your daughter now?" He asked. Pretending to care.

"She'll be turning sixteen in September."

"So hopefully the investigation will be done by then, and you can still invite him. If he *isn't* our guy, of course."

"I'm only seeing middle-aged to older men on this board, Henry. Care to explain?" Norman glanced over his shoulder at him, raising his brows in an urging for him to respond.

Sighing, already returned to his thoughts, like a child resurfacing from the depths of a lake with salt stinging their eyes and the back of their throat, his voice as gravelly and rough, yet sharp and distinct as black sand, Henry's eyes tore from the papers and a small, "huh?" Escaped his lips before he met Norman's anticipatory expression. Then, slapping the folder shut, popping up from the chair such as a spring to a ballerina figurine once trapped beneath the lid of its box—nearly sending the piece of old wood back against its heels and to the ground when he jumped down—he tossed the folder onto the conference table and moved to the whiteboard, quickly making sense of what Norman was asking with rapid twitches of his head up and down, then from side to side.

These actions made Norman wonder if he powdered his nose before coming to the Station that morning, creating a creeping suspicion toward how energetic he seemed as opposed to the usual callous, murky and sourness usually inhibited by the Agent—the only warmth ever emitted from him following the lingering scent of bourbon or honey scotch—and after a few more seconds of silence, he repeated himself. "Why aren't we looking at people Ethan may have known? Or any of the other victims?"

"Did he not know any of these men?" Henry repeatedly clicked the pen he had pinched in the place of a cigarette. Norman didn't even know he had it until the annoying *click! Click! Click! Clickclickclick—Click!* Punctured his thoughts like if Henry were to actually be stabbing the inked, metal point of the object straight through his temple, the black bleeding into the gray matter of his brain tissue.

"He *did,*" Norman exhaled, "but what I'm saying is, why not look at maybe his friends? Other kids at the school? It was oddly suspicious how quickly those kids we spoke with at the bowling alley were to get over the death of apparently their closest buddy, right?"

"Mhm…" Henry slung one arm over his chest, lifting the pen to his chin, leaving a knick of ink against the curve of his freshly shaven jawline.

"So?"

"That's because they didn't kill Ethan, Luke, or Andrew." Henry stated, pressing his lips to a fine line that curved upward into a smug cock of his brow and drawing in an agonizingly slow breath.

Watching him turn back toward the table with a swift twist of his heel and flick of his bony wrist, black hair sparse over his exposed forearm as he had rolled the tailored cuffs of his white shirt to his elbows, Norman took note of how there was a more lax presence to the Agent today—a direct contraction to his behavior—reflected in how he ditched his usual smoothed black tie for popping a few buttons down his chest and leaving his black hair ruffled, revealing that it had a brighter sheen of grey over it than what was shown under the stiffness of wet gel. It almost exuded a... Confidence—different from the self imposed cockiness Henry continually inflated by stroking his ego with sly comments and the general predisposition for believing he was the smartest person in the room—alongside stronger stench of... Sex.

"May... You elaborate that?"

"The reason you're only seeing middle aged to older men—specifically from the ages forty to fifty-five, is because there's repression in these acts of murder that would lead me to believe this is a man who has lived his life... Double dipping between reality and a fiction. This is a man that has repressed... Aggression toward the same-sex, Norman." His cologne strong and black eyes reflecting the gold light that flooded the room as dawn steadily approached, flecks of a macchiato brown glinting in the darkness, he reached for the navy blue mug of coffee he made himself and took a long sip. Tasting the bit of ash left from his lips around the rim before lowering it back to the table.

"So, what. He's gay?"

"Not necessarily, because there wasn't any evidence of rape or molestation before or after the murders, so we aren't looking at a sexual need or gratification that would lead to the killing, the sex isn't the drive. But we are looking for someone with a fragile sense of masculinity.

Someone divorced or a long-term single, who hangs around younger men, maybe even younger girls and tries to insinuate himself in their livelihood."

"So… Midlife crisis gone wrong?" The smile that had begun growing against Henry's lips suddenly dropped and he blinked at Norman until he shook his head, waving away his comment. "Sorry, never-mind. Keep going?"

Squeezing his jaw before continuing, Henry turned to lean his hip against the edge of the table. Planting his palm on the surface, his legs crossing in a bent fashion. "Maybe he was rejected, socially, sexually, whatever. So there's this hatred toward the younger men around him, these boys who are surrounding themselves with girls and succeeding in placing he never could."

"He kills them out of jealousy for what he can never have."

"But here's the niche: heard of Reaction Formation? One of Freud's defense mechanisms?" Henry paused, leaning forward.

"What's that got to do with anything?"

"Freud believed that in an attempt to ease the internal tension being experienced by the force of the ID's impulses on the Ego, finding no other acceptable way to express these impulses or desires, the Ego creates the defense mechanism Reaction Formation, yada-yada, and that makes it so the person will act *completely* opposite of how they really feel."

"Alright. But isn't that a little out-dated?"

"It's a good fucking jumping off point for how this guy would be acting. You're looking for someone that will most likely not even acknowledge or remember killing Andrew, Luke, and Ethan. Someone who's all jolly cheery and goodie-too-shoes."

"Well, then, how are we supposed to CATCH him if we don't have a pinch of tangible, reasonable cause?"

"First we have to find him. *Then* we'll worry about that." Henry's shoulders dropped when he sighed, silence cutting through their conversation when the ringer of Norman's phone went off. Henry turned back to the table, paying a single glance to him when he picked up; pressing the phone to his ear after checking the caller ID.

"Everything okay?" Henry could hear the sound of an agitated, light-toned woman on the opposite end of the line. *Stacy,* but couldn't make out what she was saying. "Okay, honey, I hear you, but I told you that when I'm working and you have a police matter you need to go through Abby—" She cut him off. Norman turned so his back was facing Henry. "Fine. I'll take care of it. Okay? Yeah, I love you too. I'll see you tonight... No, I'll be home for dinner. Okay, bye." Then, he hung up and shoved his phone back into his pocket.

Henry scrunched his nose. "What was that about?"

"There's apparently some teenagers making a ruckus in the woods behind our house and... Well, Stacy... Is... Stacy." He let out a breathy chuckle. "She wants us to go take care of it." Grabbing his keys, Norman then headed to the door while Henry lingered behind. The memory of floral perfume and milky kisses making his shoulders tense. "You coming?" Norman opened the door, and Henry cleared his throat.

"Sure."

"By the way, Stacy asked me to ask you over for dinner. Nothing special, but it's kind of a tradition of ours. She has me grill up whatever veggies we have lying around the house and makes this mean veggie bowl out of them. Think of it as her welcoming you to the Town but also making sure you're... Alright." Norman pulled his glasses—the ones he used when he was driving—from where he had them resting against his chest, hanging from the collar of his acid-washed charcoal grey t-shirt; sweat seeping into the fabric from the top of his spine as they made their way out from the air-conditioned Station to Norman's patrol car. "It's probably the only night the kids actually enjoy hanging around us." He smiled. Sliding the clear plastic frames up his nose.

Looking at him from over the roof of the car, with his fingers wrapping around the handle of the passenger door, Henry asked, "and am I?" Wondering also that it was a little late for a welcoming dinner.

"Are you what—alright?"

"Yeah."

Norman chuckled. "Just don't talk about the murders or... Say anything weird. And try not to get excited about anything. Then you *should* be alright."

"Good to know."

"And… Can you give me a smile?"

"Why."

"Just do it, will you." Norman sighed.

Henry released a forced breath, reluctantly cracking his lips open like the shell of an egg crumbling apart, the glint of coffee and ash stained, pearl white teeth oozing out and contrasted against pink gums. Baring his teeth with an uneasy twinge across the gauntness of his expression, a look of strain to the hardness and perpetual malnourishment of his cheeks that Stacy would no doubt make a comment on.

Waving at him, Norman furrowed his brow, dismissing the request with, "uh… Never-mind. Don't do that," while quickly ducking into the car, the engine rumbling soon thereafter.

Entering the edge of the woods, shadows curling around the thick roots of trees and bleeding against crumbling soil that had been pressed into compact footprints from the search party—cooled where the sun neglected to hit—the two men stepped away from the car, instantly becoming drowned in hues of stone, cerulean, and berry blues with the reflection of forest and olive green. Just as quickly, they were able to make out the distant sounds of what seemed to be roughly five voices. All male, except for the bubbly screeches of one particular; the screams sending a hot flash of searing alarm down Henry's spine. Nonetheless, he straightened his tensed shoulders, puffed his chest with a deep breath, and continued Norman toward the noise.

Parked in a small clearing that veered away from the path, hidden between that and the steam which ran higher due to the melting of snow that had covered the ground and hung ice from tree limbs that winter, was Blossom: standing on the bed of a 1977 Dodge Power Wagon, the exterior a polished wheat color and the interior a worn brown leather, surrounded by four boys who all pressed their bodies against the surrounding walls. The tailgate unlatched, she teetered on the edge of it before dancing back against bare feet—pink heels laying not far away— as soon as one of the boys attempted to snatch her with loud laughter making her head tilt back.

The boys all yelling along the lines of *don't make us come get you! Be a good girl and hop down for us, come on! We don't bite!* While throwing back more lukewarm cans of mediocre beer, Norman was the first to attract their attention with the clearing of his throat. Elbows pointed outward, he rested his hands on his hips, then smiled at the boys while Henry rushed forward to collect Blossom.

"Now, I thought I had made myself clear the last time in telling you boys not to come out here and cause a ruckus, but here we are."

"We were just trying to have fun, Sheriff."

"And I suppose a good time to do that would be when boys like you are getting killed." Norman snapped back, taking a step forward. "A little fun and games never hurt anybody before, Tommy. And I get the need to blow off a little steam. But they've started to. And by coming out here, you boys have disrespected my work to try and prevent any more *hurt* from happening. Not to mention making the conscious decision to disrespect the last three *times* I've told you to knock it off."

"We didn't mean any harm—"

"You could have very well caused it, though. Now," he motioned toward the truck, "who's truck is this?"

"It's mine." Jonathan, a lean seventeen year old who had just over the summer begun to bulk up, his lengthy arms hanging by his side before he shoved his hands into his pockets and stepped forward.

"Have you been drinking, John?"

"No, sir."

"Not one drop?"

"No, sir."

He tipped back on his heels. "Then I don't suppose you'd be willing to prove that to me?"

"I wouldn't mind, no."

"Alright then, great."

"Are you gonna—" Tommy began to speak up again when Norman shifted his eyes toward him and cut him off.

"Am I going to charge you with M.I.P's?"

"Yeah." He responded weakly.

"Well, that all depends on whether you boys believe you've done something to be punished with. Got a guilty conscious? Or can you all take this experience and learn from it? I'd hate to inflict punishment if I don't have to, because one, I should think reflecting on the risk of being brutally murdered should be enough, but two, I really, *really* don't want to have to deal with *more* paperwork."

"We understand, sir." Jonathan nodded, looking around the get approval from the other two boys—one red head and the other a tan, short boy with a buzz-cut, who kept to the back, as if Norman wouldn't notice them.

"Well, that makes my job a whole lot easier. With that, can I trust you boys *not* to put yourselves, and others —" He referred over to Blossom, who still stood above Henry, her hands clasped in his, wavering back and forth but refusing to get down "—in danger from now on?"

"Yes, sir."

"Good. Because this is your last warning and next time, I might not be so forgiving. Understand?" Norman paused, then sighed once they all nodded. "John, come over here for a minute and let's get that breathalyzer on you." Escorting the young teen to the back of his patrol car, while Henry leaned the hardness of his hips against the edge of the tailgate and held Blossom in an upright position, the bulging vein on the side of his neck exposed by the way his looked up at her.

"Get *down*." He spoke from clenched teeth. "*Now.*"

"I don't wanna—" She groaned, tugging on his hands.

"Blossom, if you don't get down right now, then—"

"God, why does everybody want to tell me what to do all the time..." Bouncing with the beginnings of a tantrum, Henry tightened his grip on her hands, his fingers pressing to her pulse. It was erratic. She stumbled forward, her knees nearly buckling, then leaned her head back. Her brows furrowing while she pushed the slowed words from open lips. "Get down, do this, drink some more... Take your shirt off... Be nice... Shut up... Listen to me... Do as I say... But they never just... Fucking... *Listen* to what I have to you—you don't... Listen, Henry... I just want you to listen for a second can you list —"

"You can't keep doing this, alright? You're going to get hurt." He urged. "Now get down."

"You're not *listening,* Henry." She pouted. "I wasn't gonna let them do anything, I *promise,* I was just plaayyingg..."

Before she could finish her spiraling thoughts, however, Henry wrapped his arms around her shins and muttered, "of course you were," before taking a step back, causing her to tip forward and collapse like an unstable lawn chair over his shoulder.

She yelped with surprise, her hands clawing over his hip for stability while he began to carry her toward the car, then giggled, "you're so *strooonngggggg...*"

Excitement suddenly lacing through her. "Are we going back to the hotel?" She asked. "*Please* tell me we're going back to the hotel—we don't have to go back to the hotel though if you don't want to but—wait—before you take me... You need to know, Henry I'm... *Totally* consenting. I know I've had a *little* bit to drink but I promise I *want* this, okay? Okay Henry? I mean not that *that* would have like stopped you *anyway* since you just do whatever you want—still, oh! Henry? You know what we should do? Henry we should go to the *schoool*... You know how we talked about going to the school because— you know..." She snorted, sighing groggily, "because..." Then, forgetting what she was about to say, Henry— continuing to step over tangled weeds and thick, fallen branches—almost twisted his ankle when he accidentally stepped into a rut; forcing a burst of laughter to push from Blossom's lungs, just as it had done before. She then made a point to lower her voice, mocking him. "I'm not as clumsy as you think, Blossom. I swear... I'm not clumsy! I'm this hot shot FBI agent... How could *I* be *clumsy!*" And Henry felt his nerves pinch, the unease building under his skull, pushing and throbbing at the back of his mind like a clumping, knotted tumor he was no long able to ignore.

He wanted to ask what had suddenly happened to make her act out, go behind his back and put herself at risk, after everything had been so... Good. Still, he knew it was naive of him to expect it to have lasted forever, and, when they finally neared where Norman was finishing up his lecture on the dangers of drinking and driving (though Jonathan had come back in the clear), Henry put Blossom back on her feet. Watching Norman usher Jonathan off to collect his friends and go home, repeating, "*straight* home." Before exhaling and attempting to ease the strain from his voice. Hoping he wouldn't notice how Blossom was behaving.

"Suppose we should get her home as well?"

Closing the trunk and peering at them from over the bridge of his nose, with the lift of his brows, Norman responded. "Might be a good idea."

Pulling up along the curb in front of Blossom's house, Norman gnawed on his bottom lip, leaning his head back and letting the engine idle while Henry stared out the front windshield. "Do you want me to walk her up?" He then asked, quietly saying, "Sophie may be more forgiving—" When, if he were being honest, *he* didn't want to deal with Sophie. *She already hates you,* he thought. "I mean—"

"It's fine, Norman. I got it." Henry could hear the apprehension in his voice and glanced toward him before opening the door, noting over his shoulder, "she already hates me anyway." Passive aggressively, then walking to the back, where he helped Blossom from her seat.

Much to Henry's dismay, Sophie opened the door only seconds after he rang the bell.

"Well, look what the cat dragged in." She sassed, leaning her shoulder against the doorframe, looking at Blossom for a few seconds before her eyes shifted past Henry's shoulder to Norman. "Norman send you up here to save himself the grief?"

"We received a noise complaint before finding her with four boys in the woods." Henry ignored what she had just said, tightening his hold on Blossom, who stared up at him, beginning to come out of her fog, evident from the way she kept quiet.

"Classy." Sophie looked back at him after Norman gave her a nervous smile and a half wave. Then, letting out a sigh, with a reluctancy that made Henry scrunch his nose and his hand linger against Blossom's hip, she took a step back, then to the side, allowing for her daughter to stumble past her. A tired, wine-laced "well, thank you, Agent Williamson, for bringing her *home*," lingering with the scent of crisp green apple and chestnut even after she closed the door.

Swallowing down the aftertaste of their interaction, still standing there—only, his arms now empty—Henry released the air from his lungs. Shaking his head and replacing it with the aroma of freshly cut, damp grass before finally turning against his heel. Reaching into his pocket to shove a cigarette between his teeth, his eyes trailing the ground, he made his way back to Norman with slow, easy steps. Halfway across the sidewalk when, lifting his head, Henry quickly caught something moving out of the corner of his eye and snapped his head toward it. Whitmore's face flashing across his mind.

"Everything alright?" Norman leaned over the center console once seeing Henry's movements had halted. Henry blinked, not quite registering what he had asked, but glanced at him, reached out, opened the door and slid back into the passenger seat. "What was that for?"

"Does Whitmore live around here?"

"No, he lives across town. Why?"

"We may want to add him to the list."

His words hanging heavily between them, unwavering, they choked Norman and made his chest constrict. "What exactly are you saying, Henry?"

Back at the station, soggy white cardboard boxes spilled cold takeout Chinese food on top of crumbled papers in the trash can alongside an open box of doughnuts going stale from the night before. Dressed in a pencil skirt and white, frilly blouse—her hair up in a high pony-tail—Abby walked into the conference room, moving over to the trash and collecting it before beginning to walk back out of the room when, nearly colliding with Norman as he stormed in from outside— his features as grey as the Agent's smoke that shot out from forceful breaths behind him, clouding the ceiling and his eyes as rumbling as the storm clouds that gathered along the edges of town—her back hit the doorframe in the attempt to slip by. Norman reached out to steady her with a hand on her shoulder while shaking his head, but was too elapsed by the thoughts running through his head and the piercing of Henry's voice in his ears to say anything before Henry slammed the door behind him, leaving Abby in question—alongside curiosity—to what was happening.

"You've had it out for him ever since you *got here.* Now, I know we're desperate, Henry. *I'm* desperate. But —"

"I'm simply asking for us to look into him. To put a picture up, bring his file out and fucking look into it!"

"Just because you saw him walking around the neighborhood? We can't go around accusing people without just cause! Maybe he had some tutoring lessons. Maybe he was out for a walk and decided to take the long way home."

"Sure, maybe Blossom has nothing to do with it. She probably doesn't! But maybe he was out and about looking for teenage boys to mutilate."

"Why are you so bent on Whitmore being our guy? Do you know something I don't?"

Henry walked to the back counter and put out his cigarette, looking at the smudges of ash with flashes of Blossom crossing his mind. Grabbing one of the foam cups and stirring three packets of white sugar into cold coffee leftover from last night (Abby had brought in the machine from the lounge after watching them trek the distance for another coffee well over ten times before lunch) he then lifted the cup to his lips and took a large gulp of the bitter black liquid; cringing slightly against the slight twinge of granulated sugar scrubbing his tongue. "I'm just saying that there are plenty of places to walk without having to pass by where Blossom James lives, Norman. And we should look into it."

"She doesn't fit the profile." Norman shot out, the impulse to scold and berate Henry swelling his tongue, constricting his throat with the development of a fat lump.

"So we're just going to let it go? Forget about it and wait for something to happen?"

Norman looked to the ceiling and closed his eyes for a moment. Biting his tongue. "I'm just going to ask you this one time Henry—" Beginning to long last irrevocably expressing, or as close as he could get to expressing, the qualm which lured him into a general mistrust toward Henry ever since his drunken bout of neediness. However, he was cut off.

"You don't need to." Henry took another sip of his coffee, walking over to the table and focusing on the glossy photograph that he pinched between his fingers, finding a comfort in the horrors of Ethan Cooper. "I've got it under control."

"So you had it under control when you were drinking the whole *bar* and asking me to go grab a teenage girl from her house?"

"What?" *He didn't remember.*

"Or maybe how you apparently crashed one of her parties? You wanna tell me what happened with that... Or why the two of you then left together? Or maybe why you've been calling it a day earlier and earlier through the past few weeks? I'm sorry, Henry, but I wouldn't think you knew the definition of *control* if it smacked you in the *face.*"

The anger that burned inside him crisp, as harsh as the sting of cheap and commit-inducing tequila, Norman pushed himself from the table as Henry looked away from him, back to the photo and muttered, "you don't know what you're talking about."

"I hope to *fuck* I don't."

The abrupt slam of the door cutting through Henry's ears behind him, his shoulders dropped and he set the photo down, looking to the whiteboard as the heaviness in his chest returned.

Sitting at the counter in the Diner, his head hanging slightly forward, Norman closed his eyes and sat there in silence for a few minutes. Taking slow, deep breaths, attempting to avoid the blooming headache that throbbed at the soft spots of his temples. He recognized he would need to continue working with Henry as best he could until the case wrapped up, or, worst case scenario, fell as stiff and cold as the bodies of Andrew Clemmington, Luke Roberts, and now Ethan Cooper. And because of this, he was starting to understand Henry's infatuation with new bodies, since it wasn't like they could go out and arrest Michael based on mere paranoia, though Norman almost wished they could, just to have a prime suspect.

Nonetheless, if they brought him in, it would most likely cause a witch hunt, and also cause the killer— whether or not it was him—to go on a spree, make a show of it, then disappear, or just disappear in fear of getting caught. If he hadn't decided to stop already.

With the lack of fresh evidence since Ethan, the Town was growing restless. Frustrated. And so was he. They needed to be strategic with their next move, but Norman didn't know where to even start.

Grabbing the glass of white wine she had set down before answering the door, grasped by the cupping of her palm, fingers pressing into the bowled shape of the tall cup, Sophie continued to sip on the white grape like a fish puckering its lips and suckling on water. Her hair, remaining in its ponytail from when she returned home from the diner, fell with thin strands around the sides of her face. "You wanna tell me what you were doing in those woods with those boys?" She inquired, turning to Blossom, who leaned her back against the wall.

"They... They invited me to come hang out. I didn't think we'd... Get *told on.*" Her tone flat, she leaned her head back and Sophie laughed at her response. It was a bubbly kind of laughter.

"Don't fuck with me, Blossom." She countered.

"I don't know... What you're *talking* about."

"You really don't think I haven't noticed you sneaking around with that Special Agent? Gone in the middle of the night not to return until late the next morning smelling like cologne and ash? Him stopping by for quick little *chats* with you in his car?"

Regardless of whether it was true or not, when Blossom began to protest with, "I'm not-" Sophie waved her hand, cutting her off.

"You think he loves you?" She quickly spat, exhaling with a sweet, apple-spiced tint of grapes. "You think by running around with these boys you'll make him jealous enough to run to your aid?"

One glass was always enough for Sophie to melt into the hatred and disgust she harbored toward her daughter, a sort of jealousy and resentment she held over her as kind and gentle as any mother's wishful desires of a life once lost. But Blossom didn't know how much she already had before she arrived and pushed herself up, smiling at her mother as if to say, *well, isn't that what just happened?* Despite the fact that making him *jealous* was never what it was about.

"I *told* you to stay out of it, Blossom. And, you know what?" Sophie sneered, walking toward her. "What you do—" She waved her hand in the air as if to emphasize what she was saying, her wine nearly spilling over the rim. "Reflects back onto ME." She then tipped the glass against her lips again. "So whether it's running around with these teenage boys and getting yourself into trouble or hanging around that FBI agent—"

Blossom rolled her eyes, feeling her drunkenness become replaced by resentment. "Like anything I do could possibly ruin your little reputation, *Mom.*"

Now, she stood right in front of Blossom, taking one step closer to her from the other side of the hall and leaning forward enough to whisper, "Pain that deep? The pain you're trying to cover up with all your stolen pills, the booze to drown out the thoughts, the running around? The recklessness? You'll never be able to get rid of it. And that Agent? You're going to find out pretty fucking soon that your actions have consequences because he isn't a damn *child.*" Before spitefully taking a long gulp of her wine, turning her shoulder and disappearing in her room, leaving Blossom to the shadows.

Twenty Five

After stopping by the Diner for a single cup of coffee to make sure that Sophie was on the clock, making up some excuse to borrow a few hours from Norman away from the Station, Henry arrived at Blossom's house, entering through the back door.

Littered on the countertop were triangle cuts of peanut butter, jelly sandwiches alongside steaming ramen with a plastic fork—purchased from the gas station—dripping with diluted hot sauce next to a black wire basket where flies buzzed around rotten fruit. Passing the kitchen table, where a glass of milk—imprinted by the shape of Blossom's lipstick—alongside plate of tangerine slices and a stale, half eaten beef sandwich remained untouched, tomato slices drooping over the sides and melted cheese solidified in globs of yellow.

Looking toward the fridge, Henry noticed that the pictures of Blossom stopped when she looked around the age of fourteen. Dressed in dull colors, her hair long and falling over her shoulders, she gleamed for the camera, but looked nothing like how he knew her. Now, she wouldn't be caught dead in the bunched, stiff fabric of the green and white flannel she wore or jeans that did nothing for her figure. Four years later, and she was hardly recognizable. Still, there was a kiddish innocence to her that had dissipated from her eyes, replaced by the harsh coldness, numbed gaze she held now. He pressed his lips into a fine line. Wondering what happened to make her so… Hard.

Moving toward the nearest room opposite the kitchen once he entered the hallway, Henry pressed his shoulder to the closed door, calling out, "Blossom?" Before his knuckles tapped against the surface.

Leaning his head forward and catching the grumbled, *"go away"* that followed, his fingers then slid down to the knob.

"It's just me." He spoke softly, waiting for another response. After a few seconds, when no such thing occurred, he opened the door.

Lost in the swirl of pink pillows and buried in a pink duvet, a fur throw tangled around her shoulders, Blossom had cocooned herself, laying with her back toward him. He could just see the back of her head, and quietly closed the door behind him before moving toward the bed, sitting against the edge. The springs squealing, still, Blossom didn't move, and with careful—hesitant—fingers, Henry then buried them in her hair. His palm cupping the back of her skull, he proceeded to stroke the blonde strands down, as if petting the head of a rapid animal, observing her, a captive creature under his hold, a beautiful, pure rarity. The image of cracking open such a perfectly round skull returning to him with the idea that if he were to tug the blonde away, he'd find a hollow, bloodied hole. Allowing him to reach into the oozing darkness and sift through her brains. *What are you thinking? What are you hiding? Who are you?*

"Blossom…" He tilted his head to the side with soft brows after successfully coaxing her to look back at him, her cheek melting against the faux pillow under her as she clutched it to her chest. "What's going on?"

"I just want to stay in bed." She whined. A harsh reminder of her age. Henry blinked.

"It's been two days. You need to go to school."

"What are you, my *dad*?" She emphasized, causing Henry to grimace, his eyes rolling with dismay. He realized he didn't know much about her father, or where he was, other than what Sophie had mentioned when he first arrived, and that was that he had skipped town on them. But for him, it had always been just her and Sophie. His hand fell from her head to the pillow.

"Did I do something?"

"What?"

"Did I do something to upset you, and that's why you went out and--"

"Jesus, no, Henry, not everything is about you. There's just… Some things that I do that I—I just—" She sighed. "Sometimes I don't even know why I do things. I can't explain why. But I do know that I don't want to fight with you right now. Okay?" Her voice just above a whisper, Henry then felt her fingers reach back to his thigh. "Can we please just not fight? Isn't it enough to be here with you now?"

"I don't want to fight with you either." He mumbled. "But I need to know if you're okay."

"I'm fine." Pinching the ironed black of his trousers, her hand then began creeping its way up the dangling end of his tie. "Be here with me."

"That's not why I came."

"You don't want to be here with me?" Meeting his gaze while knotting his tie around her knuckles with a pale, numb expression and a sharp gaze, biting down on her plump bottom lip, Blossom tugged Henry down over her so his other arm fell around her waist.

"Stop twisting my words… And answer my question." He pushed, slowing his words.

"I did."

His lips grazing hers, when she pushed her mouth up against his in a forced kiss, she felt his face harden against hers as he scrunched his brows in conflict, his hand brushing hair from her cheek before he cupped it. And in a moment of raw vulnerability, he let himself melt into her persuading touch, feeling the darkness seeping from such sweet dwindling of fingertips down his spine, causing a ripple of shivers to bleed down his limbs. However, her tongue warm to his gums and a slight whimper pushing from her lungs as she tasted the lingering ash of his last cigarette, with the sinking of his stomach and the fogging of his thoughts, the smell of her perfume, the taste of her lips still fresh, making flowers and vines bloom in his chest before wilting and rotting like those with poisoned roots, Henry then pulled away; peeling her arms from where they had wrapped around his shoulders such as peeling the claws of an animal from fresh wounds.

When Blossom fell back to the bed, he saw that beneath the sheets that trapped her in the heat from her body—the heat he so badly wished to be enveloped in and to wash away the cold ache of his age through—Blossom was dressed down in sheer, peachy-pink, champagne base, lace detailed lingerie; the thin spaghetti straps loose over her shoulders, her hair sprawling over the pillows with bounds of loose curls ticking the nape of her neck.

Looking away and smoothing out his tie—his palm running from his chest to his abdomen—before pulling her hand from where it hand fallen to his lap, Henry pushed himself from the bed. "I can't stay. And you need to go to school."

"Are you really still angry with me?" Blossom shot up, sitting with a look of bewilderment.

Bringing his palm to his forehead, he rested his other hand against his hip and exhaled, stopping with slumped shoulders and his head bowed. "What do you want me to do, Blossom?" He then asked, turning back around to meet her gaze. "Just when I think things are good, you go behind my back and do something like *that*. Then, you don't even care to explain why and you won't tell me how you're really feeling."

"I told you I'm fine."

"You went out and got drunk in the woods with four teenage boys, without even telling me—"

"What was I supposed to say? Hey, Special Agent Henry Williamson with the Federal Bureau of Investigation, I'm going to go out into the woods with boys and booze, catch ya later?"

"Well, then I suppose that's a pretty could teller that you shouldn't have done it in the first place."

"I thought we weren't going to fight."

"Yeah, well." Henry pressed his lips together.

"Come back over here and kiss me."

"I already kissed you." He protested.

Blossom kicked her legs from the sheets, swinging them over the side of the bed and leaning forward. Henry's heart skipped a beat. The lingerie outfit she was wearing was a transparent babydoll blouse, the bra in the shape of two fur hearts with the fabric flowing down her abdomen, stopping just below her hips; showing her matching, cotton candy pink lace panties and a garter belt cinched around her belly that also squeezed her thighs.

Closing his eyes and fighting back a close-mouthed smile, he tilted his chin up, letting his head fall back before his other hand fell to his other hip. He stood there for a few seconds with a slightly bent knee, his eyes returning to Blossom while she flitted her eyes down the length of his body, making a point in the way she squirmed with the tightening her fingers around the edge of the mattress, tugging gently at the sheets. Teasing him with the pulling at the corner of her mouth, knowing he wouldn't last much longer.

"I want you to choose to kiss me. Then, I want you to fuck me."

"That's not fair."

"You can't stay mad at me forever."

Suddenly Henry's voice was no more than a whisper, thick and breathy as he swallowed the lump in his throat and looked at her in a daze, the sharpness in his expression melting as a thin perspiration pricked at the back of his neck and his chest tightened. "I'm—I'm not... Mad at you." He pushed, his breath slowing. It almost looked like he was about to cry. "I never was. I was *worried.*"

"Well, you were awfully mean to me before."

"That's because…" He paused. "I can't… I can't do this… Thing with you around Norman. I can't… Do the *things I want to do to you* around Norman and that's why we gotta be careful, Blossom. I thought I made myself perfectly fucking clear with you before but, besides the obvious risk—which you tend to not even care about—do you know what that does to me?" His voice cracked. He surged forward with long steps, closing the distance between them with an urgency in his words alongside the way he leaned his shoulders forward, pinching his fingers out in front of him. The vein that traveled along the side of his neck popping with the force of which he repeated, "do you know what that fucking does to me? Not being able to touch you? To get close to you? Having to just *hand* you *off* like that and act like I didn't care? Not being able to care for you in the way that you needed me to?"

"I'm sorry—"

He was scolding her. His tone that of one speaking to a child. "*Stop apologizing if you don't mean it* and for Christ's sake, Blossom. We have to be so *fucking* careful. Do you understand? I thought we were good—"

"We *are,* Henry."

"But can I *trust* you?"

"Yes, daddy." Blossom then reached out, her fingers looping against the leather of his black belt. "I understand. And I'm sorry, I really am. I didn't mean to upset you, I just… Do stupid things sometimes."

"Stop—stop fucking calling me that." Henry sneered, but she just tugged on his belt, forcing him to take another step forward so he was practically standing between her legs. "Blossom, no. I already told you, I didn't come here to—"

"To what?" His jaw loosened, his lips parting, no words formed and his hands soon fell away from where he lifted them to her wrist, about to force her hand away. But it was too late. His knees weak and the throb in his groin growing steadily, when she spoke again, simply saying his name, his eyes snapped from her body. Her shoulders leaning back, exposing it to him, splaying it like a bloody steak to a ravenous, starved wolf, Blossom then narrowed her gaze and smirked, hanging down toward the bed by merely the strength of his hips. *"Tear me apart."*

A harsh contrast against the pink duvet covers of her bed and the faux fur of her equally as pink pillows, with sweat still damp against his muscles, fingers knotted in her hair as she rested her head on top of his chest, Henry twirled the delicate strands between his knuckles. The smoke that trailed from the cigarette he pinched in his other hand bitter against his lips, which pursed firmly around the paper, lifting his head slightly, he then pushed a rogue hand through the disheveled mess of his hair that had been yanked and pulled on by Blossom's greedy fingers during their frenzy; a give and take of unequal proportions as Henry found his muscles sore, his joints aching and his skin left burning.

With Blossom tucked against his chest, the smell of *her* was all around him, constricting, pulsating like an illness, too much of it making him felt his stomach twist with queasiness as he smoothed out the loosened strands that curled over his forehead. His head falling back against the wrinkled, soft cotton pillow propped behind his shoulders, he closed his eyes and swallowed, Blossom's voice melting into the air of her bedroom, warm from the sun that streamed in from the open window.

"You scare me." She whispered, the thought coming out of nowhere while her fingers began grazing his chest in small, butterfly like, circular motions of her nails nicking the tender flesh of bruises and bite marks.

Henry blinked. The questioning of, *what do you think about? What's going on inside your pretty little head? What does that mean?* Returning to him as his brows tugged together and he responded with a sigh before reaching over to the nightstand. Tapping the ash from his cigarette with the flick of his wrist against a small pink tray she had gotten for him. "Is that so?" A smile twitched at the corners of his mouth and he shook his head, falling back while adding, "you know, you did ask me to tear you apart. I was only doing as I was told."

"That's not what I meant." She mumbled back toward the snark lacing through his teasing comment.

"Anyway, I don't think I, or anyone else for that matter, could cause such a strong effect on little miss Blossom James. But I appreciate the sentiment."

Tracing the ashen trail of his chest hair, her lips met the hardness of his jaw, but she didn't say anything more. Henry's eyes shifted back to the ceiling, watching her fan swirl with passing shadows until he smoked the length of the cigarette to a small nub. Flicking it to die out against the rest of the discarded cigarettes at the bottom of the tray, a few minutes passed and he finally broke the silence.

"What did you mean by me choosing to kiss you?" Tucking his chin, pressing his cheek to her temple so he could look at her, he then whispered a promise that he didn't even know the implications of. "I will *always* choose to kiss you."

"Promise?"

Henry didn't respond. Rather, he showed her with the interlocking of his mouth around the buttery smooth, blush of her full pout. And that's when she realized what was so terrible about him: the vulnerability of him kissing her *gently, carefully,* that made the numbness within her suddenly wash away.

But the worst part was that she *let* it.

Feeling as raw and as sensitive as an exposed nerve, her flesh turning cold and tense, she took a deep breath, kissing him harder as if to make him feel what she was feeling: exhilaration, a giddy, teenage love affair-type feeling that slowly became replaced by—not necessarily fear—but surprise and apprehension as she found herself tied to him in ways she hadn't anticipated.

This was *different.* And a part of her was okay with that.

Twenty Six

Standing against his car in the lot of the gas station, pulling a fresh cigarette from the plastic, crinkling wrapper he had partially torn from the white and red Marlboro pack, Henry snapped the cap of his metal lighter open. Scrunching his brows and holding his breath while flicking his thumb over the serrated, hardened steel wire of the spark wheel until the white turned to yellow and a solid flame licked the end of the tightly packed tobacco.

His teeth biting down gently against the foam filter until his lungs filled with the bitter mix of nicotine, menthol, and the hint of chocolate flavoring, he then pursed his thin lips around the indentations left by his teeth and shoved his lighter back into his pocket. Taking a long, slow inhale and looking up from the beige-grey, smooth cement ground in front of him. Waiting for tank of his car to finish filling so he could continue on his way.

Now, cursing himself for agreeing to dinner with Norman and his family, he stared into the surrounding darkness that reached forth from the edge of the woods on the opposite side of the road, smoke dissipating above his head with the neon glow of the flickering lights glowing from the interior of the square, white-brick building behind him. A part of him wanted to merely flick his cigarette under the heel of his shoe and walk into it. Let the pitch black take him. Do whatever it wanted with him, then bury his decomposing corpse in the rain-soaked dirt, let the flowers and roots and worms and darkness seep into him, overtake him. Let himself just… Vanish. But then, yanking him from his thoughts, the gas line jumped with a heavy clank, forcing Henry's head over his shoulder and causing him to jump slightly.

Norman's house was located on the edge of the Town. Bordering the woods by a measly pathway of rubble and overgrown weeds, a wire fence kept the shadows at bay from their backyard with a sweeping cul-de-sac making the orientation of his house diagonal to the ones surrounding it.

Henry drove down the street before mouthing the numbers of the houses that passed him and pulling up behind where Norman was parked; a sloped driveway curving downward from the asphalt street and leading to the garage, which was left open. Moving down it, when he reached the front door, he rang the bell; waiting not five seconds before hearing the thudding of footsteps and the door opened to reveal a short-statured woman with mud brown hair, nearly black, curled in toward her round jawline. Soft features and round lips a soft calamine that matched the tint of her cheeks, she reached out and took Henry's hand in a firm shake.

"You must be Henry."

"Special Agent Williamson. But yes. Henry."

"Pleasure to finally meet you. Come in." She stepped to the side, opening the door wider for him to enter. "I'm Stacy."

"Pleasure's all mine, and, thank you."

Norman walked out from the hallway with a foaming beer in hand. "Hey!" His welcome was cheery and frantically friendly, it bubbled with the lingering bitterness of cold beer. This wasn't his first. Henry took off his coat and slung it over his arm, observing his surroundings and taking note of the fact that it had the same layout as virtually all the other houses he visited during his time in the Town, including the Clemmingtons, Roberts, and the Coopers, while Stacy walked by Norman and he extended a snaking arm around her waist. Pressing a firm kiss to the top of her head. She squeezed his arm. "The grill is all prepped." Norman then led Henry outside. "Got the veggies all cut up and ready to put on, but first, let me introduce you to the kids."

For the next hour and a half, Henry successfully played buddy-buddy with Norman and shone a gleaming light of pleasure over reminiscent, grandiose memories extracted from maybe one or two of their shared experiences, even going as far as to ask Maggie and Nathan questions, including what they had planned for after high school and what their favorite subjects were and what kind of hobbies they liked. The rest was just filling.

After dinner, the kids retreating to their rooms and Stacy making her way through the plates of leftover food, storing them in the fridge before moving to the sink and beginning to clean up, Norman and Henry sat outside by the small, rectangular pool he had built two summers ago, drinking lukewarm, raspberry and chocolate flavored beer.

"You did good." Norman lifted the amber-brown glass to his lips, taking a large swig. "Didn't think you had it in you. To be normal." While Henry looked into the sparkling blue waters, taking a deep breath with a raise of his brows.

"It's not about being normal, it's about adhering to what other people want to hear. What they expect you to be." He said.

"You didn't seem to concerned with that when meeting me."

"That's because I don't give a shit about what you *think* of me. Now, your wife? I'm sure she has many connections in town. What she thinks of me matters."

"Fair enough." Norman laughed gently, looking away.

Henry took a sip of his beer, mulling over the heavy, dark berry undertones with a melting twinge of mead to his tongue. It ran smooth, compared to his usual choice in booze. "So what's with Blossom?" He then asked.

Norman's eyes widened for a hard breath as if to say, *don't even get me started on that girl.* Nonetheless, he cleared his throat and clarified, "what do you mean?"

"Sophie said her dad skipped town?"

"Yeah, just a few months after her fourteenth birthday."

"Do you know why?"

His breath catching, Norman looked back at Henry almost solemnly, the muscle of his jaw clenching before looking back to the pool and bringing his beer back to replace the words he was afraid to speak. Finally, however, he let up. "He used to work for the hotel."

"The Evergreen?"

"Yes."

"And?"

"One day, before he got off his shift, one of his colleagues and his wife arrived a little early for dinner. That's when the colleague—Claude Miller—decided to follow Blossom upstairs."

"What?"

"At least, that was what Blossom told us. Sophie, she… She doesn't think that's what happened. She says that Fredrick just wasn't ever ready to be a father, and when Blossom decided to put out those rumors, he did what he was always wanting to do. Leave. An easy out."

His throat closing and a heaviness in his chest, Henry felt his muscles wind tighter and his temples throb. He set the back of his head against the chair. "What do you mean… Rumors."

"We checked everything out. We questioned Claude about it and he said—"

"He denied it."

"Even his wife was able to vouch that he was down there with them the whole night."

"So, you didn't do anything."

"There wasn't anything *to* do."

Henry's nerves pinched. He took another swig of his beer, almost wishing it was stronger. "And what happened to Claude?"

"He resigned from his position at the hotel the next month, but his wife and him ended up moving about four hours south of here two years ago. Not many people wanted to have him employed with them after it spread."

Silence then transpired over them as Henry didn't say anything, instead becoming lost in his thoughts, in the imagining of what he would have done to Miller if he had chosen to stay.

When he arrived back to the hotel, the alcohol already wearing off and hungry from not eating that much while at Norman's, Henry took a shower, then looked at himself in the fogged mirror once finished; gripping the edges of the sink while letting out a soft exhale, his whole body aching with coldness despite the fact that the Town had burst with a surreal blend of colors as the pine tress turned a bright green and the sky a harsh blue since his arrival. And all the more painfully apparent due to the heat, the scent of Blossom's perfume clung to his coats and pillows, lingering in the seams and cracks of his consciousness and reality. *She was everywhere,* infecting him.

Shaving the stubble from his chin, washing the slathered, foaming cream from his cheeks and brushing his teeth, he then slowly moved from the bathroom and replaced the damp towel that hung from his hips with a fresh pair of boxers before downing a two-finger glass of cool whiskey, finishing the cigarette he had lit after his shower and falling asleep on the top of the mattress, hugging one of the pillows Blossom had rested her head on to his chest, burying his face in the fabric, breathing as much of *her* in as he could. Wondering how... She fit into all this. Why, despite how much time they spent together, how he had practically memorized the smoothness of her skin, the curves of her body, the feeling of her warmth—but also, her cold—he felt as if she was the biggest mystery of it all.

Twenty Seven

Blossom felt as if she was coming undone; made of plastic, only, whose stitches had been torn open, letting all the darkness and rage that fabricated the tissue of her muscles spill from her body as thick and black as coagulated blood, oozing from the crevices of rotten flesh and leaving pieces of her everywhere she went, the feeling as if she had been chewed, then spat back out by a hungry wolf seeking to satisfy any resemblance of food overwhelmed her while she walked down the hallway into her room, where she hoped the sound of his voice would be waiting for her on her answering machine. Providing at least a small solace for the emptiness that seemed to be sinking through her, pulling her deeper, that somehow, *he* would be there to pull her out of the abyss.

Yet, seeing there were no new messages, as if all at once, the pain, anger, frustration, the emptiness had burst inside her chest, she lifted her chin. Sucking in a harsh breath as acidic as chemicals eating away at the spongey, soft bloat of decay and clenching her fists so hard her nails indented her palms. Realizing with disgust that she had begun to cry—*why was she crying?* Henry said he doubted anyone could have such an effect on *little miss Blossom James*— She then scowled, wiping her puffy eyes with her palms until a hoarse choke of her breath caused her to whimper and hide her face in her hands again, as if suddenly unable to face what he was *doing* to her, as if suddenly questioning everything she had allowed him to do, how she had enjoyed every second of it, too.

Taking in a sharp inhale, looking up again, she then shook out her hands. Forcing the air from her lungs and proceeding to nearly stomp her way to the kitchen like a child when sent to their room after being grounded; a numbness soaking through her while she brazenly opened the freezer to where her mom kept a crisp, fogged over bottle of strawberry lemonade flavored vodka in the side door. With sharp twists of her wrist and choppy breaths, Blossom unscrewed the cap. Squeezing her eyes shut, quickly tipping her head back and letting the sweet, soggy bits of strawberry that floated in the pink-tinted liquid clog her throat before she painfully gulped them down without hesitation, washing down the itch beginning to build, prodding and pulsating, at the back of her mind. These were the itches that never stop, that can never be ignored—for long, at least—because once you start scratching them, like a swelling, blistered spider bite oozing clear venom, they only get worse, and worse, until you've scratched and burrowed a hole so deep inside yourself you can see the bone. And even then, the itch doesn't cease, so you pick at your tendons and ligaments and brain tissue, just trying to satisfy that clawing need for relief.

Ethan.

Her heels falling into the dampened grass, once deep inside The Town's cemetery, under the cool glow of the moonlight with her nose blushed a deep scarlet alongside her cheeks, Blossom slowed. Feeling her vulnerability to the stare of empty, sorrowful statues of angels that had become stained and eroded by the elements over the years, overtaken by the weeds that thickened into vines and blooming flowers emerging from deep cracks, spilling from their chests, cheeks and outstretched fingers.

"You know, it isn't safe for girls like you to be out here at night, wandering around all alone, especially in cemeteries... *Blossom.*" Ethan Cooper, a long-legged and muscular chested quarterback for the football team, blinked at her with the beginnings to a smirk. He had followed her from the other side of the street. "And especially not after the recent events..."

The hair on the back of her neck standing on end and goose-eggs rising along the back of her arms, with a soft exhale and her palm resting on the cool surface of a tombstone, Blossom turned so the small of her back then hit the edge. Taking this, alongside her silence as an invitation, Ethan pulled his hands from the pockets of his varsity jacket—denim blue sleeves matched with the pine green that surrounded The Town and characterized the High School's colors—walking toward her and stopping only few inches away. Reaching out to flick a loose strand of blonde hair from her neck.

Blossom pushed herself back and onto the rim of the tombstone so one foot dangled on the edge before slipping her palm under the heat of Ethan's jacket, feeling his excited heartbeat under the thin white fabric of his t-shirt. "Cut the crap, Ethan." She purred, giving a tantalizing, shy smile with the gentle lifting of one brow as her words lingered between them. "It isn't girls *like me* that are getting *killed,* Ethan… It's boys. Like *you.*"

Not catching the luring edge of sharpness to her tone such as the melody of a screeching bird, Ethan chuckled, "oh… I'm so scared…" And leaned closer to Blossom; the stench of his cologne filling her lungs when he kissed her, his lips tasting of the citrus mead to the beer he had stolen from his dad. His fingers then slowly coming around the back of her neck, he moved his wet mouth down her jaw and Blossom let head fall back, snaking her arm around Ethan's shoulders and closing her eyes, engulfing him.

Twenty Nine

Taking plunging bites of succulent, silky, fatty tissue and indulging in the buttery, melting cut of tender thigh, with a starved inhale, saliva mixing with the blood that splattered onto his chest and smeared across his cheeks, Henry successfully tore muscle from the bone. Chewing, hurriedly on the flesh with the hard snap of his jaw before gulping it down alongside the chocolatey and dark fruit-laced bitterness of dry red wine.

He didn't drink red wine often and didn't know why he was drinking it then, only that it paired spectacularly with the meat. Closing his eyes for a moment, his chest rising and falling heavily, he then reached across the table, burying his fingers into an open pomegranate, tearing the seeds from the shredding fabrication of its glistening, wet insides just as he carved the thin matrix of protein fibers from between the organs belonging to the delicate, figure of which laid a few inches away from him.

Using his nails to then gruffly plop the fruit after the thick flesh and taste the acidic, rich and heavy flavors envelope his mouth, making his cheeks itch with the craving for more.

In front of him, surrounded by blooming pink, white, and red flowers, butterfly wing soft petals brushing her breasts and hips, the stems stuck between her arms and supporting her neck, fattened grapes draped over the open cavern of her cracked—separated—ribs with bloodied rosemary and basil leaves accenting the squishy, tender innards that lay exposed from her belly, Blossom rested flat against the crimson red tablecloth.

Looking at her, a deviant, sweltering and frantic snarl then escaped him as Henry took another bite, and another, and another—devouring her—hunched over the table with red seeping a dark, bruised purple down from the front of his white collared shirt. Feeling this impulse, this greed... It was the first time he truly felt hunger, a morbid... Depraved feeling that made him feverish with a cold sweat sticking to his shoulder blades, sliding down his spine and rolling down the sides of his temples.

The ropey muscles of his forearms twisting as he squeezed white knuckles around the hilt of a carving knife, reaching deep inside her and tearing at her insides, spooling as much meat as he could from her, he fed on Blossom. Taking everything she had to give him until there wasn't anything left, until all he could do was lick the bones clean. And even then, un-satiated, he would

*snap through the brittle pink marrow until shards stuck
between his bared teeth and scraped the soft epithelial
tissue when he swallowed them. He would gnaw on
cherry-sized, rounded curves of milky cartilage,
crunching the stiff material under his back molars with
audible pops until all there was to Blossom James was
him.*

*Her blood sticky to his fingers, turning gummy as the
red blood cells clotted, when he reached back into her
again, however, instead of feeling the soft, slick exterior
of muscle and squishy fat, warm and comforting, Henry
buried his hand into a cold, deep pit: a nest of hatching,
baby spiders that suddenly raced up his arm, climbing
over themselves and bouncing up the sleeves of his shirt.
Yelping, he yanked himself back, tripping over his heels,
beginning to fight them off, but then, his left arm was
yanked forward by a stiff, cold grip and squirming and
convulsing, Henry met Blossom's iced over blue eyes—
fogged over by death and turned grey—her hand wrapped
tight around his wrist. Keeping him from falling as she
sat up. Henry screamed, feeling the spiders crawl into the
crevices of his ears and fill his mouth, pushing themselves
beneath the lids of his eyes and tickling beneath the
surface of his skin while Blossom's cracked lips peeled
open, revealing grey gums and blood-stained, yellow
teeth. The furry legs of a larger spider reaching from the
darkness.*

*Then, shivering with the lingering feeling of spiders
running down his arms and legs, Henry blinked, finding*

himself looking up at Blossom's house. Already walking, he tossed a cigarette to the cement and smoothed out his tie, lifting his knuckles to the surface of the door and tapping twice. After failing to hear of any signs that she was making her way to answer him, he tried again, knocking more forcibly, then wrapped his hand around the knob and looked over his shoulder—his chin tucked— to make sure no one was near before twisting the knob. It was unlocked.

As if tied to a string, barely opening the door enough to slip inside, with one foot in front of the other, Henry called out her name into the spruce blues shadowing over the empty living room that turned into darker navies the further he looked down the hall. However, met with silence, his nerves pinched and he squeezed his jaw, closing the door behind him with the lock slipping easily between his fingers.

There was a slight hue of pink—emitted from a single lamp in the corner of the far wall in Blossom's bedroom— that seeped from under the doorframe, and for a moment, Henry stood there, hoping she'd come running into the hall from the pink light, falling readily into his arms, safe and sound. Wearing that tulle dress he saw her in at the Diner. The twinge of unease, of restlessness and agitation he found in her voice when she called echoing through his mind, making the hair on the back of his neck stand on end, he continued imagining the scenario of her pressing herself to his figure for comfort and let out a slow exhale. Proceeding down the hallway with hesitant steps; knowing he would be there for her. That he'd help clean her up with a tender care and understanding that with the killer still out there, tension had ripped through the seams of the Town. Of course she would be worried. Of course she would be scared. And with everything she had gone through already... But he would be there, always. Just as he promised.

If he were being honest with himself, there was a side to Henry that wanted to watch what Blossom looked like when breaking down. When falling apart, that extra coating of polish coming off layer by layer until she was as raw as an exposed nerve, twitching and in need of numbing. But now, venturing closer to her bedroom, Henry felt he was the exposed nerve, his flesh stripping away, and that just as she was the cause of this, she was also the only anecdote.

The image of a ripe, plump, bright red pomegranate whose seeds—popping in his mouth and crunching beneath his teeth, staining them and sticking between his gums like tar—were filled with poison, flashed across his mind.

Stopping in front of her door, Henry leaned in close and once more, he called her name—his hand wrapping around the knob with the familiar scent of her perfume tingling his senses—the only answer he was granted, however, being that of gut-wrenching silence, he slowly opened the door. Greeted by the sight of blood.

It was everywhere. Splattered on the carpet, soaking the slightly green-tinted fibers in red, over her sheets and flung over the walls. Her cheek pressed to the floor and a knife lay discarded only a foot or so away, her bookshelf was thrown to the floor, its contents spilling with bent and torn pages of unfinished stories.

"No—" Henry choked, falling dizzy to his knees before he crawled with unstable palms toward her. Tears beginning to blur his vision. Grabbing her face, pulling her limp body into him, he cradled her. Trying to wake her at the same time he fumbled over her body to find any wounds. "Blossom? Sweetheart, come on—please open your eyes. You gotta open your eyes." He stuttered, burying his face in her neck, her perfume filling his lungs like a burst of color and the warmth of her skin making his shoulders rake with terrible sobs. Just like that, Henry's whole world suddenly came caving in, and all he could see was black. Black, and red. Blood. He didn't know what to do. "I'm so sorry. I'm so sorry." He hiccuped. This wasn't the way it was supposed to be... This was different. It was supposed to be different. He was supposed to be better. He was supposed to be able to save her. Nonetheless, wiping his face angrily while Blossom's head hit his chest, blood mixed with the tears that dripped onto her cheek, and his fingers followed. Grazing the flushed skin, he wiped them away, his joints stiff and a headache pounding against his temples.

Still clutching onto her, with a shaky hand he then reached back into his pocket, lifting his phone up from his jacket—about to call Norman—when, with a ringing laughter bubbling through the room, Blossom's hand snatched his wrist. Again. Only, this time, as she cackled,

"Jesus CHRIST! Henry you actually fell—" He realized with unprecedented horror that she was very much alive, which, was almost certainly worse.

Henry jumped back, but Blossom continued to laugh, crawling up the side of the bed and beginning to walk toward him when he dodged her with the spin of his heels. Falling to the edge of the bed. "What the FUCK--Why the fuck would you do that?" He spoke into his palms, his elbows falling to his bony knees. When he looked up at her, he saw that her laughter had faltered and her smile had dropped. Hunched, urgency in his wide eyes, which were puffy and rimmed with red, he then angrily wiped his face. His clothes were soaked in red. It stuck to his hands, and stained his face. Black strands of hair falling in front of his eyes. "Why—why would you do that? Why?" He pleaded. "What is this fucking need to destroy everything around you, Blossom? Do you feel good about this?"

"Henry—"

"Answer me." He hissed. "Does it make you feel good? Tearing those around you apart? Destroying those who care about you?"

Silence suddenly warped through the room, pulling at her spine. Her legs burned to move, but she kept still, merely watching until he looked away. Then, Blossom hurried in front of him, grabbing his hands with a delicate touch. He let out a painful breath before pushing her hands away and wrapping his arms around her waist. Burying his face in her belly, she bent down and pressed her lips to the top of his head, feeling his shoulders shake as she rubbed her palms against the stiff muscle, his knees pressing around her thighs.

"I'm sorry."

"No, you're not." Straightening his back, he twisted his jaw, then shakily reached into his pocket and pulled out a cigarette. With the snap of his metal lighter, he let out a cloud of smoke. "You never are."

Blossom frowned at him, pushing herself onto his lap so her arm wrapped around his shoulders and her side pressed to his chest. He could even feel beads of the blood that smeared against her hands clotting in his hair, sticky like glue, as she began brushing her fingers against the base of his skull. Henry's forehead then fell to her chest with deep breaths expanding the tenderness of his ribs and she pressed a firm kiss to the top of his head again.

Looking down into her lap and noticing that some of the ash from his cigarette—which he pinched between two knuckles—had flaked on her thigh, Henry shook his head with an absent mind before brushing them off, blinking tiredly. A part of him wondering if it could be real blood, if she had kept a bucket or two for this very purpose, but the consistency was off. It clumped under her nails and between her knuckles. Corn syrup.

Closing his eyes, her touch was cold, firm, but he leaned into it. Letting out with a shake to his words, "what are you doing to me…" As his bottom lip began to quiver. Then, when she grabbed his face, Henry let her kiss him, a bitterness to the sweet, a sharpness to her tongue that he hadn't noticed before. He felt vulnerable. Weak. Shaky. Unstable. Had he forgotten to take his medication this morning? *He couldn't remember. Instead, he clung to her for support and felt his shoulders begin to shake as the tears streamed down his cheeks, staining them with the indescribable heaviness he felt. Still, even as he cried against Blossom, no matter how hard he clung to her, how hard he pressed himself to her or buried himself inside her or gave into her like giving into the temptation of washing his thoughts away with liquor, he didn't feel… Safe.*

The image soon turned to Blossom on the floor in a heap of pink lace and the bunching of her puffy skirt beneath her. Like a slaughtered Disney princess, she wiped the blood over her face with the back of her hand, tucking red strands of wet hair behind her ear, then reached under the bed, sparking a bedazzled lighter under her thumb and taking a slow drag of a cigarette before letting the heavy, burning air from her lungs with a slight cough at the end and slumping to the floor. Turning her hips so she lay flat on her back, the carpet squished with wetness under her, blood bubbling and soaking even further into her outfit while the smoke lingered above her lips.

Henry was laying next to her when he realized that's where he had been the entire time, from watching himself enter the room to sitting on the bed, to now looking down at himself. Unable to breathe, his eyes widened at the sight of his torso drenched in blood, his ribs exposed and his organs spilling from his belly, littered in stab wounds. Coughing, blood sprayed from his stained teeth as he gurgled on it from the ripped tendons and cartilage of his throat. His head falling back to the carpet. It was all his blood. Looking back to Blossom, he then saw she was staring at him, the cigarette being held to her chest, and with almost a sympathetic twinge to the way her lashes fluttered, she gave him a wide, cold smile before it twisted into a horrified, fearful sneer. "Are you going to hurt me like you hurt her?" She asked. "Do you want to hurt me, Henry? Do you want to kill me, too?"

Sitting up, frantically searching the room with wide eyes until he was sure he had been dreaming, Henry's head then fell back to the pillows and he let out a slow exhale, attempting to calm his racing heartbeat with his hand coming to his face, attempting to rub the exhaustion from his system when three sharp knocks sounded through the room, jolting adrenaline through his body like a flush of heat and a spark of a fire.

Pushing himself to his elbows and looking to the door, after a few seconds of silence, he kicked his legs from the edge of the bed, barely catching sight of the clock—which read that it was nearly 1:30 in the morning—before grabbing his gun and making his way over to the door. Tightening his finger around the trigger.

His bare shoulder pressing against the door while he looked out the peephole, through which he spotted a head of white hair alongside blurred, glazed over blue eyes looking up, Henry then looked down at himself, realizing he was still lacking a shirt and in his underwear with a curse under his breath before he reluctantly opened the door.

Staggering forward and nearly losing her balance, however, his arms catching her weight, Blossom pulled herself to her feet and let out a hearty giggle, her nails digging into his forearms as her forehead hit his chest.

"Blossom-" Henry grunted, supporting her against him while kicking the door closed. "What is this?" He then asked, not referring to a specific object but rather her state, catching the sweet aroma of fruitful intoxication oozing from her pores and clinging to her clothes while leading her to the bed. It masked the sweetness of her perfume.

"I-I'm… I'm sorry." She whimpered. "I had-I didn't-"

"It's okay." He responded quickly, instinctively setting her down on the foot of the mattress and crouching in front of her, setting his gun down behind her while watching her eyes search confusingly over his and her body wave back and forth. She still held onto him, her hands now at his shoulders, smelling like the summer. But sick, and sticky.

"I had to see you... I'm... Sorry."

Brushing back loose strands of her hair, Henry frowned slightly. She looked so... Fragile, melting into his touch, and he clenched his jaw before, with a huff, pulling Blossom's hands from his shoulders. Going to set them in her lap before standing.

She tried to reach towards him again, but he had already stepped away. "No-Don't leave, please don't leave... Don't-I don't want you to leave." She slurred her words together. "I'm sorry... I... I'm sorry. For everything, I'm sorry-please." She continued, muttering with her hand coming to rub her face while he walked over to the counter and filled a plastic cup with cold water. Plopping a fizzing electrolyte—grape flavored—to the bottom then grabbing a discarded black t-shirt from the floor on his way back over to her.

"Drink this." He lifted the rim of the cup to her mouth, his free hand slipping behind her ear in order to help steady her, and he wrapped her fingers around his wrist, taking a few hesitant sips before falling back against the mattress; a burst of giggles escaping her that almost looked like she was crying.

Henry pulled the t-shirt over his head and stood there for a moment longer, he watched her run her hands over the sheets, the room spinning, before setting down the cup against the nightstand and sitting down at the other edge of the bed with his forearms against his knees, leaning forward to pinch the bridge of his nose. A certain sense of relief washing over him that she had come to him. Despite everything, she had still come to him.

He thought Blossom had passed out when her voice filled the room, uncharacteristically steady for someone whose veins ran heavy with alcohol. "Men are so small minded." She sighed.

Henry looked up. "What?"

She didn't repeat herself, but the words then came running from her tongue quicker than she could even think of what she was saying. He could feel the anger in her tone. It trembled through the sharpness of her words and he slowly turned, using his hands to push himself higher onto the bed. His eyes glued to her while she pulled her brows together and smiled slightly with astonishment.

"They always look at girls as these delicate little creatures... Things they can destroy. Use then spit back out. Objects. But the second you open your mouth and say something worth listening to, or something like, *hey! I didn't like that. Because I have thoughts and feelings and preferences too*, they call you a whore, a slut, just... Just for wanting things—the same things they want—yet, they call you controlling and overwhelming, loud, mean, a bitch, even if you look at them for too long, give them a smile, they think, *oh yeah, she wants to fuck me. She wants me to fuck her!* Because every man wants to think they're so fuckable. Even if we shoved it down their throats or screamed it in their faces, all they'd be able to see is the idea that we're just going to sit back and take it, take it like good little sluts and beg for more, then we're going to go into the kitchen and make them a little snack, light their cigarette, kiss them and say 'thank you for shoving your cock inside me—'"

"Blossom—" Henry began to reach out to touch her, but pulled away such as a moth when realizing they were getting too close to a lit flame. The heat scorching their wings. She didn't notice.

"—And pulling my hair and slapping me and scratching me then cumming on my stomach then asking me if I came, even though you didn't take two seconds to touch me if it wasn't to direct where you wanted me to put my mouth or to hold me down like a fuck toy. But oh yeah, thank you. Thank you so, so much. Thank you!" Her voice began to crack under the weight of her words. Henry looked away, realizing with a tremendous heaviness in his chest—guilt—that she was, in that moment, speaking from experience.

His eyes closed, he pictured the way she had looked to the boy coming out of the bathroom when he showed up at the party; how the blush in her chest had greyed in a pale, milky grey and the pink of her lips had become more distinct, as if she had seen a ghost, the way her eyes were rimmed red and the bags under them slightly puffy —like she had been crying—how desperate she was to leave her own house, her own party—despite the rage that had consumed him that night—and the fact that she had gotten into his car in the first place. He let out a deep breath through open lips.

"You did great, for five fucking minutes. That was life changing.'" She continued, then paused. As if out of breath. "And us girls? We've been taught, *conditioned* to think that this... Behavior, is a fucking compliment. You're lucky to catch a dick so good, bitch. Be thankful he's even paying attention to you."

"Is that really how you feel?"

Please say no. Or don't say anything.

"I-I'm just... Im so fucking sick and tired of men thinking they can tell me what to do and touch me and use me like I'm some toy."

"You don't really put yourself in a position to stop them, Blossom. Don't you think you..." Ask for it? Classy. He didn't finish his thought, but she got quiet and Henry rubbed his palm over his eyes.

"Someone needs to teach them a lesson, someone needs to show them." She dipped her words just beneath a whisper, almost to the point where Henry could barely hear her.

"What does that mean? You want revenge?"

Blossom then pushed herself to her forearms, looking at Henry with an iced over gaze, sharpened like the edge of the blade, her words cutting through the air like a hot knife to cold butter. Her cheeks were flushed with heat and there was a moment of clarity when he wondered if she was indeed drunk. "I want more than revenge. I want them to feel what it's like to be used and spat out over and over again until all they become is this rage that's boiled inside of them, that's consumed them. That's been inside of them for so long they can't remember a time in their lives when they weren't filled with this—this hatred and... Sorrow, guilt and this... Shame." Between her words, Blossom drew her lips back, revealing her teeth like a snarling dog as her chest heaved and her fingers continued to twist in the sheets. Blotches of white over her knuckles. "I want them to feel what it's like to feel weak, small, left questioning their existence as if they were born to do this, if being an object for destruction and pleasure, made of flesh and bone and only known for one part of them was what they were meant to be—to do —all along, just put on this earth to suffer and be used, to be chewed on and bitten and clawed at and destroyed, over and over. I want them to know what it's like to be manipulated. To not know what's real, to not even know themselves, their emotions. To be powerless. At someone else's mercy, like a lamb waiting to be slaughtered." She fell back to the mattress with a slight bounce of the springs, nausea making her shiver with goosebumps. Needing the room to stop spinning, Blossom then spoke more carefully. "I want to say to them, look at what you've done. What you've made me. And I want them to be able to see what they've made me—because while they fuck, and take, and fuck, what they don't know is that they've created weapons out of women."

Henry swallowed the lump in his throat, the growing desire to touch her turning less from wanting to comfort her, but instead... The want to coax every bit of this hatred from her, milking it from her and seeing it in his hands, of tasting it like grain fermented into an aged whiskey from when she was first... *Used*... Bitter and unforgiving, burning his chest, these thoughts caused him to blink heavily, still ridden with sleep. He then stood from the end of the bed and walking over to the desk, grabbed a cigarette; flicking the razor edge of his lighter before a flame sparked, burning through the paper.

Making his way back over to where Blossom glanced at him with the softening of her brow, as if sympathetic, he proceeded to breathe in lungfuls of smoke. It felt wrong, gross, even, as he stood above her, but he didn't move. Instead, staring down at her spread out figure, her hair splayed over the musty sheets as it had been so many times before, the blonde contrasting against the faded red, green and orange-yellow plaid (he had gotten a new pattern at the beginning of nearly each week when the room was cleaned out, despite him specifically telling the front desk to skip his room due to sensitive, case-related information) he began thinking about how, with her in this state, he could do anything and she wouldn't be able to stop him.

Noticing that her bottom lip was glistening with the spit that sprayed from the force of her words, she licked it off—before he could—and disgust then twinged through Henry while he sucked in another deep breath, relaxing the ache in his joints with nicotine. His knees nearly grazing the side of the mattress between her legs and his shoulders gently leaned back.

"You will never understand, Special Agent. But what I'm talking about... Is the female rage." *Sounds fucking made up to me.* "When I woman isn't afraid to kill to take back her power—the power taken from her as soon as she had tits and an ass. A body that was... *Ripe.*" Blossom lifted a brow and stuck out her hand towards Henry with an open palm. He exhaled the lungful of smoke, turning so he could sit back down next to her before handing her the cigarette. His leg bumped into hers and ash dusted the sheets between them.

"So," he watched her lips curl over where his had been and her chest expand, smoke kissing her the way he wanted to. "Would you kill? To take back your... Power?"

Blossom lowered the cigarette to her collarbone and let out a smile, her head falling to the side so she could look at him. His gaze flitted down to the way her free hand had begun to trail the space between them, pinching the thin fabric of his boxers between her fingers as she then teased, "oh, how you would like to know..." A string of giggles following.

Henry's stomach knotted and he felt the blood began to pool between his hips. Then, silence spread between them, as thick and hard as the outer coating of sour candy, sticking to his back molars and stinging against the inside of his cheeks. Lost in the swirling smoke, the lingering buzz of whiskey in his belly and the equally as intoxicating alcohol that laced her breath, her presence dizzying him like the feeling of being crushed under the sea-foam green of a massive wave holding him under salty waters, before he could stop himself, he was leaning down onto his side and letting her reach up to wrap her arms around his shoulders; the cigarette still clenched between her knuckles nearly burning him as he met her in a strained kiss.

Deepening the movements of his lips, drawing out every drop of what he identified to be strawberry-infused vodka, it worsened his cravings and his hand snatched her hip, a tight growl rumbling deep in his chest when a shockwave of pleasure rippled through him from the way he impulsively ground his hips against the mattress.

Just as quickly as it had begun, though, Blossom pulled her face away from his. Turning as to take another puff from the cigarette with the fighting back of a creeping smile. Henry glared down at her for a brief moment, out of breath, his whole body tense and hot, sweat tickling the back of his neck before reaching back up from her hip and plucking the cigarette from her teeth; shoving his face into the crook of her throat, breathing her in before clamping his jaw around the curve to her shoulder and feeling her heavy pulse throb against her tongue as a wolf does when gnawing at the throat of its prey.

Lifting her chin, she buried her fingers in the tuffs of disheveled hair at the back of his head with taut curls wrapping around her knuckles like vines; the gasp that emitted from her throat quickly turning to a groan and tearing from her open lips as he shoved his hand between her thighs, which fell away from each other easily, allowing Henry to press the lit end of the cigarette into her soft flesh and causing Blossom to grip him tighter. Yanking on his hair while fighting back a scream.

He wanted her to scream, not caring if the rooms that bordered them could hear. He wanted her to hurt, to feel the burning of the embers against her pinked skin and be marked by him, to be reminded of this... Pain even when he wasn't there. Pressing harder, pinching the cream-white paper so hard his the sweat on the pads of his fingers softened it, nearly twisting the length into two halves, her whole body tensed beneath his and the veins in her neck strained while he bit down on them harder.

Smudging the hot ash toward where the magenta pink hemming of jean shorts that ended just below of the crook of her hips, the length making his heart skip a beat, in the next moment and to Henry's obliviousness,

Blossom reached her arm above her head. Fumbling around the folds in the sheets for the gun he had laid down in his efforts to get her situated and cared for; something he instinctively longed to do since the night at the station, a twisted, maternal-like pride coming from the fact that he now had her there, helpless and in need, needing him. Like an injured, wailing lamb. However, not entirely lost and still very much Blossom, she forced his teeth from the now red-tinted indentations of her neck with the muzzle of his semi-automatic, 9mm Glock G19 pressing into the soft space against the inside of his jaw bone. Her hand wound tight around the grip.

The now defused cigarette rolling to the carpet from between her legs, Henry lurched away from her body, falling to the side with his palms exposed, hands lifted and muscles rigid while Blossom—her movements still slowed and clumsy—climbed over him, the gun nearly falling from her hold in the process before she shoved it back into his jugular; her knees hugging his ribs as she sat on him.

"Bl-Blossom. Blossom put the gun down." He whispered, his sharpened voice now unstable and hoarse. "Put the gun down."

"You wanna know if I would kill to take back my power?" She mumbled back at him and Henry gulped, closing his eyes. His head resting against the mattress. Taking deep breaths, attempting to cease the tremble in his fingers, his brows pulled together. He could feel his heart racing and feared for a moment he'd have a heart attack.

"Put the gun down? Just put it down. Please." She merely giggled, biting her lip down at him and rolling her hips into his abdomen. He could feel her heat, repeating his words slowly. "Blossom. Put the gun... Down."

"You're so fucking hot when you get angry..." Her shoulders falling forward, her free hand fell to the space above Henry's shoulder as her mouth pressed to his temple and she giggled again, snorting. Still, she didn't listen, and clenching his teeth—a single smear of her blood across his bottom lip—his throat closed and his breathing restricted, Henry snapped his hand up. First grabbing her wrist and yanking her arm back before twisting the weapon out of her hand. Kicking his left hip up so he could flip her weight beneath his, rendering her weakened.

Tightening his bruising grip around her wrist, he hissed, "don't ever fucking do that. EVER." Before pushing himself off her and standing away from the bed, the blood that pooled in his stomach boiling into a cold anger. Picking the gun up from where it had fallen from the bed, he then checked the safety, realizing he forgot to unlatch it in the first place before setting it on the nightstand closest to the small kitchenette and running his hands through his hair; beginning to yell at Blossom while she pressed her palms comfortingly to her chest, squeezing her fists. Not comprehending what he was saying, instead looking up to the ceiling fan and watching the blades whirl steadily.

"This untamed rage, is sweet, delicious. It's the petals of the delicate flower than men so callously dig themselves into and wish to be enveloped by... Held by." She began murmuring to herself. Henry turned back to her.

"What the fuck are you saying?"

She sniffed. Tears trickling down the sides of her cheeks. "It's the arms you go home to at night and the honey that drips from your tongue, it is poison, it is love, Special Agent."

Henry frowned, realizing she was referring back to what she had been saying before, then licked the blood from his bottom lip, tasting the sickly aftertaste of iron before shaking his head. "I don't believe love is that cruel, Blossom. I think there's more." He pushed. The hardness of his body reflected in the strain of his voice.

Is this love? Is that what we have, Blossom James?

Would you want that?

This violence, is this what you crave?

"You seem to be the hopeless romantic. It's cute." *Cute.* "But what I... What I'm saying. Is that men want to control everything. But you're so afraid of being out of control that you've never taken the time to realize that you've never even been in control."

"Control can be cruelty." Henry stated. He was exhausted.

Blossom wildly shook her head. "No, no, love can be cruelty, Special Agent. Control is less destructive. Control is survival."

"Is it? Wouldn't it be less painful to let yourself... Feel? Let go? Love?" *To love me? Would that be so bad?*

"Sometimes I want to let go..." She whimpered, taking the Agent by surprise. Staring at her with sadness, he then looked down at the carpet. Silence transpiring once more between them until Blossom whispered, "I don't want to keep doing this..."

Regardless, Henry hadn't heard her. And when he looked back up, he realized she had slipped into a deep sleep, her head falling to the opposite side of the room with the relaxing of her hands making them fall closer to where he could see the now crusted, smeared blood diluted—thinned—by his saliva, a darkened shade of red and purple from where his teeth had broken the vessels beneath the surface.

Carefully draping the knitted throw—which had been pushed to the corner of the bed—over her body and looking down with the softening of his brow, taking the time to guide a few strands of blonde hair from her temple, Henry pushed them behind her ear before retracting his hand. His fingers grazing the soft blush of her cheeks, causing the corners of his mouth to twitch into a gentle smile while looking down at her and observing such gentleness in the way her lips—the cupid's bow indenting into a gentle curve that led to the point of her thin-bridged nose—remained just slightly agape. Soft breaths audible and her chin tucked toward her chest.

Taking one of the pillows from the top of the bed, he then turned off the light and moved to the leather armchair at the other side of the room for the rest of the night.

Thirty

Waking up, first thing Blossom noticed was the stench of ash and fresh pine coming in from the window, then the feeling of someone's hand on her shoulder. The blinds drawn, the room dim, she slowly realized where she was while turning upward to meet Henry's attentive gaze.

Seated against the edge of the mattress, he looked down at her with concern, asking, "how are you feeling?" And waiting for a moment before pulling his hand away after she didn't respond. Letting it fall to his knee before clearing his throat, he continued with, "I have to go, but I uh... I went downstairs and grabbed you some food. Just... Some hard boiled eggs, waffles and fruit. I didn't know what you would have the appetite for."

Blossom blinked up at him and quietly responded, her brows pulling together. "Thank you—but, Hen—"

Looking away, Henry shook his head. "Don't."

"You shouldn't have been looking out for me last night. That wasn't fair." Her brows curved upward and she turned toward him, grabbing his hand, pressing his knuckles to her lips. "I'm sorry. I didn't know what I was thinking coming here."

His shoulders and chest heavy, his pale, gruff features were illuminated from the dust-filled and smoked out streams of sunlight. She saw he had already taken a shower, blow-dried his hair, and redressed in a fitted light grey cotton poplin shirt that was currently folded just above his elbows. Tucked into his black, fifties-style trousers, he wore a dark grey, nearly black tie that was knotted just beneath the protrusion of his sharp Adam's apple and matched the same shade of iron as his pants alongside the jacket that was slung over the desk chair.

"It doesn't matter." He muttered back at her following a long pause. "Because…" he squeezed her hand back. A sadness in his voice she wasn't prepared to hear. "I need you to know that when I said I would always choose to kiss you… That wasn't just—" Henry was never good at communication; the skill of being able to form words in an intricate, appropriate way to convey emotion escaping him into bitter, spitfire words that cut into the air such as a hot, silver blade cutting through thick cuts of bleeding steak, salt melting along the edges, the meat sizzling along the corners and the blade hitting with a heavy thud on the wooden, wet cutting board beneath. Nevertheless, he persisted. "I wouldn't have wanted you to go anywhere else last night. Okay? I'm glad you came to me, and that I could be there for you. But the thing is—"

"Henry…" Blossom whispered, but he didn't hear.

"The question for me becomes whether or not you're willing to choose *me*." His words falling flat, Blossom scrunched her nose and huffed in a slight scoff, dismissing the flutter in her stomach. "I know that's a lot to ask, and that's why I want you to think about it. But… I have constantly chosen you. To put my job alongside the investigation at risk *for* you. Do you get that?"

"I never asked you to do that."

"You didn't have to." Henry pulled his hand from hers. Lifting it to rub the crease from between his brows, feeling a headache blooming in his temples as tender as the bruise that yellowed her skin, blotching all the way down to her clavicle with the faint seeping of red dots. He didn't realized just how hard he had bitten her. Thinking now that if he had just pulled up, he could have torn a chunk of meat from her, consumed her, just as he had continually fantasized of doing. Lost in these realizations, he blinked softly, his lips opening slightly as his hand fell away from his face, nimble fingertips reaching out graze the wound. She flinched slightly, the recoiling of her from him bringing him back to the room. He hadn't even checked the burn mark left by his cigarette yet. Frankly, he didn't want to. "That night of the party…"

"I chose to get in the car with you. I *chose* you, Henry."

"No—and when you asked me to tell you *why* you got in the car, at that time I didn't know. I couldn't see. But you weren't choosing *me,* you were choosing to run *away* from something—I was just the getaway. And I think last night you running, too. It wasn't because you actually wanted to be with me."

"I want to be with you." Blossom choked. "Please—Henry, it's different *now.* I want to be *here,* with you—I wasn't running... Nothing happened."

"It's okay." Henry didn't give in, urging, "let me *help* you."

Her eyes widening, she could feel the words bubbling in her throat. "I can't."

"*Why.*" He was cornering her, trapping her under the will of his affection, suffocating her. She didn't respond, and Henry shook his head. "Blossom... I'm asking you to think about whether or not you're willing to make the choice in the *same* way I have. Not to run to me in order to get away from something else. But because—"

"I... Want to."

"I know."

But can you? Can you really give up all that... Control? After everything?

Refusing to make eye contact with her again, his head bowed, Henry stood up and walked over to his jacket, unrolling the cuffs of his sleeves to his wrists before shrugging it on. Then, snatching his keys into the middle of his palm, tightening his fingers around the jagged edges, he quietly made his way over to the door when Blossom worked herself into a seated position and called out a small, "H-henry?"

Yet, despite the opening of her mouth again, no words came. So, she closed her jaw again. Doughy eyes wide and pleading, speaking the words she couldn't seem to form.

Henry turned back to her with the letting out of a quick exhale, as if making the decision on the spot, thinking through it as the words left his mouth. "You can stay here. Rest, have something to eat, drink some water, maybe take a bath... Clean up." He nodded, inhaling and finishing quietly, "if you need me, I'll have my cell."

Blossom nodded back, her shoulders slumped back against the frame and watched him slip from the room. Then, staring at the door with the sudden, stark loneliness making her head throb and the blood rush into her cheeks, she noticed out of the corner of her eye that a wrinkled, misshapen pillow had been pushed into the slick black cushions of the arm chair diagonal to her. Furrowing her brow at the idea of Henry not just residing on the other side of the bed.

Attempting to recall what just transpired between the two and why he hadn't accepted her back into his arms— why he was making it so damn hard just to move the fuck on—the weight of his request made her limbs feel heavy and her body feel shaky. As if she still had alcohol her system was attempting to expel.

Blossom slumped back down against the pillows and closed her eyes for a few minutes before sliding from the bed and walking to the bathroom, where she stripped of her stiff clothes, allowing for the billowing heat of the shower to fog in her lungs as thick and consuming as the nicotine from the Agent's cigarettes.

Lifting her face, feeling the water spray down her chest and soak her muscles, her eyes closed and her hands resting against her sternum, a deep breath left her lungs. The scent of him consuming her until the heat of the shower stripped her skin raw, becoming almost bruised by the stinging red blemishing her figure from where the water hit. She wasn't one for hot showers, always taking cold ones—but the heat helped with the shaking of her limbs and the itch she could feel coming on. There was also comfort in the pain she knew Henry subjected himself to, standing beneath the scalding waters. She wanted to understand. *He* wanted her to understand. But what he didn't realize in asking her to *truly* choose him, was that—in order to create that, there would have to be a final sort of destruction—so, smelling of blackberry and almond—Blossom then redressed, pulling back on her velvet one-piece before re-buttoning the high-rise waist of her shorts, which she pulled a piece of cinnamon from the back pocket of her shorts and chewed the rubbery texture into a ball of sweet spit.

Thirty One

Seated against the curved plastic of a basil-green chair behind a dark, wooden desk with the slow and steady tap of the pen against the blue-lined paper she had 'borrowed' from Jake Stephens, Becky's older brother, who—for the past five minutes—proceeded to stare at her, Blossom slowly turned to her right and pointedly made eye contact with him. He looked away, but even then she still fought back a smile, lifting her brows and pretending to care, knowing full well he could see her out of the corner of his eye.

Then, the bell rang through the room and cut off Mr. Whitmore, forcing him to stutter through the last of his lecture before giving up and shuffling the papers on his desk into neat piles while shaking his head. Watching him, Blossom slung her legs out from under her desk.

"Mr. Whitmore?" She asked, small, lifting the edges of his name while moving toward him.

He looked up, pulling his brows together with intrigue. "Ms. James… What can I do for you?"

"I just have a few photos I wanted you to look over… For the end of year project. Since you'll be gone next week. Well, I heard you were taking the week off. For catching up on grading." She held her hands behind her back with a slight lift of her shoulders. He could see the indentation beneath her ribs as she breathed, outlining the slope of her pressed breasts beneath the thick, soft fabric of her cami top.

"Oh, yes—" He shook his head, looking as if it was the first time he was hearing about it, but quickly regained his composure. "I'll still be here, so don't you worry about that." Blossom bit her bottom lip, her jaw still working on the gum and smiled when he motioned to her hands. "Do you have the photos?"

"Well, actually…" She released them and leaned forward against his desk. Her fingers slowly crawling atop the laminated plastic of his school ID, which was connected to a coiled, plastic scrunchie. Red. "I was wondering if you'd be able to come by? Maybe this afternoon?"

He paused, sitting back against his seat before smirking. "Oh?" And that's when she knew—where others would have recoiled from her invitation upon the regard of teacher student relationships, he would only push further—that her assumptions about him were correct. That everything was going to fall into place. "And... Shall I bring something?"

"What did you have in mind?"

"Just a delicious bottle of red wine waiting to be cracked open."

"I like the sound of that."

"What time should I come by?"

"How about... 4:00?" *That would give his mom enough time to find him. Given she works until 3:30 every Thursday.*

"So early?"

"I don't believe there's such a thing."

"*I like the sound of that.*" He echoed her words with a smirk and Blossom slipped her hands from his desk, clasping them back behind her while slowly moving away, Whitmore's gaze lingering.

"You *should,*" she said before exiting the room with a single skip.

Back home, Blossom sat slouched against the couch in the living room, her hair falling to her shoulders with slightly disheveled waves. A glass of blueberry-infused red wine in her hand, one of the only blends her mom kept since her collection was mostly made up of hard liquors, pinot blanc and chardonnay, the undertones of mint, dark chocolate and baked prunes created a sharp aftertaste; like bitter milk chocolate as she held the rim of the glass to her lips, inhaling the bone-dry scent and staring at the red glow of the tv, which buzzed in granule distortions of a nature documentary found by flicking impatiently through the channels.

Having sought the comfort of a crumbling, cold cranberry lime pie with stiff pecans cemented in the glossy, maroon sauce, she ate the cinnamon-dusted crust first, breaking it off with her fingers before scooping some of the creamy filling onto the top and sitting back, chewing softly. Licking the red from her fingers and tasting the metallic undertones of blood that lingered beneath her nails.

Washing it down with the wine, Blossom then turned over the glossy finish of a newly printed polaroid, still warm under her touch. Looking down at its contrasting colors and the exposure of the camera's harsh white flash when, on the tv, a lone wolf began charging through powdery snow toward a pack of elk that dispersed into slowed gallops. Their hooves sinking deeper into the earth as if it were reaching up and grabbing them, holding them down while they bounced with desperate leaps, soon, more wolves followed. Nipping at the heels until the strength of their jaws finally caught one with strings of saliva snarling from grey and white-blotched gums, successfully toppling it to the ground—going for the kill —while up ahead, the rest of the pack stopped running, quickly finding out that their time had yet to come. With that, they turned back to watch the destruction unfold.

With a glazed-over look to the way her brows lifted, Blossom imagined herself there, too. Hidden by the ivory of her skin with only red to show for the flushing of her pasty flesh, naked, her nipples hardened by a biting breeze, standing in the snow while snowflakes kissed her auburn blushed cheeks, burnt from the ice blue sun and observing the way the wolves buried their yellowed canines into the ligaments and muscle tissue of their prey. Tearing the elk to pieces with growls vibrating up the bruised cartilage of its esophagus all the while blood— hot and bubbling—melted into the white like syrup drizzling from vanilla-bean ice cream.

Her soft hair, as white as the snow that numbed her skin, tickling her shoulders and blowing over her face while breaths, as tender as the hot meat that filled the wolves' bellies, fogged in front of her lips, looking up into the crystal white and blue-streaked sky, Blossom imaged *she* was the elk, having the wolves digging into her, legs cruelly twisted, held down by the clamped jaws with slick tongues lapping at open wounds and hot breaths misting her body. The soft, squishy, elastic fabrication of pink and red organs exposed for snow to delicately fall.

After the documentary ended, as if mocking Blossom with bright pink and polished plastic, the catchy tunes of synthesized music dubbed over a monotone woman's voice then walked through a cheery, pedaled manuscript toward preteen girls with the showcasing of a new line of Barbie toys in a commercial decorated by white-painted smiles and blue eyeshadow, puffed, glossy blonde hair combed by tiny brushes in tiny, plastic doll houses. The all-American production of perfection making her jaw clench and her stomach knot until she reached her hand to the left, fumbling for the remote, and turned off the tv. Silence filling the room as she finished her wine with large gulps.

She thought that time would have been easy. That the rage blooming in her touch and leaving bruises against his flesh, that leaving him with the same irreversible damage she felt rotting from her core, would have allowed this time to be easy. Still, that gnawing, pained feeling hadn't gone away and she instead found that each time chipped at her more and more, until her throat closed and her fingertips trembled and she gritted her teeth against the memory.

Looking to the clock, she took a deep breath, the only solace coming to her that everything was in order. It read 3:00 p.m.

Thirty Two

After leaving Blossom in his hotel room, Henry had made his way to the Station, meeting Norman there an hour later, when he and the other officers, some even coming despite not being on duty, hung around in the second conference room to the right; eating the cherry, raspberry and blueberry filled cream donuts Abby had brought for them alongside drinking pulp-clumped orange juice and milk that was nearing its expiration date. The acidic, curdled aftertaste still lingering against Henry's tongue even as he attempted to wash it down with another gulp of the coffee Sophie had refilled for him just thirty minutes before, he could feel the sensation of the liquid burning in his chest radiated up his sternum as he lifted his hand from the countertop, turning his wrist just slightly to see that it was 3:36 p.m.

Thinking of how the teenagers would be filling in soon, he carefully set back down the mug, letting out a sharp exhale with a slump of his shoulders. He couldn't tell if it was from the pain that lingered at the back of his throat, but there was a bubbling anxiety he could feel, cold and pressing against the back of his ribcage, his heart beating heavy.

He had been there for about an hour and a half when the woman who had given him his first cup of coffee, Jenny Madison—mother to one of the boys he interviewed with Norman at the very start of the investigation—exited from the back of the Diner. Her hair was the same sandy blonde as her son's, pulled into a bun of loose waves reaching around the curve of her rounded jawline, and he watched her spin back around after pulling open the front door with the ringing of the bell overhead, waving back at Sophie, who called out a quick, "see you tomorrow, Jen!" While a single, curled strand of her hair bounced against her forehead. Her smile still evident when she turned back around, the door closed behind her with another ring of the bell.

After noticing the Agent was low on his third cup of coffee since he arrived, almost fifteen minutes later, Sophie grabbed a quarter-filled pot of coffee from one of the burners put to medium heat and walked around the counter to where he sat, reaching over and beginning to pour while he tucked his hand into the pocket of his jacket, one elbow still propped on the counter and pulled out his cell. Checking the home screen to see that he had two missed calls from Norman alongside a single voicemail that had been sent three minutes ago.

Shrugging off a fleeting apprehension, Henry pressed the device to his ear and listened to it over the sound of the coffee filling up before Sophie pulled back the pot; a couple of droplets splattering against the counter when she did, just as Henry felt his stomach sink.

Upon his arrival, red and blue lights staining the walls of the house and blaring from the tops of the cars that surrounded the yard, an ambulance parked diagonal across the street with two policemen redirecting traffic on either side, Henry walked with long strides up the sidewalk and met Norman in front of the entrance, proceeding in getting quickly briefed on the situation, which, wasn't much considering he had just arrived as well, while they took the stairs two steps at a time; gripping the rail and passing the scattered members of Norman and Frank's small but efficient team before entering the scene, located directly to their right and down a narrow, dimly lit hallway.

Immediately, Norman halted in the doorway, wiping his hand over his mouth. "Oh... *Fuck.*" His voice cracked. His other hand coming to rest on his hip as Henry walked ahead of him with his shoulders slumped and his head tilting.

There was a new body.

Kyle Madison was found shortly before Norman called Henry, after Jenny had come home to notice that his things were still by the door and his car was still parked on the driveway despite having watched him leave for school before her shift.

Lying face up on his bed with one hand tied to the headboard in pink ribbon, his throat slit and an indiscernible number of stab wounds littering his bare chest, his eyes stared up at the ceiling dry, bloodshot and fogged by the white glint of death. Empty.

Henry looked over the boy's corpse with a grim disgust over his face.

As if a blender had been turned on without a lid to contain the mess, red soaked into the sheets, pooling in the center and trickling through foam padding, staining the floorboards beneath. His limbs bruised a pale yellow, turned grey, rigor mortis locked his jaw and eyes into an eternal state of shock. Shock that reflected the fact that the killer had severed the tendons of his throat while he was still breathing, leaving him to gurgle and suffocate on the curdling, spouting gushes of red that sprayed onto his face and crusted in the fibers of the bunched rag shoved between his teeth to keep him from making too much noise, considering this had occurred outside of his normal hunting grounds. Choking him to death, as if the twenty something stab wounds weren't sufficient.

Henry crossed his arms over his chest, inhaling the stench of rotting meat, the thick aroma of a butchers shop where salt-cured meats hung to dry and a rattling A.C failed to the rid the bloodstained floors of their sick residue. It was the same stench he experienced in the shack when finding the rotting corpse of Ethan Cooper; two flies—hungry and twitching—frantically swirling in dizzying bouts through the air before dipping their barbed limbs into the gaping tears of shredded flesh peeling outward of Kyle's chipped sternum that resembled fresh liver, mushy, sticky with syrupy blood turned to a paste.

Henry let out a deep sigh.

This wasn't about the next body. This was rage. This was unpredictable, unorganized.

No more excitement in the lax of his figure due to a reason Norman, who now walked up to his side, knew very well of, nonetheless, he looked at him wearily, and asked, "what does this mean?"

The light flashing from Frank's camera, shutters going off every few seconds while he diligently recorded the crime scene at hand before allowing for the evidence to be bagged and collected, even he knew that the killer had decided to try a new game and was testing the capabilities of the FBI agent and the Sheriff. He had done this practically out in the open and in broad daylight—a stark difference to the sanctuary of the woods that he had found before—and that meant, if he could get away with this, if they couldn't nail him right then and there, then there wasn't so much hope as to wait for the next hit, all the while he gained more confidence.

Frank lifted himself away from the body with his camera close to his chest, looking to the FBI Agent, expecting him to jump into a rant made of fanciful verbiage neither of them, being small-town folk, would necessarily understand right away, but would trust with the background of his experience. Still, this time, Henry didn't respond. All he did was make eye contact with Frank, then tuck his chin to his chest and look down at his shoes. His expression hardened. Leaving the question to linger as stiff and cold as the corpse in front of them.

Gnawing on his bottom lip, apprehension in the way he continued to document the crime scene, when, carefully stepping back against his heels in order to get a wide-frame shot, Frank noticed something sticking out from beneath the bed, he blinked, pulling his brows together, then crouched down. Reaching forward to pull the object out while muttering, "uh—guys? You might wanna see this." And standing back up.

"What is it?" Norman asked, eagerly.

After both Henry and Norman had made their way to either side of where he stood, Frank turned his shoulders and lifted his hand to show them what he had found. Henry exhaled a forced, aggravated breath before nodding for him to grab a small, clear evidence-labeled bag and drop the laminated school ID into it, finally answering the first question with the utterance of, "what *this* means, is that our *killer*—is getting a little too confident," while twisting his heels, a newfound sense of energy lacing through the sourness of his tone, driving his movements. "He's getting *cocky*. And when that happens? *Mistakes* are made."

Exiting the house, ducking under the yellow caution tape that had been connected to either side of the porch, Henry crossed the lawn toward where he was parked, Norman hurrying close behind him; passing Kyle's parents who were at the moment being walked through the rest of the process that would require Jenny, his mother—who Henry had just seen leaving the Diner, still dressed in her uniform—to come down to the station and give a formal statement. Tears streaming down her puffy face while her husband wrapped his hands around the back of her shoulders, he held her back to his chest and nodded occasionally at the instructions being laid before them.

Nonetheless, his attention being pulled away from the distraught couple, feeling his phone begin to ring, Henry lifted it up to his face and knitted his brows, reading the caller I.D.

Blossom.

"Blossom, I can't—" His voice fell flat with an agitation lacing through the sharpness of his breath. Then, he heard her.

Something *was wrong.*

He turned back to Norman, who halted in front of him with widening eyes. "Blossom?"

"He-Henry—please—"

It sounded as if she was hyperventilating, choking on her own breath before gulping it down. Henry's heart dropped. He spoke louder. "Blossom, tell me what's wrong."

"He-he—Whitmore—Whitmore, he tried to—and I—oh my god, I—"

"What *about* Whitmore? What happened—"

"Henry, what about Whitmore?" Norman stepped forward, but Henry waved him off.

"Blossom where are you?" His heart lodged in his throat, restricting his breath at the sound of her nearly incomprehensible speech, he lifted his hand to his forehead and closed his eyes. "Blossom, you need to tell me where you are. Are you still at the hotel?" Nothing. "Are you home? Are you at your house or the hotel—Blossom you need to tell me so I can come get you."

"M-mine—I'm at mine... I went home, and he was—he was there—I tried... I tried to get him to *leave* but *he just*—"

"Just." He cut her off. "*Stay there.* Do not. Move. I'm coming. Okay?"

"Henry—" She hiccuped.

"Just stay there." Hanging up and dropping his hand back to his side, Henry then looked back to Norman, trembling. "Whitmore went after Blossom."

"Is she okay?" Norman stepped closer.

"I don't know."

"Where's Whitmore now?"

Despite the calm facade over Henry's face, there was a slight twinge in his voice, and Norman saw the pain glint in his eyes. "I don't *know*."

It wasn't supposed to feel like this…

Blood crusting on her hands, her arms, splattered over her cheeks and drenching the front of her blush velvet cami bodysuit, soaking into the front of her pink shorts and trickling down her thighs, Blossom sat in a pool of blood; slumped in the kitchen, her back resting against the wall, her chest ring and falling with shaky breaths while tears dried on her cheeks. Next to her, her fingers gone numb, they wrapped limp around the slick handle of a carving knife, and she looked down at it, her bottom lip quivering as she fought back the urge to continue crying.

Her chest felt empty, ripped open and filled with maggots, rotten flesh eroding away at her thoughts. And she could feel *everything.*

She didn't even realize it when Henry ran through the hallway, his voice echoing through the thin walls as he yelled her name, but with his hand wrapping around the entryway, he swung around into the kitchen, skidding to a stop above her before crouching down.

Her eyes wild, blurred and full of tears, Blossom held her bloodied hands out in front of her, her brows curving upward while she met his gaze and murmured, "I lost control." There was blood in her hair. Bits of flesh under her nails. Choking on her next breath, she then cried like a child does, coughing and wheezing in front of him until Henry grabbed her, pulling her into him. "I lost control— I lost control—" She almost yelled, muffled and filled with terror, wrenching from her chest as she clutched at him, her face buried into the crook of his neck, arms wound tight around his shoulders.

Out of the corner of his eye, Henry could see the tangled, heap of flesh belonging to the corpse of Mr. Whitmore. But with a shaky breath and Norman already on the phone with the hospital, sirens drowning out Blossom's sobs, the blue and red from the patrol cars that followed them flooding through the windows, Henry just turned his head so his nose buried in her hair and closed his eyes, feeling the blood seep into his clothes.

Thirty Three

Seated in the stiff chair he had pulled to the side of Blossom's bed, his elbow propped against the arm rest with his chin against the top of his knuckles, Henry's gaze was unwavering as he watched over her; a lack of composure to the way he crossed his legs in front of him and slouched back, the bags under his eyes—grey and blushed pink—contrasting against the black of his eyes. His expression painted with a certain discontent, an anguish while he attempted to piece together the rest of the puzzle pieces, nonetheless, even now, the picture on the top was malformed and distorted. Some parts missing, the rest sloppily put together, and he couldn't seem to make sense of it. His shoulders slumped, he wiped his hand over his face before Blossom—her throat still raw from crying—attempted to say his name, reaching her fingers toward him.

Blinking, Henry leaned forward, taking her hand back into his, and whispered, "you're okay. I'm here."

"I…I'm sorry—Henry."

Henry squeezed her knuckles and shook his head. "You don't need to apologize. Just rest. Okay?"

She had a large bandage on her forehead covering the laceration that resulted from face planting into the edge of the countertop during her attempt to flee through the kitchen and out the back door, the bruising reaching down to her temple. Treated by thick glue to the open wound before the slightly swollen flesh was pushed back together to minimize scarring, thick gauze tightly wound around her abdomen as well to cover the gash along her side and stab wound Whitmore had managed to inflict during their struggle, the thick, woven stitches stiff and making her breathing shallow despite the pain medication the nurses had given her. Unable to shower, blood still crusted over her skin and clumped in her hair, lingering under her nails.

Giving a light knock at the propped door, causing both of them to pick their eyes up, Norman stood in the doorway and asked Blossom, "you holding up alright?" Before she gave him a weak smile, and he nodded with a quick, "good," while Henry stood from his seat.

Carefully placing her hand back down, walking around the bed, the harsh white lights of the hospital brightened his features and made him look even paler—more tired—than usual, the tip of his nose slightly blushed. Norman wondered if he had been crying. "Is he dead?" He asked as soon as he stood in front of Norman, leaning close so Blossom couldn't hear.

"Yes, and I already have guys at his house and combing through his car."

"Anything?"

"All clean."

"But?"

"We found photographs at the *school.* Pink ribbon in his *desk.*"

Henry let his head fall back slight with a smile pulling at his lips and a gentle chuckle. "Okay, great, that's great." Then, he blinked. "What were the pictures of?"

"Let's just say Blossom was his muse."

"She was the pink ribbon."

"What do you mean?"

"I've been thinking about it, and it seems he was doing it all *for* her, sending her a message with each of them, that they would never be as worthy as..." The words rolled from his tongue, venomous and bitter, "*him.* Those boys didn't deserve her because she was always going to be his. The pink ribbon was the message. And he was going to make sure of it. What his goal was—"

"Do you think he really wanted to kill Blossom?"

"When we get her statement we'll find out."

"I can't believe you were right about him this whole god damn time."

"Don't be too hard on yourself, we didn't have what we needed to go after him anyway."

"Still, I just wouldn't think he'd keep stuff at the *school.*" AKA *I should have looked into it, like you said. Then maybe, it wouldn't have gone this far.*

"But that's *why* he *kept* it there."

"Sick son of a bitch..." Norman ran a hand through his hair. "Well, now that the case is closed, are you going back? To Quantico?"

Henry shrugged. "With the paperwork I need to get done with what happened and the fact that I also need to get Blossom's statement..." The grey afternoon light shining gently over her delicate features, when he turned so his back hit the door and looked back to her, he saw she had closed her eyes before glancing back to Norman with a fleeting smirk. "Well, don't be expecting to rid of me so easily."

"How could I ever?" Norman patted Henry on the shoulder once with the flat of his palm, then exiting the room, left him to walk toward the window; looking out at the afternoon fog that followed the gentle tap of rain, settling over the Town and wrapping grey around the visible tree line. It seemed as if everything in the Town had calmed after the sirens had died down, an eeriness to the way even the pine now stood motionless, apart from the slight bobbing of branches when restless birds, who sang sharp, piercing melodies, jumped from their wet, twisted and mangled arms.

Walking to the vending machines from Blossom's recovery room, Norman spotted Sophie, who pressed the button B4 for a double espresso iced coffee with milk and a caramel flavoring. Dressed in a thin yellow, short-sleeved collared blouse tucked into blue jeans, she had her hair down and her back toward him, allowing him to sneak up on her.

"Not nearly as good as anything you make." He leaned his shoulder against the illuminated glass cover as the machine whirled, dropping Sophie's drink with a blinking *thank you!* Across the green pin pad where she had stuck her card just before he arrived, successfully making her jump with a soft gasp.

"Shit, Norman." She huffed, reaching down to grab the cool metal can before snapping back the metal cap. Her posture relaxing again, she then crossed her other arm around her abdomen and motioned toward where he had come from. "How is she?" While taking the first sip.

Norman, a wide grin dissipating, turned so his toes propped behind him and leaned his head back. "Why don't you ask her yourself?"

"Like she'd tell me shit, Norman."

He dipped his head in acknowledgment, waiting another beat before responding. "She's fine, Henry's watching over her."

"Oh, well, of course he is." She raised her brows, proceeding to gulp down the coffee like it was alcohol.

Watching her, Norman rolled his eyes to the side with a blink. "He did his job, Sophie. And he's in there, looking after your daughter who was almost murdered, comforting her, while you're out here with me."

"What exactly are you saying, Norman?"

"I don't know... Maybe... Henry is what she needs right now." He closed his eyes, sighing.

"Like you'd know what's good for her."

Then, opening his eyes again and glaring at her while she took another sip of her drink, Norman abruptly pushed himself from the vending machine—about to excuse himself back to the station—when he hesitated, turning back only to ask, "was it true? What happened?"

However, Sophie's expression went blank and she left him in silence.

Thirty Four

In light of the investigation, the dance had been pushed back two weeks, past the Senior graduation, which was held indoors with double the amount of parents and teachers on watch—so happening to include Whitmore himself—as well as a number of on-duty officers from the Sheriff's Station. But now, with glitter covered paper-cut outs of hearts matching the other white and red decorations alongside the pastels of pink hues and blues that lined the walls, a video loop of a cupid angel—a fat baby with a bow and diaper with rosy cheeks and a wide smile who bobbed up and down, shooting arrows into various people who then fell in love with each other, hearts popping like tiny balloons into the air between them as they began kissing—was projected on the far wall. The theme being love, really it just looked more like a Valentines celebration than an end of year formal.

The dance floor populated by boys wearing red ties, pink suits alongside girls dressed in red and white gowns with flowers pinned to their wrists using trimmed pink ribbon, taking a large gulp of spiked, sugary punch from a red solo cup she had brought to her lips, Blossom stood next to the dessert table—which held assortments of cupcakes, pink-frosted cookies and red velvet cake with whipped cream decorations alongside globs of syrup-coated red strawberries—her eyes darting back and forth from the crowd to the gymnasium doors; her wounds for the most part healed, the cut on her forehead a thin scab. And though plenty came up to ask her to dance, others too cautious in light of hearing what had happened, Blossom merely kept watching. Waiting. The pit in her stomach growing larger than even she would care to admit.

Nonetheless, the clanking of metal echoing through the gymnasium, perking back up, she finally spotted him.

Flashbacks of his own high school years itching at the back of his neck and making the hair stand on his arms, when Henry entered, he looked around the crowd of teenagers huddled in the center of the room, bubblegum pink and purple lights shining over him—dimming the atmosphere to match that of the theme and soaking shadows of couples in red—while squeezing his fingers into tightly clenched fists before flexing them. The anxiety bubbling in his stomach making his heart lodge in his throat and his heart beat painfully. There wasn't a doubt in his mind that it was a good thing he had skipped his own dance—all of them—back in the day, but with his eyes grazing over the crowd, searching for the only reason he had come in the first place, butterflies immediately swarmed in his belly when he finally found it.

Blossom was already walking toward him from across the gym when he laid his eyes on her. Cutting through the dance floor as the beats of *Stupid Cupid* played as frilly and fluffy as the tulle of her dress, Henry scrunched his brows, the relief he felt seeing her washing away into something... Else.

Despite seemingly always wearing pink, she was instead dressed a blue, sleeveless ballgown, compared to the theme of the dance and the girls that had followed such colors; embroidered overlays of floral lace decoration covering the lace-up corset that hugged her chest in a scoop neckline and exposed the soft dip of her breasts, accenting the fluffy waistline. When the lights shone just right Henry could see the pink of her legs beneath the multi-layered skirt. Her bounds of white hair bobbing in shiny waves over her shoulders, spilling from her scalp like a golden fountain, she looked like Cinderella with glitter dusted over her cheeks as she stepped through the crowd from seven-inch silver high-top heels, platforms on the bottom. Compared to having to duck his chin to look down at her, Henry merely shifted his eyes. The top of her head coming just under his nose versus shoulder.

"You came!" She said, light and fluffy. She was *fluffy*. That was the best word in his mind for it. She was bright and fluffy and *blue* and *cute*. He smiled back at her with a quick lift of his brows, wondering what enraptured him so much with her, and why every time he saw her it felt like the world would fall out from under his feet.

He concluded it was the music and the way his chest grew warm and his stomach knotted and how much his affection for her made his head spin. Just like the animation of the cupid that played over the DJ, it was like Henry had gotten a damn heart arrow in the ass. Knocking him flat on his face. His widespread lips creating deep indents of his cheeks, with a blink he tucked his hands into his pockets, not because they were cold but because he needed to keep himself from reaching out and touching her.

When Blossom finally stopped in front of him, inches away, he took a breath full of the perfume she had smeared over her skin. She smelled as she always did, of flowers and sweetness, but there was something to the way it nauseated him tonight. Like powdered sugar, it dissolved against his tongue, coating it like honey, and infected his veins with a rush of adrenaline. It was like even with all that rage and resentment that filled the spaces between his marrow, there was still room for her. For the sweet poison of her taste, her scent, her touch, which stained everything —even the black of his ash and the rot of his insides—pink.

When she began again, the song had ended and instead the soft lullaby of Paul Anka's *Put Your Head On My Shoulder* played, signaling for couples to sway along with the intoxicatingly melancholy melody. "Do you like my dress?" Blossom asked, her nails sending shivers down

Henry's spine as she wrapped her palms around the back of his neck and pressed her body to his. Swallowing the lump in his throat with a shaky exhale, he took her in his arms, careful not to hold her too tight, cursing the musical choices of the dance in making the butterflies in his stomach multiply at an alarming rate, and how much it all felt like a dream.

Henry was never that good of a dancer, but dancing against Blossom, he forgot he wasn't and they moved together naturally without a second thought.

"It's blue." He looked down at her, pressing his fingers into the exposed small of her back, feeling the softness of the dip in her spine between the laces while pulling gently on them and stroking his thumb in small circles, making her blush. From the sidelines, parents nudged elbows and watched with confused stares.

Blossom began twisting and tugging at the edges of Henry's hair, dipping into the black and brushing against greyed roots. It was getting long, the waves in its thickness barely keeping tamed under the gel. "I thought you'd like it." She responded in a light, hesitant voice, more like an exhale.

He dipped his head down to hear her better over the music, her cheek grazing his when he emphasized, "it's *blue*."

"You told me your favorite color was blue, so I just thought, maybe..." The two of them spinning gently, the skirt of her dress curled around his pant leg and Blossom wrapped her arms fully around his shoulders. Wishing this moment would never end, for the last minute of the song they stayed in silence and Henry closed his eyes. Feeling one of her hands slip beneath his folded collar as she rested her head against his shoulder.

Nonetheless, the DJ turning up the volume to a song Henry couldn't name, he pulled away from Blossom, taking her hands in his and holding them to his chest. She stopped swaying and looked up at him when he whispered, "let's get out of here."

"What... Are we running away together?"

With Blossom squeezing her fingers over his knuckles, Henry caught himself thinking about how Whitmore had planned to steal her for himself. The idea of him succeeding blooming a deep rage within him, alongside a deep sadness that made his chest heavy and the music fog in his ears. Swallowing the lump in his throat, there was a slight crack in his voice. "Would you?"

And in the next moment, Blossom's glossed lips pulled into a gleaming smile.

The engine of his Chevrolet buzzing beneath the walnut brown leather seats, Blossom sat pressed to his side, having gathered her dress in her hands with her blonde hair blowing in the wind. The night sky littered with dazzling silver stars, driving up Evergreen road to the hotel, she then maneuvered herself to the opposite side of Henry and stuck half of her head out from the open window. Feeling the cool

kisses of the night air against her face and breathing deep
the pine-scented gusts of passionate winds.

As if to keep her from falling out, Henry grabbed her
hand, turning his head to watch occasionally, admiration
numbing the aching of his joints.

The entrance of the hotel barren, the fire turned low, the
length of Blossom's dress dragged behind her and she
allowed Henry to guide her to the elevator, where he stole
his first kiss. Cliche and frantic, he pushed her to the wall
and tasted the lipgloss—a faint lingering bubblegum
against her teeth—holding his palm at the back of her head
before the elevator dinged at the fourth floor.

After tugging her the rest of the way to his bedroom
and continuing to kiss her through the door before it shut
behind him, he began loosening his tie with a gruff hand.
However, just as Henry thought he had her all to himself,
she pushed her flattened palms to his chest, causing him to
stumble back and choke a quick, dizzy, "wh-what. What's
wrong."

Her hands not leaving his chest, instead she wrapped
her fingers around his tie, tugging gently. The knot loose, it
still pulled around his neck, and he tried to go back to her,
but Blossom held him at arm's length. "I want a drink." She
teased. "Get me a drink."

"What? No."

"Get me... A *drink*." She teased him. "Don't worry...
I'll share."

Huffing, Henry looked to the ceiling. "Fine." Then, turning around, Blossom fell back in a puff of blue and blonde. He pulled out a bottle of cooled vodka, grabbing two glasses that clinked together; pinched from his fingertips.

Watching him, Blossom propped herself to her elbows before reaching out. "Just bring the damn bottle over." She argued. It was *annoying.*

"Blossom-"

"Didn't you want to kiss me?" Planting his hands on the countertop, Henry bowed his head. Then, snatching the bottle and unscrewing the cap, he took two swigs. Watching Blossom closely while situating himself in front of her, between her knees and looking down.

"That's not the only thing I had in mind."

"Oh really?" Blossom reached her fingers up just enough that they caught the leather edge of his belt. Tugging him forward, he landed to her side with a huff, and she began kissing his alcohol laced lips as if trying to intoxicate herself on his breath. Her manicured hand cupping the side of his face, scratching behind his ears. Then, slumping back, she took the bottle from him and lifted the rim to her mouth. Henry rested his chin on her shoulder as she gulped down the poison, a cold sweat beading at his brow.

The two continued kissing until their words slurred together, their lips became numb, muscles melted together, and they other didn't know when one person stopped and the other began; mixing, swirling together like thick batter that clumped and solidified until Henry pulled her onto his lap, his arms resting on her thighs while her knees hugged his ribs. Blossom wrapped his tie around her knuckles and drank more than he would have liked her to, her weight against his abdomen making him filled with the need to touch her. He wanted to rip the blue from her body and bury himself in her pink. And began to—hiking the fabric of the dress up to her hips—when Blossom's face fell under his jaw and she bit his Adam's apple, just as she had done in the car, the soft vibrations of her moaning making him clench his jaw before falling to the mattress like a dying soldier falls off the top of a horse.

Giggling, she then slipped toward the edge while Henry attempted to grab for her, sitting up quicker than he was capable in the process then falling back to his forearm, dizzy, his cheek resting on his shoulder with his disheveled hair falling in front of his eyes while he struggled to focus on Blossom. "What are you doing?" He mumbled.

Blossom set the bottle of vodka to her feet, waves of blonde falling in her face while proceeding to use just about every fiber of her being to reach down and carefully undo the straps of her platform heels. Kicking them off, she then walked—stumbled—toward the door, leaving Henry to fall forward from the bed. "Bl-Blossom st…Come back…" He huffed, trying to move his legs as fast as they could carry him—which just ended up with him palming the walls for supports as—in her utmost determination (only worsened by the stinging taste of booze against the back of her throat, burning her tongue) Blossom exited the hotel through the side door after taking the elevator—the doors closing before Henry caught up to her—then walked to the side gate to the pool, which had closed about two hours beforehand.

Henry wondered how she knew about that entrance, but the thoughts quickly washed away when his blood pressure rose as she climbed the locked fence. Fabric of her dress catching, there was a gentle ripping sound, but she just tugged it free with a harsh yank of her arm.

"Blossom!" He hissed. "Blossom, please sto—*stop.*"

Swinging his leg over the fence before pushing himself up with a grunt, however, he wasn't as graceful as her and ended up falling to the other side. Hitting the cement with a harsh smack of his hip, the alcohol managed to numb the sharp pain to a dull throb when he pushed himself back up, but he cursed under his breath, fully aware that he'd be left with a tender bruise along his side. When he looked up again, Henry watched in horror as Blossom neared the edge of the neon-saturated blue and pink, purples of the pool lights, holding her arms diagonal and tip-toeing along the curved cement and tile. He really, *really* didn't want to have to dive after her. Still, just like no amount of protesting had stopped her from getting this far, the pull of gravity finally won and with a single mis-step, she fell into the swirling colors. They engulfed her with a heavy splash and foaming white bubbles.

In that moment, Henry had sobered.

Running as fast as his legs could carry him, he fell to the side of the pool, locking his hands over the edge before peering into the water.

The red lights that shone through the waters diluted by teal and cerulean, sapphire and berry shadows, they turned to shades of magenta, raspberry and carmela. Coral oranges turning to mango and paprika, greens melting into her dress like sea-foam. The colors seeped into Blossom, saturating her skin, her bright ivory lemon hair moving in the water like swirling tendrils; twisting and curling. Scattered strands like seaweed flowing alongside the gentle current. He could see the shape of her, warped and nearing. Fragmented. But it looked as if she was a part of the water, her dress billowing and blooming out from the waistline, and as Henry watched her, his chest squeezing, he imagined if he were to reach into the depths and try to grab her, she'd simply dissipate into a hazy fog, swirling around his fingers.

Resurfacing, she moved back to him with small doggy paddles and a wide smile, her face dripping and large breaths pushing from her lungs as she attempted to ease the burning deep from within. "Come in!"

"No." Henry shook his head, whispering, "Blossom, please. You've had your fun."

"I'm just getting started…"

"Can we not do this? Please, let's go. Let's just go."

"It feels so *good* though… Come in."

"I'm sure it does but..." He squeezed his jaw. She looked so beautiful, like a mermaid, shimmering and breathless and alluring. "It isn't safe." He urged. "Please just get out."

"Kiss me." She huffed, swimming with the paddling of her hands under her chest until she was under him again. "Kiss me."

Her right hand reached up, twisting in his tie like a leash. "Blossom..." He warned, his knuckles blotching white as he leaned his weight back. "Stop. No."

"Kiss me..." She moaned, chanting it, "kiss me, kiss me, kiss me, kiss me..." Like a witch's spell while pulling herself up so her lips grazed his just before he curled forward, crashing into the waters.

He could hear her laughter underwater.

Muffled.

Not sure if he was drowning, or if he was already dead, everything was blue. Then red. Then pink. Then orange, yellow, green, then blue again, and Blossom pulled him against her by the collar of his black suit coat. Kissing him.

The taste of chlorine mixed with vodka.

Doused in changing lights, Henry melted. Dissolved into the water, into Blossom, and kissed her back. His hands wrapping around the sides of her face before he turned his head and wrapped his arms around her waist. Her legs tangling with his, they sunk deeper into the water until all the oxygen had left their lungs, which burned and contracted, and they were forced to come back up.

Blossom clung to Henry as he pulled her to the shallow end. Drenched, the dress hugged her and dragged heavily around her legs, shaping her hips and her breasts, her whole body practically visible beneath the thin fabric. She was shivering, but as they laid against the stairs, wrapped around him, Henry held her close and they kissed again. Wondering in the meantime if it was the alcohol making his head spin, or if it was her.

He didn't care about being caught, but he was sick of having to touch her through the now soaked fabric of her dress. Her *blue* dress, and bit her bottom lip, tugging the corset loose from her back. She clawed at his chest, and in the next moment, her hands found his belt. *Are we really about to do this? Am I doing this?* Henry asked himself. His heart fluttered, his cheeks warm and his lips numb, hair wet and dripping into his eyes, Blossom's straps loosened from her shoulders and Henry kissed her jaw, then her throat, then the nape of her neck, then turned her under him so her hair submerged in the water and she was splayed beneath him.

"Why did you choose *blue-*" he yanked the skirt from the water, slipping his hand underneath the tulle, then the slip, and feeling the goose-eggs scattered over her thighs.

"I don't... Know..." She sighed, her eyes fluttered closed and her lips pulled into a crooked, goofy smile. He angled his hips up against the side of her leg, feeling himself becoming lost within his heat. Their lips meeting again, Henry slipped his hand around the underside of her jaw. Making her look up at him.

"I want to fuck you, Blossom." Henry growled, his grip almost leaving bruises. He stopped at her knee, pressing into the underside and feeling the sensitive flesh alongside tendon against his fingers.

She giggled again, hiccuping. "Then… Fuck me."

"Do you *want* me to fuck you?"

"Yes…" Her fingers buried in his hair, he kissed the corner of her mouth.

"I want to hear you say it… Tell me how much you want me. *I want to know you need me.*"

Her chest weighing down, her jaw slackened and her legs falling away from him as she sat up, Blossom's expression went numb and she opened her eyes. Henry at first kept trying to pull her toward him, thinking she was laughing, and kissed her shoulder, attempting to bring her back to him. But then, furrowing his brow and finally pulling her chin, she yanked herself away from him again, letting out horrid, wrenching sobs.

"Jesus christ—Blossom—" He fell away from her with his palms raised.

"I-I don-don't know what. Happening—I don't know wh-what's happening to me—" She pushed.

He looked at her with worry, his mind flashing with whatever Whitmore could have done to her—the bruises left on her thighs and wrists, the now-healed cut on her forehead—before she fought him off. How much Blossom James let herself endure before she finally defended herself. Choking on water, booze, and air all at once while speaking faster than her drunkenness and blubbering tears would permit, she hid her face behind her hands.

Only, when Henry fell to the next step down and waded his way in front of her, reaching out to place his hand on her back before bringing her to his chest, something neither of them could admit was just how much—the same as how she had molded him into what she wanted, he had begun to splinter her exterior—morphing her into someone she hardly recognized in the mirror. "I don't know what's wrong with me... Something's wrong with me—"

"Nothing's wrong with you, Blossom." He urged. "Hey-" He pressed his lips to the top of her head. "Nothing's wrong with you... Okay? It's okay to feel these things. You went through something no one can understand. But what you're feeling right now isn't because something is *wrong* with you." Pause. "Listen to me!"

Muffled, her words were acidic, heavy as they curled with a childish whine. "You can't even *see it,* Henry, but I could destroy you—no one would ever know—you can't even see it, you don't even understand—"

Like a crack of a whip echoing through a hall, a hot knife cutting through butter, a pin needle dropping to tile floors, the only thing he could hear was the blood in his ears muffled by the splashing of water and the gurgling of the filter. He felt her grip on him tighten, and a nearby owl, hidden by the trees, hooted. Closing his eyes and pinching the tulle fabric of her dress between his fingers, Henry let out a heavy sigh, then muttered, "you already are."

Thirty Five

It was the hottest summer the Town had experienced in the past three years. Nearly a month since the dance, after all the files had been locked in storage cabinets in the back of the Station alongside the reports and crime scene pictures and Norman had returned to his usual, day-to-day activities, catching up on the speeding tickets, parking tickets and curfew fines he had neglected to touch since the arrival of the FBI to his doorstep, Henry —wearing one of two short sleeve, navy button ups he owned, tucked into his usual trousers—following a late brunch at the Diner, drove up the road to Blossom's.

He entered through the white picket fence into the backyard, the cool, rusted metal lock slipping easily under his thumb when he slowly pushed the gate back into place. Turning, that's where he spotted her in the middle of the lawn; the sun beating down from clear blue skies and making her ivory skin glow like a marble statue tinted by hazelnut and cherry blotches on her kneecaps and shoulders, on her thighs and blushed across her cheeks. She wore a strawberry pink bikini, laying on her back on a white, plastic pool-side chair, a frayed green towel tucked under her.

He could tell she was looking at him from the way her head turned just ever so slightly in his direction. Still, she didn't move until he was standing a few feet away. Merely lowering her large-framed black sunglasses with cat-eyes down the bridge of her nose. "My mother's inside." She said, flat.

"Her car is gone and on the way, I saw her in the Diner. Got a slice of pie in the car if you want it." Henry sat on the edge of the chair, his fingers slipping over Blossom's knee and wrapping around her thigh. Looking down, watching his touch gently indent the softness of her skin, he traced the bruises. Then, grazing over the faded blister from where he had put out the cigarette, the blotch of seashell-pink tissue now stained with faint yellows, a glint of sadness shadowed his eyes when they fell on the pink scars of where she had been caught by Whitmore's knife. Her words echoing in his head of how Whitmore had tried getting her to pack a bag and leave town with him.

"He kept talking about me flirting with him, as if I caused it. As if I gave him an open invitation to think he had the power, the right, to pick and choose who I was with. And when I didn't choose him…" She had spoken

bitterly, her statement also being that of her relations with the Agent—"when I didn't choose him, when he saw that I was with other boys, he decided they weren't good enough and that's why he was killing them. Because they had all..." She looked at Henry through the swelling of tears. He had looked away, his gaze instead lying on the floor between his feet. *"In one way or another. I don't doubt he was going to try to kill you, as well, if I hadn't..."*

"He wouldn't have been able to."

"You still underestimate everything he's done? He killed righteously. He didn't understand what he was doing was wrong—and you still think you'd be able to evade him? It didn't take *me long—"*

"It's alright, Blossom. You don't need to say anything more." Norman cut her off with a wave of her hand. *Sympathy oozing from his words and the way he looked at her, yet covering the disdain and callousness to how he really felt toward everything she was saying. The disgust that cut his words short. Though, it was too late for that, now. And he knew it.*

Despite how talkative Blossom always was, she didn't seem to have much to say regarding what happened, and the meeting was short lived.

Blossom pushed back up her glasses, leaning her head back, chin lifting. If he were to ask what she was thinking about, she would have told him that, with the sun beating down on her like it was, occasional kisses of cool breezes whipping through her hair, she'd picture herself lying in the middle of a pond, weeds tying her to the water with her dress slick with moss and her hair tangled with flowers, floating, free, like John Everett Millais's painting of Ophelia.

Instead, Henry remained silent and Blossom just let out a sigh, re-opening her eyes, left with a sea-sick feeling in her stomach, accompanied by a shell-like emptiness. An emptiness that told her no matter how hard she tried, no flowers would ever bloom to fill her heart or soul with a sense of peace like in the springtime. So, in order to fill that pitted feeling in her stomach, she sat up, dipping her head beneath Henry's to catch his lips in a desperate kiss. Her name staining his lips, he quickly caught the back of her head, while from inside, the melody of *Everybody Loves Somebody* by Dean Martin played on the highest volume from an old radio on the kitchen windowsill, and weaved his hand through her hair while his other hand rested at the side of her opposite hip.

They sat there, continuing to kiss slowly, gently, quietly, until Henry turned his head. Breaking the kiss and squinting toward the sky, while Blossom rested her forehead against his shoulder. "I want to love you... So badly..." She pressed to his hollow cheek, her breath warm. He caught a hint of strawberry sweetness, the smell of flavored corn syrup. Alcohol.

"But?" He murmured, petting her hair down, feeling its light texture beneath his touch, the strands gliding over his knuckles while his brows pulled together and his chest squeezed, his limbs heavy with longing.

Blossom didn't answer.

Kissing her again, it all felt like the beginning to the end. *Of what, though?* He couldn't say. He was finally okay with not knowing, and perhaps, in some twisted, pitiful desire, in all his destruction, in his damage, he didn't want her to answer, and simply kissed her. That's all he wanted to do, anyway.

His fingers pressing into her spine as if to dig his nails through her soft flesh and rip it from her, she shivered against him with a low hum, biting his bottom lip until his jaw ached and the metallic lingering of blood smearing against his tongue sent his arm tight around her waist. Standing, he then swiftly picked Blossom up from the chair with an ease of lingering strength from his youth and carried her inside. Her mouth leaving blooming trails of raspberry and blackberry kisses down his throat. *It all felt like a dream, and he didn't want to wake up.*

After laying her on the bed, Blossom cupped his cheek, welcoming him with the eager wrapping of her legs around his waist. Lost in his thoughts and in the feeling of her body pressed to his, just as they had been in the pool—his hunger left un-satiated—now, tasting her sweetness, feeling her warmth, Henry's heart lodged in his throat, the mattress springs squealing with a light bounce as he moved with a frantic, unnerving edge to his sharp figure. Her hair sprawled around her head, *like a halo,* he thought to himself, Henry's lips caught her jaw and he moved down the curve of her collarbone to the dip between her breasts. Running his hands down her sides until he pressed soft, flowering bruises into the meat of her hips. His teeth grazing her skin, then, causing a burst of swarming butterflies in his stomach, as his eyes met hers, Blossom took his hand. Directing it inward.

Finally giving her what she wanted, Henry rolled the her bottoms down her thighs, her knees instinctively spreading for him while she twisted the sheets between clenched fists. He would have liked to admit he was gentle with her, but just as he had started off gentle the night of the dance and soon forgot about her injuries—a part of him wanting her to feel weak under him, scared, vulnerable, like he always found he did—with her chest lifting breathlessly and her toes curling, her heels propped against the soft tissue between his shoulder blades, Henry's touch was a bittersweet mix of gentleness and roughness. The callousness of his greed making waves of pleasure radiate up her spine; infecting Blossom with a smile. Tilting her head back, biting down on her bottom lip, she could feel herself coming apart beneath him. Unraveling. His name kissing her lips like the fluttering of butterfly wings as she began gulping shallow breaths.

With the sunlight streaming in, the birds chirping light and freely outside the open window with the music still blaring from the kitchen, there was a sense of peace. Contentment that followed the oozing of sticky cum around Henry's long fingers as he felt her walls contract around him, already so wet, *for him.* Observing the ways *he* laid an effect on her, her rosy cheeks reddened even more by the sweat that perspired at her temples, he then moved himself back over her body—the friction building between his thighs from where his erection pushed against the fabric of his boxers, making his skin hot and itchy with the need to have her, all of her—and catching his face between her hands, her lips engulfed his and her tongue ran flat up his chin, licking up the lingering stickiness from between her thighs before Henry then pushed his fingers up to the corner of her mouth.

His face not an inch away, as he ran his touch along gentle pout of her bottom lip, pulling at her gums, feeling her teeth under his rough touch, when Blossom bit down against his knuckle, he fought the urge to pull back. Feeling his skin indent with the print of her teeth like a rabid animal does the flesh of its kill. Nonetheless, Blossom's chest fell with a sigh and she suddenly pursed her lips around the smeared blood beginning to bead; mixing it with the thick strings of the creamy, cloudy white cum that globbed between his knuckles, sucking lightly, tasting herself with the swirling of her tongue along his nail.

Her eyes fluttering closed such as a baby lulled by a mother's touch and her hands came up to grasp at his palm, at this, Henry felt his stomach knot and carefully situated himself back between her hips. Finally burying himself into the soft, warm flesh of her inner thighs, into the petals of Blossom's flowering heat after unbuckling himself from his pants with a gruff, forceful hand shoved between them, a hasty exhale escaping him, followed by a low, guttural groan. In return, Blossom gave him exactly what he needed, at the same time, taking exactly what she wanted.

A perfect balance.

Thirty Six

The pink duvet sheets pulled up around his waist with his arms behind his head, the smell of *her* surrounding him, Henry listened to the muffled stream of the shower water splashing up the sides of her tub, melting with clinging, suffocating bouts of steam from the baby blue tile walls while pushing himself to his elbows. Tilting his head to the side with a tug of a smirk against the growing stubble on his hollow cheeks, she had left the door open, allowing him to see her through the reflection of the clear, plastic hot pink curtains she stood behind, her back turned to him.

Come the full bloom of summer—the investigation becoming more of a memory with each day that passed— Henry noticed he also had more color in his cheeks and had even managed to cut down on the number of cigarettes he smoked a day, replacing the euphoria of nicotine with bliss of her kisses. That was enough.

He wondered if this could last forever.

The thought spawning a bubbling excitement in his chest, seemingly nothing could have dimmed Henry's childlike infatuation, the idea of sharing breakfasts with her, keeping her in his bed, perhaps settling down in one of the houses next to the infamous park, or perhaps closer to the Evergreen hotel—deep within the trees—making him smile and shake his head.

Kicking his legs over the side of the bed, picking up his boxers from the soft carpet, for a moment, he looked at the spot he had dreamt finding Blossom drenched in the artificial blood of a cruel-intentioned joke. The spot he had dreamt she had murdered him. His heart skipped a beat and he couldn't help but imagine her scrubbing bleach against the carpet. Nonetheless, instead of ruminating on it, being filled with question toward her, Henry simply blinked and looked away. Realizing despite the number of times he had been in her room, he hadn't taken the time to look around. So, after pulling the fabric up his hips and redressing into the black tank top he had been wearing beneath his suit, Henry walked diagonal of the bed to the opposite wall, where Blossom had a white bookshelf next to her desk and vanity.

Peering down with the turn of his head to the side at the various books, the shelves were more so filled with magazines than actual literature. However, there were quite a few classics and modern stories that caught his eye. His fingertips grazing the spines of these novels, dust layered his skin in a thin sheet. He rubbed it away before moving on to inspect the contents on the top, which included a stack of old magazines, a vase of dead roses and lilies, alongside an unwashed mug of coffee that had dried at the bottom in a thick brown paint. The sides peeling away like old wallpaper. Reaching up and unclasping the golden lock of a glitter pink ballerina box, he proceeded to watch as the tutu-wearing, white figure turned with a soft lullaby, the dancer's springs bobbing side to side until restlessness led him to carefully shut the box again and continue on his search. He didn't know what he was necessarily looking for, but... His heart skipped a beat when he side-stepped in front of her dresser.

On the side were faded paintings of flowers and bumblebees. He imagined her getting it when she was a young girl, the images the same as those that would be found in child's bedroom. Gnawing on the inside of his bottom lip, glancing over his shoulder toward the bathroom, where steam still billowed and Blossom still contained herself under the shooting stream of hot water, fragrances of floral tints and citrus fruit lathered against her skin, Henry let out a nervous breath before reaching forward and pulling open the top drawer.

It was filled with shirts. He furrowed his brows and closed it. The second drawer containing her skirts and shorts and pants, for a moment he pinched the fabric of a velvet skirt between his fingers. Feeling the softness and observing the shimmering, glossy tint of pink and streaks of white from where he glided his thumb over the folds. Then, moving on, finally, with his next breath catching and his cheeks becoming hot, Henry tugged open the third square drawer to his left. Revealing mixes of tangled lace, silk, and velvet lingerie.

He reached in such as a child does when reaching into a drawer full of candy, sifting through the fabrics, his eyes widening at the intricate, small, scandalous sets of bras and frilly panties before his nail caught the edge of something folded, shoved to the bottom of the drawer.

Curiosity prodding at the back of his mind, he pushed the lingerie to the side and looked in, pulling a plain, cream-white folded envelope into his hands with a gentle frown.

Popping the triangular flap open in the expectation of finding a wad of green, crumbled bills, a plane ticket or love letters, however, Henry found that its contents were instead, pictures.

They were pictures of bloodied, torn slabs of flesh, chipped teeth, bright purple and black bruises, pink ribbon, alongside the glazed, empty eyes of Kyle Madison, Luke Roberts, Andrew Clemmington, Ethan Cooper, and even Mr. Whitmore; all staring up at Henry with fear stretching open their loosened jaws, dirt staining their gums, blood trickling down their chins, and their forms rigid. Death oozing from the exposed innards of their abdomens and shattering the marrow of their bones.

They were crime scene photos, resembling the ones back at the station, locked away for what Henry had thought would be forever. But these were also... *Different,* from any of the ones he had spent hours staring at. They weren't copies.

The realization clamping down around his senses, as overwhelming as the pain of a wolf's bite, it shackled Henry to the roots of the Town quicker than he could process what was happening. And with a shallow, pained exhale flowering open his lips, feeling them weave their way around his ankles—bloodthirsty and destructive— revealing its sickening, true form, he finally tore his eyes away from the pictures just as the nuanced, fullness of Frank Sinatra singing *You Make Me Feel So Young* blasted through the room from the static, old speakers of Blossom's pink stereo.

Looking like a doll dressed in her delicate, thin, macaron-pink tulle dress, it was past noon, and she sat amongst the chaos of families gathered in the park. Watching, observing, peering through pink framed heart shaped glasses with her back against a chipped wooden bench. The corner of her mouth twitching into a smirk as her eyes settled on the figure of a young man who clicked through his music playlist with sweat glistening on the back of his neck and his lungs filling with burning air, he passed without notice to the way Blossom ran her eyes over him. The hint of aftershave and sweat tickling her lungs. Nonetheless, standing, just as Adam Hall turned into the wooded pathway, Blossom followed him into the darkness.

BLOSSOM

Made in the USA
Columbia, SC
03 May 2021